"Dreadnought was a very real presence back in those days, when David Mathew first cautiously introduced him to me. You could feel him lurking there in the pub with us, glaring and muttering virile threats, peeling off notes from a grenade of fivers, as roseate and raw with pressure as a phimosis. The terrible ideas he had, the appalling decisions he made, the *crisp* deterrents he meted. Unyielding, sentimental, complex, simple; a force. A paradox. An enigma. A cunt. Let David Mathew introduce you to Dreadnought Flex. See how *you* do."

Paul Meloy, Author of *Adornments of the Storm*

"Let's say *Dreadnought Flex* is a weird crime combination of time-travel and casual violence, or perhaps *Dreadnought Flex* is an SF novel replete with bar room anecdotes running an East End vibe, or maybe *Dreadnought Flex* is the prelude to a master criminal's cook book where the recipes – and also these definitions – should be taken with a pinch of salt. Then let's say Bone is a better condiment, a gateway to access alternate versions of the novel and its characters, where Mathew has cooked a fast-paced hybrid with a distinct voice and a twisted heart. If that's what we're saying *Dreadnought Flex* is about, then we might just be getting close."

Andrew Hook, Author of the Mordent neo-noir crime series
(The Immortalists, Church of Wire)

"*Dreadnought Flex* is written with such clarity and insight that it gets to the heart of broken masculinity. A thrilling and savage read."

Jonathan Oliver, British Fantasy Award-winning
anthologist and writer

"You won't be able to take your eyes off Dreadnought Flex. And you'd be wise not to – he's as unpredictable as this strange, original, exhilaratingly funny novel."

Mat Coward, Dagger and Edgar nominated crime writer

Montag Press
ISBN: 978-1-940233-58-1
Cover art © 1982 Steven Stapleton
Design © 2018 Rick Febré
Author photo © 2018 Jo Hatcher

Montag Press Team:
Project Editor – Charlie Franco
Managing Director – Charlie Franco

A Montag Press Book
www.montagpress.com
Montag Press
1066 47th Ave. Unit #9
Oakland CA 94601 USA

Montag Press, the burning book with the hatchet cover, the skewed word mark and the portrayal of the long-suffering fireman mascot are trademarks of Montag Press.

Printed & Digitally Originated in the United States of America
10 9 8 7 6 5 4 3 2 1

DaVid Mathew

–DREADNOUGHT–
FLEX

Remembering

Anthony Mathew (1945-2005)
Sheila Furnell (1931-2012)
Joel Lane (1963-2013)

DAVID MATHEW

DREADNOUGHT FLEX

MONTAG

Contents

BOOK ONE:
PRESSURE POINTS

I. Crisis Work

i

EVEN AS A BOY, BEFORE A second language had started to pound in my head, I was developing an interest in genealogy. Absorbed by the potency and beauty of family lines, I was happier with a pen and a piece of paper than I was with toy guns, board games or friends. I had a talent. And an idea that I might be able to set the world straight – back on kilter – through the action of familiarizing each person with his or her own dynasty.

I was brought up by an aunt and uncle, back in Denmark. Dad abandoned us; Mum died. To trace their family trees required the patient assistance of aunt and uncle. Such as I learned I presented on large sheets of flipchart paper, with my felt-tip pens of various hues sinking in deeply like a process of osmosis. Viewed from behind, where the ink had blotted through, the paper would resemble a network of veins, arteries and capillaries. I thought of it as a man's body (always a man's) – minus the limbs, the skin, the bones.

Tracing a family tree is exciting. It is also frustrating. On a daily basis, if this happens to become your job, as it did for me, you are thwarted. Leads perish into plumes of nonsensical smoke; people vanish. Despite your best efforts and your most stringent methods of research, the trail goes cold, or turns in on itself like the shuffle of a kaleidoscope's colours. A woman becomes her own aunt, her own grandmother, because the lines get tangled.

At least, that's the way it goes for *most* genealogists. But not for me: I have the talent, I have the gift – and I've never spent a day without Dreadnought Flex in my blood.

Dreadnought Flex was why I left Copenhagen and came here – to West London. Dreadnought Flex is why I'm writing these words. Not necessarily the Dreadnought Flex who is alive in the early breaths of the twenty-first century; but for now he's the easiest one to reach.

And where am I going to reach him? At the locus of one of his previous incarnations: the Church of St Nathaniel the Decisive, out Holborn way.

Wish me luck.

ii

Sighing at length, Dreadnought cracked his knuckles and picked up the receiver. The mouthpiece was so close to his lips that anyone observing might have thought that the man intended to kiss it rather than speak into it. There were no observers. Dreadnought was at home and even his wife was discouraged from being in the same room while her beloved conducted business.

'What's up?'

He was standing by the front door in black slacks, black shoes and an apple-red shirt, which was turned up tightly at the sleeves. His neckline plunged down to the fourth button, revealing a few chunky chains and a V of chest hair.

Dreadnought checked his watch: it was approaching ten p.m.

'What time's his flight? You're having a laugh, mate. I'll never make it in twenty minutes. Can you handle this one for me? I'll call up Charlie Peacock to meet you there and – what?' He'd been interrupted. 'What do you mean he's *sick*? He'll meet you there, all right? I'll turn up as soon as I can.'

He collected his cigar-cutter from the sideboard. He

slammed the door when he left the house. 'Hello, darling,' he said to his wife. She was approaching on foot, having disembarked at North Acton Tube. 'Got some business to take care of. Home as soon as I can.'

Mazza had not said a word, he realised as he turned the key in the ignition. Having recently completed a tour of duty that had involved whistle stops in Ealing, Green Park and Islington, the car was reluctant to up-tools. The engine growled. Dreadnought was obliged to twist the key extremely hard, to swear loudly, and to pump the gas as if he was inflating a tyre, before the car agreed to cooperate. Dreadnought turned his head. Mazza was standing on the pavement, her gym bag by her side; although she was smiling palely she had the air about her of a left-behind pet. Dreadnought smiled back.

The dilapidated Bentley pulled away from its allocated space. Cluttered percussion rose noisily from beneath the bonnet, and Dreadnought thought, as he had for the seventeenth consecutive day: *Better get that fixed. Take it to Bible Street. Roy'll do it cheap.* Then his attention was consumed by the roads of Acton – as he tried to remember the best way to Heathrow Airport. His sense of direction was catastrophic. He usually got one of the boys to drive him.

While dialling Charlie's number his eyes never left the road; his thumb knew the pattern to be traced.

The call was answered not by Charlie but by Sylvia, his wife. 'He's really ill, Dreadnought; he's got a fever – he got it off me.'

'I'm sorry, Sylv, I need him.'

'Have a heart,' Sylvia pleaded, and the simple emotion in her words – not to mention their decidedly nasal quality – made something shrink in Dreadnought's belly. If he wasn't careful he'd be accusing himself of sympathy.

At the other end of the line was a kerfuffle; virtually un-recognisable as it was, Charlie Peacock's voice arrived. 'What do you need me to do?'

'It's Dave Stroker.'

'What about him?'

'Done a bunk, off to the airport.'

'He's done *what*?'

Dreadnought explained. 'Mickey goes round for the monthly, yeah, and the shop's shut. Like that other time. So he goes round the cunt's flat – Hang on a second.' He needed his left hand to change up to third. 'Mickey goes round the flat to give him a tickle. Fucking *Mum's* there.' The disgust was palpable. 'He'd left his own mother to take the flak.' Dreadnought did not much relish the thought of what Mickey had had to do to make the woman talk, but needs must. 'Mickey had to get crisp before she gave in. He had to say sorry afterwards.'

'What terminal?' Charlie enquired. 'Where's he going?'

'I didn't ask! Call you back, mate.'

His left thumb touched Mickey's number. 'Got him?'

'Nah. But good news: flight's been delayed.'

'Excellent. What terminal?'

'Three.'

'And where's he going?'

'Melbourne. That's how scared he is.'

Dreadnought rang Charlie Peacock's mobile. From the swarming rush of traffic-noise, Dreadnought knew Peacock had already taken to the road. 'Terminal Three. Running back to the mother country.'

'No he ain't, mate. I'm on it.'

Dreadnought parked illegally in a passenger drop-off zone. Minutes later he was skipping through crowds, in search of Mickey. Impatiently he scanned the departures board, but his eyes weren't certain what to look for.

'Information' he spied, in the distance. In a flurry he headed for this oasis. The woman behind the counter asked if she could help him – the sweetest words he'd heard all day.

'I'm sure you can,' said Dreadnought, catching his breath. 'Someone I know's just gone through to catch his flight to Melbourne. But he's forgotten his insulin. I've got to get to him.'

The woman nodded. 'I'm afraid you won't be able to go through if you haven't got a ticket, even if it's an emergency. But I can contact the gate.'

'Would you?'

The message was relayed by telephone. 'What gate?' Dreadnought asked, endeavouring to hold back the cadence of panic that was threatening to unleash itself. He dashed away.

At the gate, Mickey looked like a second left shoe. He had no idea how to proceed, and Dreadnought felt (simultaneously) a flush of self-importance and a greater wave of weariness, knowing that again the burden fell squarely upon his own shoulders. No greetings were necessary.

'What you gonna do?' Mickey asked.

'I had the security girl pass on a message,' said Dreadnought.

'But he ain't gonna come out, is he?'

'Not the point. Want him to know we're here, get him scared.'

Mickey frowned. 'But Dreadnought, he ain't gonna *come out.*'

'No.' Dreadnought would have to go in. His eyebrows pinched together. His brain computed the pros and cons. 'You're gonna think me rash,' he said. 'But where's the desk, mate? For the airline he's travelling on '

Once more, Dreadnought sprinted off.

Wielding a credit card minutes later, Dreadnought sniffed and said, 'A one-way ticket to Melbourne, my good man. On *that* fucker. Now. Any price'll do.'

Silently the desk-official complied with the customer's wishes and the transaction was begun. In due course Dreadnought stood in yet another line, handing over his boarding pass and getting his neurons nuked by the metal detector. The threshold squealed, and Dreadnought raised his arms routinely. He was frisked.

Even as the security guard found it, Dreadnought remembered he'd placed his cigar cutter in his trouser pocket. 'Sorry,' he said, 'I was in such a hurry I forgot to take it out. Flight's gonna take off in a few minutes.'

Allowed to proceed with the cutter in hand, Dreadnought knew he had received his three pieces of good luck: the flight's delay, the securing of a ticket, and now this. He raced for the departure gate.

The flight had not boarded. Anguished travellers had been stalled in the lounge and a few passengers had taken to complaining to the gate personnel. Dreadnought's eyes scanned the crowds. Some kids were napping, head to toe, across three seats. A lot of holiday-maker stubble was on show. The room stank of frustration.

There!

Five rows of seats away, and with his back to the desk, Dave Stroker was reading a broadsheet. From a distance he appeared nonchalant: he believed he'd got away with it. He hadn't taken Dreadnought's sense of maniacal fair play into consideration. It was *business*.

Dreadnought approached, his fingers on the cigar cutter in his pocket. Not wasting a second, he dropped to his knees in front of Stroker and shoved the broadsheet at the man's face.

There was a grunt of perplexed disapproval, but Dreadnought paid it no mind. Simultaneously he used his left hand to grab hold of Stroker's right wrist, then pushed the cutter over Stroker's ring finger. The digit slipped in easily, and not for another second would Stroker comprehend.

His face was a portrait of fear. As he glanced down at the chunky new jewellery he'd been donated, his green eyes melted and Dreadnought said loudly: 'Airport police, sir. Come with me if you would.' And he stood up, slowly, expecting Stroker to do the same thing, which he did. To the sound of mumbles, Dreadnought led Dave Stroker away from the lounge. 'Not a word or you lose it. Not messing.'

Dave said nothing. Dreadnought breathed his sweat. They were passing a knickers-and-socks shop when Stroker finally asked, 'What now?'

'Now we're leaving. Have a nice little chat about responsibilities.'

'I'm sorry, Dreadnought. I didn't know what to do '

Dreadnought was not sympathetic. 'Tell it to your mother,' he said. 'You should be ashamed of yourself, leaving her to fend for you like that. You're a disgrace!'

'What you done to her?'

'Nothing, no thanks to you. How do we get out of here, I wonder.'

'I don't think we can.'

The only way out was the way he'd come in – and Dreadnought couldn't imagine fulfilling this chore without needing to explain himself. In fact, as he approached, shackled to Stroker, the guard who had questioned him turned and subjected Dreadnought to a vile and meaningful stare.

The only thing to do, Dreadnought reasoned, was to cut off the guy's finger – endure the screams – and escape by way of the airport constabulary, in the back of a marked van, with a sky of cloudy bruises on his features.

'This,' he said to Stroker as he turned to face him, 'is going to hurt *me* more than you.'

Dave Stroker felt the initial pinch of the cutter on his ring finger.

Dreadnought leaned towards his victim. 'Don't leave me, darling,' he said louder than before. He sucked his lips onto those of Dave Stroker, and eased his tongue into the other man's mouth.

As Dreadnought curled his free hand onto Stroker's backside, to give it a squeeze, he waited. He waited to be told to stop; he waited for a chance for them both to be allowed back out, in order to give their relationship one more chance. They had both seen the errors of their ways.

Dreadnought felt Stroker's tears as they ran into their lips.

iii

Despite being within Dreadnought's orbit for the better part of a month now, as I've been securing this humble bolt-hole in North Acton (at a ridiculous monthly rent) and generally getting myself ready by learning the lay of the land, I have realised that there is only one sure-fire way of getting close to Dreadnought and of attracting his professional curiosity: I'll have to hire him. Somehow I'll have to earn his respect by paying him for it, for a job completed. I wonder what he'll cost.

Finding Dreadnought was a piece of piss. (I love this expression.) I can only take a leap-in-the-dark guess here, but what I felt must be close to the sensations twins experience, when one of them is hurt, lonely or afraid. When you've been with someone (or your earlier versions have) for at least four hundred years, and will continue to be for longer than that, you form inexplicable bonds. So as soon as I landed in London I knew exactly what part of the city to head towards. I could almost dream my way there.

West London is stuffed with pubs, of course – as is East, North and South London. It was simply a matter of making some routine enquiries about the great man: some of which were met with shrugs and sighs, others with nods of the head and helpful directions to different pubs. So it was that late one afternoon I ventured into The Bloody Chamber, and I knew I had found my man. Not that he was present; but he'd been there – I knew it. A head-to-toe queasiness engulfed me, and the barman looked worried.

'If you feel sick, mate,' he said, 'I'm not serving you.'

I tried to smile. 'Just gas,' I said. 'Pint, please.' I had two before I thought it safe to test the waters. 'Do you know a guy named Dreadnought?'

'Sure. Drinks here a couple of times a week.'

'Any idea where I might get in touch with him?'

'You can leave a message here if you like. Leave your number.'

'Sounds good. I need him for some work.'

I made it outside before I vomited.

The phone rang as I wasn't having breakfast but should have been. Countless doctors have informed me I must begin the day with at least a piece of toast, but generally speaking I ignore them. I take the pills for my high blood sugar, I roll a cigarette, and I read or write – that's if I haven't been up all night, riding the insomniac's waves, and don't feel dreadful.

It was seven o'clock.

'Is that Mr Haabjoern?' a voice mispronounced.

'It is.'

'This is Dave Peacock, landlord at The Bloody Chamber. You were here a couple of days ago.'

'Hi, Dave. Any news?'

'Are you free at four this afternoon?'

I typed the directions as he gave them. Then I thanked Dave Peacock, said goodbye, and felt hungry enough to keep down half a piece of toast. I went over to my old-fashioned wardrobe and tried to choose what to wear.

iv

The venue was not a pub. As it would turn out, Dreadnought holds such clichés in high disdain. Instead we met in a butcher's shop called Beef Encounter – in an office at the back. I had to wait to be served. An old girl was buying pork scratchings – the real deal. I didn't realise that this sort of crap still occurred; I was pleasantly appalled. They were handed to her in a mangled polythene bag: a collection of rind and gristle, with pieces the size of finger bones. As she turned she had a crock-of-gold gleam in her eye. 'For me dog,' she explained, although I'd heard her say as much to the butcher.

'I have an appointment with Dreadnought,' I announced to the butcher, assuming that the two men were not the same.

'You Mr Haabjoern?' he asked – with a rare accurate pronunciation.

'Yes.'

He nodded his considerable head. 'Go through that door, to the end of the corridor, it's the last door on your left,' he said, and I was about to thank him when he added, 'And if you spy a spotty little herbert, tell him to get his arse out here and do some work. His break was over five minutes ago.'

'Will do.'

A few seconds later I was knocking at a door. The spotty

herbert wasn't spotted, although I was aware of a figure lurking beyond the fire escape: his restlessness was kicking up shadows as he booted stones around, and strings of smoke were coming in from the cold. From within the office I heard no invitation to enter. The door opened.

The shaved head to disguise the retreating hairline; the bustle of two heavy lips; the unshaved wattles – he was perfect, I thought. He was exactly as I'd expected him to be. The track suit bottoms and the brown leather jacket over a creased rugby shirt. Perfect.

But he was not Dreadnought Flex. He was the muscle.

'Come in, Mr Haabjoern,' said a voice from a place beyond the security guard's torso. 'Take a seat.'

I entered. I sat. A woozy air of expectation was about my skull, and then – something worse. A quadruple dose of nausea. It was the not the first time it had happened, but it was, I think, the first time it had occurred so powerfully: that I slipped – I skidded through time.

Flashes of light beat into my eyes, and between them I saw Dreadnought at various points in history: at Pressure Points – where the lines can snap and where the structure can fall apart: where the spine might break and the bones splinter, to rain to the floor with the floppy old organs, all throbbing.

What I saw was Dreadnought, with tea-coloured skin, accompanied by sidekicks of similar hue, in a futuristic-looking gymnasium; or Dreadnought – I am certain – in black with a highwayman's pistol; or Dreadnought in a maze of filth-ridden alleyways, overlooked by washer-women and smeared children; or Dreadnought ingesting a balloon's worth of white powder – not cocaine – called Bone. Like a monkey on ice, my imagination veers up and down the timeline, scoring through hundreds of years.

A voice dragged me back to the office. 'I believe,' said Dreadnought, 'in a system of fair play and honesty from the beginning.'

The nausea took a few seconds to disperse, and for the next two hours would float my way in ever decreasing waves.

'This is Charlie Peacock,' said Dreadnought. The man who'd opened the door nodded. 'And my name is Dreadnought Flex. I'm here to help.'

I nodded across the desk. 'Rene Haabjoern,' I told him, wondering if I should shake his hand.

The fact that Dreadnought had pronounced my surname correctly the first time had passed me by; but it didn't on this next occasion – as the man said, 'And what can we do for you, Mr Haabjoern?'

'I need a pulse. I need some crisis work conducted.'

'And may I ask why?'

'It was a business transaction. He left me out in the cold.'

'I understand. I understand the need for revenge.'

'Good.'

'I understand its language. I speak it fluently.'

'Good,' I repeated. 'This is not about money.'

'It's about face. But if you want us to lean on him for the cash, we can build that into the price.'

'Thank you. But the punishment's what I'm after.' A pause. 'On the subject, though, of money,' I said.

Dreadnought held up his hand. 'All in good time, Mr Haabjoern. What's his name, what's he look like, and where can we find him?'

'His name's Chris Martin. Do you know the Dolphin Hotel? Tiny place, near Acton Mainline – mostly for refugees.'

'I can find it,' said Dreadnought.

'Well a hop, skip and jump from there is the Church of St

Nathaniel the Decisive. He'll be there, in the graveyard.'

'Why?'

'He has a hands-on attitude to his drug deals,' I explained. 'I'm going to set up a deal he won't be able to turn his nose up to. If you see what I mean.'

Dreadnought leaned back in his chair. 'And what would you like us to do?'

'Kick his teeth in.'

'Literally?'

I thought of the victim I would also have to hire. 'No, not literally.'

With a frown Dreadnought said, 'You'll have to be specific, Mr Haabjoern. We aim to give the customer exactly what he wants.'

'Okay. What I want is for you or one of your team to punch him around for a while. Don't break any bones and don't cause any permanent scars or internal bleeding.'

'The face?'

'Leave it alone.'

Cocking his head to one side Dreadnought said, 'If you'll forgive me, that don't sound like much of a punishment. How much did he fuck you out of, if you don't mind me asking?'

I'd anticipated this question. 'Three hundred,' I told him.

His face remained expressionless.

'Just out of interest, mate,' said Dreadnought as I was standing up, putting my coat on. 'You wouldn't know where I might buy a Persian rug, would you?'

It took me a second to comprehend that there was no code.

'Me anniversary soon. Mazza wants a Persian rug for some reason. As well as some knickers and bras and that.'

I still don't know whether the question had been intended to comfort me, flatter me, or disarm me. It did all three.

'I'd imagine a carpet shop could order you one,' I said.

'Cheers.'

I fastened my coat. 'How many years?' I asked politely.

'It's our third.'

'Congratulations.'

'Cheers. You can go out the back way if you'd rather avoid the smell of raw meat. It gets on my tits sometimes.'

'Thanks.'

Three years he'd been married. But you're wrong, I wanted to say. You've been married to Mazza or someone like her – one of her drafts, her versions – for at least four hundred. When I do my maths, it might turn out to be longer. Which is not bad going in these days of easy divorces.

I decided to refresh myself with a cigarette; then I discovered I was not alone out there in the staff car park. Another man was present. Young. Big built, sandy-haired, he was noshing his way through cigarettes, as opposed to doing any work. We nodded at each other. Not wishing to put the young man ill-at-ease, I even pretended that I needed a light, the better to strike up a conversation. In Northern Europe we are not afraid of silences, but I know in England, discursiveness is the game.

'Do you work for the butcher?'

'Unfortunately. Trying to get out of it.' A good London accent, with the mouth moving like that of a crap ventriloquist. 'It's a Job Centre deal, mate. Can't leave. Fucks me benefits.'

'I see.'

'You couldn't put in a good word in with Dreadnought for me, could you? That's what I wanna do.'

'I don't know him on that level,' I said.

The young man nodded. 'Fair enough,' he told me, and

then I thought that would be the end of that – but the need to confess seemed enormous. 'I got an interview with him in a minute. That's why I'm waiting out here,' he explained.

We drew on our cigarettes with impatience. Having started his earlier, he finished first, stamped it into the gravel and said, 'Well all the best, mate.' Meaning it sincerely, I wished him luck, and took out another smoke – this one to enjoy on my own. No sooner had I taken a drag on my second snack than the door opened again (startling me slightly) and Dreadnought walked out with his hands in his pockets.

'I'm going to get fags,' he said. 'I'll walk you to the taxi rank.'

'Do you want one of mine?' I proffered the packet. With a nod and a sniff the great man accepted. We walked a few hundred metres to a row of shops that was almost identical to that we'd just left. Here in London, here in Maggotville, there is always an identical row of shops close by.

I was perfectly aware that Dreadnought was sizing me up. 'You a married man, Rene?' he asked.

'Regrettably, no.'

'Do it. Soon as you can. Best thing ever happened to me, Mazza is.'

I smiled. 'It's lovely to hear a man talking like that '

'Everyone needs a partner. And she's mine.'

And you're mine, I thought. I shook Dreadnought's hand for the third time in an hour and he watched me as I angled my body into a waiting car.

The driver asked, 'Where to?'

'End of the road and turn left. Just get me out of here.'

'You'll still have to give me a couple of quid, mate. Minimum fare.'

'You've got it. Let's go.'

I gave the driver a fiver and said, 'Cheers.' Then I sloped into the nearest pub, the same one as before: The Bloody Chamber. Desperately fatigued, I had a pint of beer, then another, all the while trying to work out how I was going to execute the next bit. I had a sandwich that tasted only of bread, thinking – I'll have to do it. It'll have to be me.

But it couldn't be. I couldn't be the victim.

A good proportion of the pub's drinkers' heads turned swiftly towards the door as it opened (mine included). In walked the sandy-haired guy from the car park. Say what you like about Dreadnought, he is certainly expedient when it comes to interviews.

As I had sat myself at the bar, as close to the door as possible, the young man had little choice but to notice me. The grin he wore widened slightly. 'This'll either be your congratulations drink or your commiserations drink,' I said.

'Congratulations,' the young man replied.

'What'll you have?'

He ordered a strong lager, and I followed his lead. I have spent the better part of my life in self-imposed solitary confinement, regardless of who has happened to be around, and I cannot explain why I chose to spend time with this stranger, other than to say –

He is part of it. The destinies and dynasties I am chasing: this man, who thirty seconds later introduced himself as Gary Brooker, is part of them all. We are linked, but I don't know how or why yet.

'Rene,' I said.

'Good to meet you, mate,' he told me.

v

Telephone boxes would be a complete waste of time; but

I tried them anyway, as crumb one on my gingerbread trail. Awaiting my attention was a risqué array of whorehouse brochures: a splayed and rearranged deck of prostitutes' cards. I took out my gum, blew my nose and dialled the first.

Martina. A wild blonde ride. All your dreams cum true.

'I'm calling for Martina,' I said. 'Is she free?'

'You're talking to her, my friend.'

I paused. As Dreadnought himself might have said, I nearly bottled it. 'I'm wondering if you do any requests.'

'Well now, darling, that would depend on the nature of the request.'

'I need a man.'

'Don't we all, dear. What you saying? There are specialist places '

'I don't know the numbers. I was hoping you might be a Madame or something. A manager. I need a man.'

'So you said.' She breathed into my ear. 'I can help you.'

'But he has to be a bit special.'

'Young?'

'Irrelevant. Accommodating,' I said. 'He's got to agree to a bit of rough. I need to hurt him a little bit. Or a lot.'

'I have a number you could dial. Are you ready?'

'I'm ready.'

'It's 9.9.9. Emergency Services. You sad bastard.'

I really need to work on my approach, I thought to myself.

vi

The Church of St Nathaniel the Decisive is like a matchstick ship: it has that appearance of vulnerability. I have always adored fat churches.

I sat in the graveyard, with a small bottle of brandy to keep me warm. I had read the stone in front of me so many times that it had ceased to seem sad. The night was plugged with stars, and I watched them drunkenly.

I hadn't been able to hire anyone to take the kicking, so I would have to take it on the chin myself. I was pleased to note that the lines of the church had started to blur. This meant that the pain, too, would be less than specific. All being well, it would hurt like a towel slap.

From somewhere behind me I heard the unhurried, unworried noise of two people approaching. Either dedicated grave robbers, I thought, or suicidal lovers. Slip her bra off in this place, mate, and she might die of frostbite.

Alternatively they were my destiny. Feeling hot as they moved towards me, I wondered if they too were commenting on the strangeness of the situation. Finally I looked up. They were dressed in black, but I'd seen that coming from miles off. It tends to be the way. The face of the one on the left was pear-shaped, hairless; he had a nose like a squashed piece of fruit. The other one was younger. A factor of ten years, I would have guessed. As I'd later discover, here was Mickey, the elder and the other guy I'd already met.

The former spoke. 'You must be Chris Martin.'

'For the purposes of tonight, I suppose I must.' I sounded weary. 'But my real name is Rene Haabjoern. I hired Dreadnought.'

'Sure you did,' said Brooker, who was evidently eager to get going. 'That's what they all say.' In the darkness he still hadn't recognised me.

'So how would I know Dreadnought sent you?'

Brooker was not to be denied the hiding he had come to administer. As a new recruit of Dreadnought's, he was keen to be seen to do well in front of the other employee. Not since my uncle slapped me around on two specific occasions – when I set fire to the hay barn, and when I became erotically interested in one of the farm's cows – had I felt such hemmed-in, smouldering, eager-for-release antagonism, aimed in my direction.

'By the way,' I said, 'congratulations again, Brooker.'

'Rene?' Surprise and indignation coincided in his voice. He leaned forward, to convince himself of his belief. 'What *you* doing here?'

'Waiting for you, mate,' I told him, as if they had just arrived and none of the previous conversation had registered. 'I'm your victim.'

'You know him?' said the other guy.

'A bit Look, I don't understand.'

The voice was wheedling and the latter sentence was directed at me. It even occurred to me to feel sorry for Brooker. How was this going to look – the fact that he knew his short-term enemy? Furthermore I felt sorry because it had to seem like betrayal, and that's never nice. I hadn't mentioned anything about the job I was hiring Dreadnought to complete, and now look at how things were going to turn out.

Brooker's voice sounded hurt as he said, 'Why Rene?'

He was asking me why I had chosen that name, not why I was here in the first place. 'You've got it wrong, Brooker. My real name is Rene.'

'Enough of this,' said the other man. 'We have our instructions. And I have mine, mate, don't forget. Do you think Dreadnought's not gonna ask how you got on?'

'No.'

'Well then.'

Well then. I had heard the conversation with my own two ears, albeit through a thickening fog of surrealism. I wasn't there. It wasn't me; it was a dream. I tell you something, it was a bloody good job I was drunk. God knows what would have happened if I'd attempted to face the ordeal dry.

II. The Crock of Gold

i

They honoured the agreement. My face is okay.

My body, on the other hand, is a swamp of bulbous bruises and deliquescent swathes. And it has to be said – I feel like shit.

Such is life. And good things have arrived as a result.

First Brooker and then Mickey, like tag-team wrestlers, set to with such intensity that I seriously wondered if I was going to make it through to the other side. All things being equal, I now realise, it could have been worse: they might have used weapons. They might have killed me. But that's about as far as I can go with my gratitude. Curled into a ball, I took the kicks and Mickey's swearwords (Brooker was silent) until the energy flagged. With a final *adios* kicking from them both, they walked away. I heard Brooker say something about needing a drink, and I took his point.

Then light flared in my head. I saw a picture of Brooker, minus his monkey-like mentor. A pub. Not The Bloody Chamber. Somewhere I don't think I've been to. He was Christmas Eve drunk, but this was no festive season. No decorations adorned the corners of picture frames, or sagged from the eaves like drooping moustaches. Brooker was alone. Made of rubber, he wobbled to his feet and I followed him into the Gents. He took a stall. Locked the door. Then he pulled a balloon from his back pocket and laboriously unfastened the knot. When he'd massaged the white powder onto the toilet seat he said, 'My beautiful Bone,' and his nose raked it efficiently.

A further flare.

Brooker is entering a shop. As the proprietress sits down, she hears the tinkle of the front door hitting its warning bell. She looks up. She appears guilty – as if his entrance has interrupted something. Brooker is noticeably older – twenty-five or twenty-six – and he has oily jeans and a packet of cigarettes in his shirt pocket. A flirtatious camaraderie is abroad.

'Hello, darling,' says Brooker.

Flare. And back to the pub – or to *a* pub, anyway. I haven't been to this establishment either, and I don't know where we are in time. On the other hand, I found I could tiptoe around the thoughts of the two men who were now entering the building. Neither of them resembled Dreadnought, but he was there. Which meant, that the other one was Brooker.

The church bell rang.

Mickey and Brooker took their leave.

ii

Events have been leading here. I can smell the stench of a foregone conclusion.

What will I be called? At the very least, an *agent provocateur* – but that's only the half of it. I'm aligned with this man. I'm connected in some way, destined to wriggle and coil my way around his history – around his drafts, his better versions.

iii

'You're a loyal cunt, I'll give you that.' This was Dreadnought. 'But thick as pig shit,' he continued. 'Can you see my point?'

'I can.'

It was two days later. For forty-eight hours straight I'd been pissing blood, wondering how to inject myself back into the mainstream.

I entered The Bloody Chamber. If I'd been worried about Dreadnought divulging the particulars of his dealings, I needn't have been. I said to Dave: 'Can I leave another message for Dreadnought?'

'He'll be here in a minute, if you want to wait.' I waited. Dave explained. 'It's Wednesday. He always comes in on a Wednesday. His missus goes to the gym on a Wednesday so he pops in and says hello.'

'Do you take a credit card?'

'Sure. You want a tab?'

I left my coat with my pint and strolled up the road to buy some rolling papers, newspapers, some tobacco. Come what may, I was going to wait. I was going to speak to the great man.

Nearly three hours later he arrived. Even though he was accompanied by people I didn't know, and seemed set for a celebratory evening, he soon made his way over to my table. Humbly I said, 'Hi.'

Dreadnought was in no mood for such erudite banter. 'The fuck's going on?' he demanded. The Bloody Chamber turned cold.

'I did this to impress you. I want to be part of your team.'

'You got a funny way of going about it!'

'I thought it would be a good way of getting introduced to you.'

'You weren't wrong.' He sat down on the chair opposite mine. 'But you could've gone about this whole affair differently.'

'Would I have got your attention?'

Dreadnought slipped his head forward. 'Probably not,' he admitted. 'But you wouldn't've got the fuck kicked out of you either.'

I thanked him and he offered me a drink. I called for lager. In due course it arrived, even though Dreadnought hadn't moved. A twitch of the eyebrow had been sufficient. 'So what do you wanna do?' he asked.

'Work for you.'

'As what?'

'You name it.'

'I will, mate.' Dreadnought examined the moment; he considered his options. 'What's your form? What's the biz?'

'Mainly pills,' I said; 'pills and dope. Rarely H, but once in a while I'd come across someone with a need. You know how it goes.'

Dreadnought was nodding. He knew how it went: supply and demand. 'I was very much small-time,' I continued. 'You won't find anyone who's even heard of me!' I raised the beer to my lips. I was playing down the non-existent life of crime in Denmark for a variety of reasons. Principally I didn't wish to be checked-up-on, and not even Dreadnought would be so paranoid as to call in an international favour.

'I never touched it myself,' I said.

After taking a long swallow, Dreadnought nodded again and said, 'Fair comment. Each to his own, like. I respect your honesty Come and meet some of the boys. Let's see how you fit in. Consider this your interview.'

Then and since I've met a few of Dreadnought's colleagues. There was Tubular Bill, Frank the Ferret (a pickpocket and a burglar, who presented his talents with aplomb: shortly after Dreadnought had warned me not to trust the cunt, he held up my watch, and wiggled it like a whore would a garter; he was grinning – it was a simple demonstration of his skills). Who else? Fat Gina, Chemo-Sebby. The names of these people! The names are said with little irony – perhaps with a modicum of pride. But would you be proud to be known as Fat

Anything? Fat Gina isn't even overweight!

Do I read Dreadnought right? He doesn't open himself up to ready interpretations. Nor does this shock me: murkiness has helped him secure a respected throne. It's intransigence that makes him the man he is. But what kind of a man is that? A voluminous man, for starters. Also diligent, generous, acerbic, tight-fisted and clean. His good qualities are always being cancelled out be the less-good qualities; and vice versa.

I have a horrible feeling he has started to see through me already. I'm not as deep as he is, and I'm going to have to work harder at this.

iv

'Training eggs,' I mumbled (apparently) and then woke up.

Brooker regarded me fondly. 'That sounded like an interesting dream,' he said, his hands on the wheel, as if he'd been waiting for the end of my nap before departing. 'You wanna share?'

Brooker is the team's dream expert – a role, however, that is not hotly contended. I have seen members of Dreadnought's crew show interest, briefly, in the subject of their own dreams – but then again, I've seen members of Dreadnought's crew show interest in the comparative merits of the breasts of film actresses. More often, though, they tell Gary Brooker to shut up; once, and once only, Dreadnought gave him a fatherly clout round the ear. This was taken in the spirit in which it had been intended: as a sign of affection.

We'd both been a month in Dreadnought's employ.

I've really got to stop being such a sympathetic listener. Shaking my head I told Brooker, 'I have no idea. There were these eggs '

Brooker nodded. 'Training eggs,' he answered confidently. 'You were saying that aloud.'

'Was I?' The dream unravelled; it gave itself a little shake. 'I remember now. I had to train these eggs to hatch. It was my job.'

Brooker shifted the position of his hands: he moved them to three and nine o'clock on the steering wheel. 'You know what that means, don't you? Means you're waiting for something to happen. That's what your unconscious is telling you. You're anxious about something.'

'Aren't we all?'

He started the engine. We'd been told to wait in the van – borrowed from a man named Wrighty – until Dreadnought called. 'Phoned when you's asleep. We gotta go do some damage.'

'Who to?'

'Pekinese Pete.'

We were driving in a new dawn drizzle. In Dreadnought's world, I had already come to learn, things often occurred at dawn, in the drizzle. With all my heart, I must confess, I dislike London; but in the midst of a rainy early morning you could almost forgive it.

'Owns a restaurant in Hanwell. Owes a few bob and can't pay up. So we have to go round and set fire to the kitchen.'

'Well how's that gonna help?' I asked.

'Insurance money, mate.'

'But he won't get that for ages.'

'That's our orders,' Brooker replied in a slightly miffed voice.

'How much does he owe?'

Brooker smiled and executed a ridiculously sharp and late left turn. 'Do you really think he's gonna talk money to a cunt like me?' he said.

'I suppose not,' I agreed.

It wasn't often that Dreadnought did deals, or made arrangements, with people who owed him cash. The phlegmatic threat and the presence of a few of the lads was usually enough to shake the moths from the wallet. Very rarely did Dreadnought execute any of that 'equivalent value' bullshit. Very rarely did he ask one of the boys to hump the guy's laptop, TV or video down the stairwell, in order to sell it at Gadgets.

'They go back a bit, do they, Pete and the boss?'

'Yeah, I think so. Why do you ask?'

I'd played a hunch. There was history in their relationship, I had gathered: and not necessarily the sort of history that they knew any damned thing about.

For the time being Brooker decided to let the matter drop. He had other things on his mind. 'You got any tattoos?'

'Nah. You?'

'Nah. But I'm thinking about it. I fancy a change of image.' He paused. 'I quite fancy getting myself a cock ring an' all.'

Behind the establishment, in a small courtyard displaying its uncollected black plastic bin bags like trophies, Brooker brought the vehicle to a halt. There was no other vehicle present. I felt colder than ever: the moment was drawing closer. Were we going to break in? As Brooker unfastened his seatbelt he changed the subject by saying: 'Here, Rene. In Denmark, you're all a bit liberal, intcha.'

'Sure. We run naked in the streets.'

'Piercing's nothing though. The birds got clit rings and that.'

'That's right. The aunt who brought me up had nipple rings.'

'There you go then.' Brooker frowned. 'This country,

Rene – honestly. Sometimes I despair. All so *stuffy* sometimes.'
He completed a rueful shake of his head.

'We should overthrow the government,' I offered, really
pushing my luck at this point. But you can't push a melon like
Gary Brooker too far, as I was later to discover – in this version
of ourselves and in another.

'How would we do it, mate?' Brooker asked.

Trying (and succeeding) not to laugh, I told him I would
have to think about that one. Brooker nodded and said, 'Do
you agree?'

'About the English being stuffy? I do, as a matter of fact.'

Brooker sniffed. 'Come on,' he said. 'Let's burn this
restaurant down and we can go and get some breakfast.'

We got out of the van. 'So why don't you just do it?' I
asked. 'The cock ring.'

Brooker shrugged as he dragged a can of petrol along a
filthy once-white dustsheet. 'Angie's not too keen.'

'Angie's your bird?'

'Yeah. Well, I'm working on it anyway. Got a wank off
it the other night, so I'm making progress. She's a hypocrite
though. I say, "What's the difference? You got your ears
pierced." And she's like – "Yeah. So? That's me fucking *ears*."
She's one of them women you can't argue with.'

'Unreasonable,' I said to keep on his side. We were making too much noise by half, I imagined. An ugly notion presented itself: that we would enter the premises – only to find
the cops there. Suddenly I was convinced that this was a trap.

The back door opened. I managed not to exhibit too
much shock. Brooker had not bothered to tell me that the manager or one of his minions would be meeting us at the site. But
here he was. A tiny, orange-skinned Oriental guy poked his
head out. 'You're late,' he informed us. 'Get in here.'

The kitchen was in darkness. It did not smell of food; it smelt of cleaning products. 'Did Dreadnought explain what I need?'

Brooker took the enquiry. 'He did indeed, Pete.'

The door was still ajar and Pekinese Pete said, 'In that case I'll be off. Just the kitchen, lads, okay? Just the kitchen.'

Yeah: because it's simple to control a fire, right?

With a flexing of his lapels – the standard forearming against a gale – Pekinese Pete slipped through the door. I said, 'What do you reckon, Brooker – can we have some lights on or what?'

'I don't suppose it'll hurt.' Brooker began to unscrew the container of petrol, using wristy, flamboyant gestures, a palpable sense of excitement on his face. 'Get to the door,' he tells me. 'This'll go up like a fireworks display. You don't wanna lose your eyebrows.'

We move to the outside door.

V

Life has taken on a new set of routines. Dreadnought is insistent on the strategic capabilities of early mornings, and we are obliged to rise with the cock. For me, a lifelong insomniac, that's no big deal; but I wonder how some of the others manage it. Especially Brooker.

Typically it goes like this. Dreadnought rings at the crack of dawn, at about the same time as I am having my final drink of the evening, and getting ready to slip into my jim-jams (if I wore such items: I must reconfigure my body clock). He says, 'Mate? Job for you.' I accompany Brooker (so far, only Brooker – the new boy) as he fetches the monthly protection money. Evidently this is seen as a no-risk enterprise. Or I make some calls or word a letter or something. I do a bit of driving

My working day, by and large, is over by mid-morning, and I'm not so certain this suits me down to the ground. As a general rule, Brooker and I will hobble into the pub: The Bloody Chamber, The Duck, or The Bottom of the Barrel (as unenlivening as you might imagine). And we chat for half a day, or until one of us runs out of money. Usually him. At the moment I have a stack, but it's not going to last long. So it's just as well I have, if not a lawful occupation, then at least an occupation. I have a job! All I needed was to get my ribs chipped. And believe me – there are no hard feelings. I talk to Brooker, and even to Mickey (a surly fucker), as though I have known them all my life.

Am I turning into them? Haven't I *got* to turn into them? You don't kill the whale from a distance; besides, the atmosphere is magnetic. Constantly I feel in danger for my life and it squirts adrenaline through my system.

Fifteen minutes ago the telephone rang: the mobile, that is, that Dreadnought has insisted I buy. It was six-thirty. I was typing.

'Did you sleep all right?'

'Not bad,' I lied.

'Come over to Beef Encounter, would you?'

'Sure. Who'm I working with?'

'You're solo on this one, Rene. You can handle it. I'll see you good for a drink, don't worry, mate. Just a bit of collection: Dave Stroker. Remember I told you about the slap I had to give someone at Heathrow? That was him. So don't worry, he won't give you shit. So much as blinks in an aggressive way, tell him I'll be over.'

Deciding to stand up for myself I said, 'I'd rather not have to fall back on your name, Dreadnought. No offence, like; but I'm assuming this is my probationary test, and if things get naughty, I'll sort it out.'

'Fine by me.'

vi

Dave Stroker co-owns a painting and decorating shop called 'I Second That Emulsion!' It stands at the end of a road off a road off Acton High Street.

I approached the premises with caution, stupidly slowing as I drew near and risking not being able to accelerate again. Although the car behind me honked, I was more concerned with the car I was driving: Dreadnought's car – the Bentley. It would not respond to the pressure I exerted on the gas. Changing down to first helped a little, but not much. I started cursing: ripe, inventive Danish curses. After an age of fruity burps from a series of horns, I managed to get the car to cooperate. Grudgingly we began to gallop off to the next intersection. Sweating. Pulling over to the side of the road served to remind me of how to breathe. I lit a cigarette. I should've gone on the Tube, I thought as I flicked the dog-end out of the window. A sallow pigeon arrowed in to taste it.

As I entered the shop, a bell ting-a-linged. It was like something out of a Cotswolds bakery, *circa* 1950. A few people browsed. A couple was deciding on the right colour for their imminent baby's bedroom. At the counter I asked for Dave Stroker, reasonably certain from the description I'd been given that I had my man. I felt as though someone had taped a grenade to my scrotum. Even my sweat was sweating. My muscles were as heavy as lead. But even in my overloaded state, it seemed, I was casting a sinister shadow over this poor sap. Or at least, I was about to.

'That's me!'

'Well you shouldn't sound so pleased about it. Dreadnought sent me.'

His face had a peculiarly dry look. 'Where's the other guy?' he asked, keeping his eye both on me and on the other customers.

'Early retirement. Are you ready?'

'You could be anyone,' Stroker protested. 'Don't take me for a mug.'

I lowered my voice. 'Do you really want it reported that you're refusing to make another payment, Dave? Cuz that's what'll happen. After we've gone out the back, that is.'

I've noticed that the characters Dreadnought hangs around with can say the word *fuck* without actually moving their lips. This, Dave Stroker did now. Elaborately, and with maximum flourish, he rolled his head to stretch his neck muscles. When he returned to me I was ready with my cold grey stare.

'Close the shop,' I told him quietly, 'before I close it for you. Or pay up. You know the rules.'

Stroker opened the till.

III. The Heart Forecast

i

Winter is deepening, and you can sense the moods of the population. When I went round last night, Dreadnought was hanging his Christmas decorations – though it's nowhere near the festive season. Yesterday was November 12th: my birthday. It was odd. You could see the tinsel in the window, and the taxi-driver was intrigued. He waited until the door opened before pulling away, making me feel like a kid on my first sleepover.

'You own a calendar, I'm right in assuming?' I said as the door closed.

Dreadnought looked baffled. 'I missed summing?'

'This stuff's more common in December,' I told him.

'I like the build-up,' Dreadnought replied, a little huffily.

'Well I'll help you. What can I do to help?'

What can I do to help? has become a mantra in these honey-moon weeks of my involvement with Flex. Helping is all I do. Even when I scrape my gums clean every morning I imagine that I'm brushing to aid Dreadnought; that I'm coughing up blood for Flex.

My induction has consisted of early mornings, and tu-multuous strikes on those whom Dreadnought deems to have deserved it; or more often, simple and routine collection of 'the monthly'. Door opens, typically, and an arm reaches out. In the hand is a brown envelope. The money is not counted: everybody knows what happens when Dreadnought is short-changed. The Heathrow Airport story is legendary: many places I go I hear versions and exaggerations of the warning. Cross Dreadnought's path and you'd better nod politely. Take a penny from his coffers, and you'd better put it towards some medical insurance – you're going to need it.

How am I shaping up? The early mornings are no sweat. In the morning I slip out of my sodden sheets like a fish, landed on the rowboat. I don't eat enough or I eat too much: the same patterns I've observed since childhood, when my mother died, and I was dunked in the cold water of clinical grief. It has occurred to me that I'll need to find a milder curry (and no doubt take the laughs from the lads!) in order to repair my ruined digestive system; beer is already giving me a gut. Shall I risk an orange squash and slimline tonic at the Bloody Chamber? Right.

Mentally I feel fine: at this precise moment. I'm home, I'm happy; but I'd be foolish to ignore the possibility that my existence around Dreadnought is doing lasting harm. How can it not be? The proximity to menace; the angels continually tutting in my face and wagging an admonitory finger.

On the other hand, errands I execute in Dreadnought's name are often legitimate. It is easy to forget – especially here in the eye of his self-made hurricane – that Dreadnought has business concerns that are *kosher*. Beef Encounter, the butcher's shop: Dreadnought doesn't run it but he owns it. And it's one hundred per cent legal – subject to the same health checks, receipt perusals and government thermometers as any other business selling meat. No bodies are blue in the freezer; no fingers get baked in a pie. Though he might not outright own several other businesses, he does have shares in them: in Gadgets, an electrical store; in Aquamarine Plumbing; in 'I Second

That Emulsion!'. Add what Dreadnought makes from these shares, to what he collects as protection money every month, to what he scores from freelance racketeering, smuggling, gambling and fighting, to what he's owed by around half the pubs in West London (or so it seems), and the picture becomes clear that Dreadnought is far from an impoverished man.

So why does he drive such a heap?

On the subject of money, I'm still not sure what salary I've been placed on. Needless to say, I have signed no contract; furthermore, to date at least, there seems to be no correlation between the difficulty of the task completed and the remuneration. A fixed rate for collections is fair enough; but I think I earned more than what I actually received for what happened ten days ago. This has scarred me.

ii

I'd known it would happen sooner or later: on that day I witnessed Dreadnought getting crisp – getting fervent. And it was over the dumbest of matters.

It lasted less than a few minutes. It followed on from our trip to Chinatown, to assist in the locating of an errant Japaneseman. The fact that the absconded one – a Mr Rakishomo – could be anywhere by now, I continued to keep to myself. It's sometimes best to keep such fancies to yourself, around Dreadnought. Especially when he's got a bee in his bonnet. But of course the search was fruitless.

Brooker took the Tube from Leicester Square. Dreadnought and I returned to the car, where two pieces of paper were fluttering like eyelids from beneath each of the windscreen wipers. With no little show of disdain, Dreadnought plucked the first – a flyer, an advertisement, of all things, for a hypnotist's services ('Want to give up smoking? I can help!') – and then the second: a parking ticket. As Dreadnought was shaking his head at the injustice, I was more concerned with the burly Samoan guy approaching.

'What do you cunts do for encores, eh?' the approaching man wanted to know. 'Where d'you leave your brain this morning?'

It was cool the way that Dreadnought took a few extra seconds to complete his reading of the parking ticket. Theatrically, then, he looked up at the accuser. 'Are you talking to me, by any chance?' he asked.

'Yeah I'm talking to you, idiot. Who else?'

Dreadnought addressed me. 'Stay where you are, mate,' he said, although I'd made no move to intercept the advance.

'What seems to be the trouble?' Dreadnought went on.

I thought at that point that the man might explode from apoplexy. It was perfectly clear what the trouble was: on Dreadnought's command I had doubleparked the car, there having been no other alternative.

'I can't get out, can I, genius?'

'Would you like me to move my vehicle?' said Dreadnought.

'Obviously!'

'Then why don't you ask nicely – before I tell my man to teach you some manners.' No mistaking the subtle change in tone.

The Samoan guy regarded me. 'Him?' I did my level best to appear as though I had a major ace in the hole. Two of me could have made up the man's bodyweight, and there would still be skin and bone left over.

'Do you know anything about martial arts, mate?' asked Dreadnought. 'Well, he does. If I tell him to jab your eyes out, he'll do it. Do you know why? Respect. Which you ain't showing me right now '

The man was backing down. 'Just move the car. I'm late.'

'You haven't apologised.'

'For what?'

'Raising your levels.'

'For fuck's sake – move it,' said the Samoan.

Dreadnought executed his stagey but cruel chuckle. 'Believe me, you worthless piece of crud,' he said, 'you ain't seen impatience till this cunt' (referring to me) 'loses his rag. I'm tempted to let him go for it, just to show you. Or shall I tell you about the time he did a karate jab at some poor fucker's chest? Knocked his heart out of place. Cunt bled to death.'

'I just want to get to my appointment,' the man said weakly.

'Which one's yours? Which restaurant?'

'I don't own a restaurant. I just wanna leave '

'Rene?' said Dreadnought. 'Get the toolbox. I don't like this wanker's tone one bit. Let's show him how to respect people.'

Throughout the altercation I had been holding my breath. Now I released it; the next thing had been made clear – and I was relieved. Violence: it was violence that was looming. What else had it ever been? But you don't think like that in such a situation.

I unlocked and opened the boot. Why didn't the big guy just lamp him one? Just give him a bloody nose – that would teach him a lesson, I thought.

I took out the toolbox. Well aware that this was as much of a test as I'd been given, I was equally clued up to the fact that I had to perform well. I sucked in an enormous breath. In my left hand I carried the metal receptacle, while in my right I held the metal claw hammer that I had just claimed from one of its slide-out trays.

No time was wasted, because I know that no time can be. As I approached the Samoan I did not ponder on how easy it would have been for Dreadnought to move the Bentley and ignore the insults. Instead I studied the pleading expression in the victim's eyes, and I swung the hammer. Instinctively he protected his face, but I was aiming much lower: at the backs of his knees. Contact. The large man fell down onto his kneecaps.

This was when Dreadnought leapt into life. His teeth bared, he got his hands on the back of the man's rippling neck and forced his head forward, saying, 'Swallow it!' The man's brown mouth opened wide. Guided by Dreadnought, his head fixed firmly over the exhaust pipe – and I was scared. This was escalating too fast.

'Keys!' Dreadnought was screaming. 'Gimme your keys!'

The man's mouth was trying to digest the bitter pill of the rusting exhaust pipe, and was held in place by Dreadnought's clammy fists.

'Hold the cunt!' said Dreadnought, and I shock myself with this – but there is a buzz to perpetrating manic viciousness. I held the Samoan's head onto the exhaust pipe with a full sense of nervous righteousness in place. Dreadnought had opened up the driver's side.

The first time I had a sense of misplacement was when the engine fired – when the big guy wriggled in earnest. But I managed to hold on.

It was horrific. The fumes burped into the victim's mouth, and leaked from his nostrils like drug-smoke. His eyes turned red. Then his eyeballs wandered east and west, and I didn't know – honestly – if we had killed him or not.

I let him go. He fell to the side as Dreadnought continued to rev.

Unhurriedly, Dreadnought then made his way back to the Bentley's passenger seat and I made mine back to the driver's. 'I hope he's okay,' my conscience could not forbid me from saying.

'I hope he's not,' said Dreadnought.

I started the engine on the tenth attempt. Not once did Dreadnought appear out of sorts or to be experiencing impatience; not once.

'Let's go back to mine,' he suggested. 'We can start early.'

iii

Sometimes it's like a juggernaut skidding on an acre of black ice, it's an evening or early morning wreck; other times it's akin to chasing a feather, or a fluff of pollen, on the breeze. There are no guarantees.

The first time I became aware of what I had (or of what had me), I was six. I was lying in bed, presumed asleep. It was late on a Friday night, and any minute now the fireworks would begin; Friday night was when my uncle and aunt became frisky. They would sit in the kitchen with a bottle of vodka and a huge hunk of meat, gouging off chunks and laughing like halfwits, as the juices oozed and dribbled down their chins. Caveman scenes, believe me; and I know how bacchanalic things got because even then I was useless at sleeping and I used to sit on the stairs and peer through the crack between the door and its jamb. Inevitably I'd be discovered and sent to bed, which I now concede must have been what I was longing for; but I can remember wondering why I was never allowed to join in the fun.

Aunt Else would sit in Hektor's lap and wriggle on his still-clothed erection. And I would listen to their drunken progress through the house. The sounds were frightening. Lying in bed, I would paint moving pictures: I could see them as they traversed the dark oblique of the rickety stairway: I could see them, printed onto the patches of darkness in front of my eyes. Aunt Else's wide *derrière*, swishing back and forth in her petti-coats and long skirts. And Hektor's face mere inches from the fabric, with his hands on her hips for balance as they climbed.

The bedroom scenes were the worst. I had to squeeze my ears with my palms, as the brass bed began to whinny and bray. Maybe it was the drink that kept him going, or held him back from his prize, but Hektor was quite a goer. Nor do I now assume that as a child I elongated the events in the way that children will. The Friday nights shared by Else and Hektor were no three minute thank-yous. They went the distance.

I couldn't stand to hear it: those grumbles and groans and spiky intakes of breath. If the headboard wasn't knock-ing dents into the wallpaper, Else's backside was – as they per-formed standing up for a while. I could see it all. Every shift of position, every thrust, every lunge, every parry; every bite, every claw, every kiss. Although the information was unbidden and unwanted – detested – it swelled in my head and scoured my sinuses. I would awake on a Saturday morning with flu symptoms, more often than not. Sometimes I would be ex-cused my meagre chores, but just as often I'd be called a shirker and told to pull on some britches.

Now – here in London – my objective is to see further both ways down the time line. I want to see how it all works out. Wouldn't you? An aesthetic but also an intellectual instinct pulses. I need to know how far back I can glimpse through the mists of time. But I want to go forward as well: fast forward, though it might end be expensive on the nerves.

Are you aware, sir comes a woman's voice – from the toaster that I have installed, unnecessarily, into the same hotel room that I checked into weeks and weeks ago: my room at the Dol-phin Hotel. My first thought is: *I've got to get out of this room.* The toaster's slit has become a mouth; its metal lips are moving slowly. *I've got to get out,* I tell the toaster's beautiful voice. My flat in a block on Fellows Road, Swiss Cottage, will welcome me home in three days' time; for now I have no choice in where not to sleep.

The toaster has not finished speaking.

…*aware, sir*…

It's an echo: a time-echo. Immediately I know what is about to happen. The carpet thins like a speeded-up tape of a man's head encountering male pattern baldness.

But we are not travelling forward: spinning quickly, mad-ly, burning. We are travelling *backwards*. The carpet has gone; my feet are on a hard stone floor. The scene is familiar: it's the one I've been waiting for. The air is like the deep-freeze at Beef Encounter.

I'm in a waiting room again.

iv

'Are you aware, sir, of the name of Leonardo Da Vinci?' Katherine asked, her eyes shining into mine.

I watched as Katherine unfastened her portmanteau. One Sunday a few months earlier, Katherine had shown me what I was certain she was about to show my brother – and a rank stranger.

'He was born in the year of Our Lord 1452 and died in 1519,' said Katherine. The paper was pressed between two uneven pieces of thin wood. 'But he produced this plan,' Kath-erine continued, 'for a vehicle called *The Seahorse*. As you might observe, his imagination was a fiery item.'

The paper was in good condition.

'What is it?' asked Edward. He was handed the flimsy article.

Katherine said, 'It is the original of Da Vinci's plans for a vehicle that travels underwater. He called it *The Seahorse*, as I say.'

'Good grief,' said Mondo. 'May I?'

As though he were handing over the Crown Jewels, Edward passed the parcel. Mondo could only shake his head.

'I have to ask you, Katherine,' he said. 'Howsoever did such an item come into your possession?'

Katherine cocked her head. 'A long story, sir. And one from which my family line, I fear, does not emerge unscathed or unsullied.'

'Do tell,' said Edward.

But I happened to know the story: Katherine had given me all of the salient details on that same occasion. Nor was I ignorant to the fact that Katherine, a spinster and only supported financially by occasional jobs in a laundry, was keeping the plan for a rainy day.

I also knew why Katherine was travelling to the capital. She had accepted a cleaning job in that expensive city in order to be nearer to her ailing sister – the mother to the nephew with the comically-advantageous ears. And I was aware that she desperately needed money to help her kind.

'My family has served for generations,' said Katherine. 'A cousin of mine was working for a German aristocrat named Hugh Bargeld. He did not treat her well, sir. When he got her with child, he discarded her onto the street – but not before Eliza took her parting gifts. Some ornate spoons, some etchings, a silver goblet – and this Da Vinci, which had been accumulating wealth in the old man's study. When Eliza died, it came to me, and I confess that I knew not what to do with it.'

'It is gold,' said Mondo. 'Goodness gracious, words fail me, Kathy.' His frown was as loud as my brother's. Quickly he added: 'I must have this.' He spoke into her eyes with his own. 'What price are you asking?'

Katherine smiled. 'Are you expecting me to discard a family heirloom, sir?' she replied.

'Someone else's family heirloom.'

'Well, yes,' she conceded.

'You cannot,' I finally offered. 'Not now, Katherine.'

Edward turned to face me. It was at this moment that I realised that silence as a natural state is bestowed with powerful benefits: when one does eventually unburden one's concerns, the telling is all the more potent for what hasn't come before.

'Lucy?' he either asked or demanded: at that moment it was hard to tell which. With holy men it often is.

Mondo was ignoring me. 'Kath, I'll give you fifty pounds,' he said.

'No, Katherine,' I interjected. Why? I wanted to be the one who helped Katherine. Ever since she had begun to confide in me, I had wanted to be the one who paved the path to Katherine's greater good. I loved her.

'Lucy?' said Katherine. The quizzical expression was love itself, I was certain; it made my heart soar, and sore.

The door opened. Rain-soaked, as sleek as an eel, the waiting room porter popped his head over the threshold to apologise for the lateness of the coach. 'It won't be much longer, ladies and gentlemen,' the boy offered.

Such warm air as was present soon evaporated, and was briskly replaced. The chill of the night raced in to pinch our noses. The door closed.

I was aware of the three pairs of eyes on me, so I said: 'I've been saving.'

Mondo was losing patience. 'Sixty, Miss Wollington,' he said, but looked at me.

'What would you want *The Seahorse* for?' asked my brother.

What could I tell him? Proof of an independent thought? A life? As a chance to give someone the sort of freedom that I personally yearned for?

'I'll give you seventy,' I said. In truth, I think I surprised myself. Where on earth would I obtain such a sum?

But it had to be me.

Edward stared. Again he repeated my name, and I almost told him to be quiet. It was only the fear of the future belt – the buckle, the strap – that sealed my lips. There was no doubt that Edward could be kind, but kindness was but a fraction of his emotional repertoire.

I faced him. 'Please, Edward,' I said.

Outside, a commotion. It was not the result of the storm, but rather of what had defied it: the coach was arriving.

'Please what, my sister?'

'The money, Edward,' I replied. 'Consider it an investment.'

'Seventy-five,' said Mondo the Magnificent.

'Please, Edward.' For the first time I was aware of the ravaging tears in my eyes.

'Lucy?' said Katherine.

'Please,' I said once more, softly, intending to convey a host of emotions, the predominant one being that of desperation. I couldn't bear the thought of a stranger owning my loved one's keepsake.

I was jealous.

Of a sudden, Edward flailed. 'My dear sister,' he said, embarrassed, 'don't cry.'

Horse-hooves clipped closer.

'Darling?'

'I'm all right, Edward,' I responded with my face imprisoned in my fingers.

His arm an anchor on my shoulders, Edward led me through the rain to the coach. Katherine and Mondo followed. The night was grim.

And then money changed hands.

Eighty pounds.

Mondo resembled a man who had had his home burned to the ground. He was seething.

'Enjoy,' I told Katherine as the horses snorted, drank the air, and pulled us forward. My skin was as cold as wine-bottle glass in a cellar. I closed my eyes and smiled.

But now do you wish to hear the truth of it all? Dear Reader, here it comes. Not once since that evening have I seen or heard of my confidante, my friend. Nor has she adhered to her promise to write to me regularly. I have yet to receive a reply to a single letter that I've written.

Never again have I heard of Mondo the Magnificent. To nobody else whom I have asked is the showman's name familiar.

And I am frightened of viewing what it was that I bought. I don't want to know.

v

'What is stronger than betrayal?' he asked me suddenly, an hour or so before we'd been to Ealing to meet the Japaneseman who wanted another Japaneseman located; an hour before the altercation with the Samoan. 'You can count the number of trustworthy cunts in your life on one hand. *You're* one.'

'Thanks.'

'And Mickey's another. Miserable bugger'll never find another governor like me.' Dreadnought chuckled. Did he suspect something?

'And Charlie Peacock?' I asked.

'Good as gold, mate,' said Dreadnought. 'But *someone's* going to betray me. Do you know why, Rene?'

'Why?'

'Because someone always does. It makes the world go round, mate. Betrayal. Believe me. The strongest emotion known to man. Now let's find this Japanese snot.'

vi

'Beef spear,' said Gary Brooker.

'Pork sword,' said Mickey.

'Spam javelin,' said Charlie Peacock.

It was eleven a.m. The venue, of course, was The Bloody Chamber. Depending on who you asked, we were having a cheeky few, a pensive pint, or a quiet couple. In other words, we were drinking heavily at mid-morning, with the daylight full of pigeon cries and traffic burps from the open door behind our backs. A workman was fiddling about with a problem on the hinges. The air was cold. Not to warm ourselves, but simply to keep the long, dead hours full and the boredom at bay, the boys were colluding and competing on euphemisms for the word *penis*, based strictly (for some reason) on a combination of meat + weapon. Eager to fit in, as ever, I offered up: 'Turkey truncheon.'

Brooker nodded approvingly, and Peacock laughed. I wouldn't have expected much of a reaction from a surly brute like Mickey (and I didn't get much of one): his involvement in such pub pranks is strictly for the sake of appearances, not for fun. Not even to kill time. Mickey participates for one reason and one reason only: it's part of the job.

But at least it seems that I've been accepted.

'Salami scimitar,' said Brooker.

Three weeks in from my hiding in the cemetery of St Nathaniel the Decisive, and we are all part of one big roguish, red-nosed family. No idea did I have at the time – no real idea – of how close I had got to the man himself; but at least the disciples were letting me play.

No one could trump Brooker's effort so we started to talk about his sex life instead. While continuing to pursue an elusive beauty named Angie, young Gary is nevertheless keen to fulfil any of fate's subtle twists. Two nights earlier, for example, he had first serenaded and then 'noshed' a Chinese-American student of Bioethic Philosophy (whatever that might be: perhaps he had misheard) in a bar called Denim Jackie's.

It was at this moment that we were joined by another circle of characters. Along came Peephole Pete (porn) and Frank the Ferret.

'You remember Frank,' said Mickey, surprisingly.

'Yeah. You lifted my watch, you cunt.'

'I did indeed.' Frank chuckled. 'Not a cunt in the world safe – not when *I* get the urge. I could steal the beard from your face, mate,' he boasted.

Charlie tipped his empty glass at my chin (it was my round, again) and said, 'We was talking about your beard, as it goes, the other day: me and Dreadnought. He don't like it.'

Inexplicably shaken by this news, I moved quickly onto the subject of my invitation to Dreadnought's home this evening, a mere eight hours from now: my first visit.

Charlie shrugged. 'He's never invited me,' he said. 'But it's simple, mate. Mind your *p*'s and *q*'s and don't spill no beans on the floor. What you think – he's gonna ask you over if he hates you? Come off it. He's got something lined up for you.'

'Are you sure?'

'Either that or he wants to *give you one*.' Charlie chuckled.

I ordered the drinks.

Not even four hours after I had entered The Bloody Chamber, Dreadnought walked through the (still wide open) door. For dramatic effect, he did so with an ambulance siren squealing behind his shoulder blades. He bid us all a warm welcome. He ordered the next drink. He apologised for being late. 'I had to go and see me mum,' he explained.

I want to meet her. But she was to die, of course, between this casual gathering and the nonsense with Mr Samoa in Chinatown.

When the general hubbub had died down – the excitement at seeing our beloved one more time – he enquired as to the progress of our various tasks. Charlie Peacock informed him that the search for the Japaneseman – whose name, it turned out, was Tanigawa – was ongoing. 'Well, what you doing in here then?' he patiently queried. 'The van's ready; Rene collected it from Wrighty. Just find the twat.'

Charlie and Mickey left.

'You, Brooker – I want you to do something else,' said Dreadnought, lighting a cigar. He polished off his brandy – a double – in one swallow. 'Go over to Denim Jackie's. There's a character there called Tommy Dwyer. He's playing in a band called The Haunted tonight.'

Brooker nodded. By now – already, so soon – he knew the score. 'What should I give him? A tickle? A spank?' he asked.

'Nothing. Just listen to what he has to say. Another one, Dave, if you'd be so kind,' said Dreadnought to the barman. Then he returned his attention to us. 'This is at the request of Bernie Acapulco. A little job he wants doing. Play it by ear, mate. I don't think it's physical.'

'So it's not a collection,' Brooker wanted to clarify.

'I didn't say that. Take your mobile. Eight o'clock.'

'Tommy Dwyer,' Brooker repeated. 'How will I know him?'

Dreadnought sniffed. 'It won't be hard to recognize him – he looks like Bill Wyman. In fact, he was in one of them tribute bands once – the Roaring Stones – and our Tommy there tried to sue the cunt.'

'Sue Wyman?' said Brooker. 'Why?'

'Well he left the Rolling Stones, didn't he? So from that point on our Tommy's not in his band. You can't have a tribute band that don't look like the original, can you?'

'I suppose not.'

'*Course* not. So he had to leave, and then he tried to sue Bill Wyman for loss of future earnings. Didn't get very far, needless to say.'

Brooker nodded. 'Do you know what? If I was Bill Wyman I'd-a paid the twat. Pay up and make him look stupid. What's ten grand to a rock star?'

'But why would you want to make an East End villain look stupid?'

'Ah! But Wyman don't *know* he's a villain, does he? Probably just thought it was some tit in a trance on the take. Which it was.'

A few minutes later, we finished our drinks. Some of the foam inched back to the base of my glass. Dreadnought's face was all business.

'We got work to do,' he told me and Brooker. 'How much you had?'

'About eight pints,' I answered.

'You?'

Brooker said, 'Ten.'

'Right, Rene – you're driving.'

I had donned my overcoat; I had pocketed my purse of tobacco and my packet of cigarette skins. We were about to leave. I had even reached the wide open door, and could hear the outside din. But one more sound claimed my attention before I ventured out.

'Oi, Rene!'

I turned. It was Frank the Ferret, with a smile on his face.

'You might be needing this at some point.'

Rotating like a frisbee, an object crossed the bar. I ducked and caught it, and then brought it to my face with full astonishment. My wallet.

'Don't ever tell a bloke like me you're safe,' he said. 'Red rag, mate.'

It was not until I got outside that I checked that all of the cards and the (limited) amount of cash were present.

'How old are you, Frank?' I asked loudly. A few heads turned.

Frank looked sheepish – and I hadn't even reached the punchline. 'Thirty-seven.'

'So why don't you stop acting like a kid?' I said. 'We all know you can steal better than anyone else, so what's in it for you to carry on proving it? Have some *pride*, for Christ's sake.'

Outside, Dreadnought was smiling. As we made our way to his dilapidated Bentley, he released the thought. 'Don't expect that to be the last of *that*,' he warned.

'Oh I'm scared,' I replied. 'A little minge like that: what's he gonna do? Arrange a hit squad? Don't make me laugh, Dreadnought.'

'He could steal the liver from your ribcage, mate.'

I snorted. 'He can have it. It's worthless.'

IV. Trite

i

Casting jealousy to the wind, I will now talk about Gary Brooker. The look of the Country Irish; his pale, nigh-on albino lips; the carrot crop; the brute ambition. Brooker got his first solo flight before I did. And at the time it really fucked me off.

ii

Neither early nor late, Brooker arrived at Denim Jackie's at seven. He was anxious. Not knowing what to expect from the encounter, he had donned his smartest clothes and shaved. 'I was told to ask for Tommy Dwyer,' he said.

'Name?'

'Brooker. For Dreadnought.'

In a back room he met Tommy Dwyer, a skinny rake of a man wearing a baseball cap and a tracksuit. He was also sporting an impressively heavy medallion and a cautious sneer that evaporated as soon as Brooker had introduced himself. 'Nice to meet you. What do you know?'

'Nothing.' A mistake, as I later told the boy. 'Dreadnought told me to listen to what you had to say.'

They moved into a back room off the back room. A smell rose up to greet them. Brooker would describe the scent as akin to an African safari – not that he'd ever been on an African safari.

Or ever would.

iii

This evening, svelte, lithe and incorrigible, Dreadnought came galloping into my dreams. He was dressed in black. He wore a highwayman's hat. Cocksure, with a pistol in his gloved hand, he has waved down a passing carriage. And he does it – he actually says it:

'Your money or your life.'

The sky is the colour of a bruised pear, but there is a purity to the oxygen that I can feel from three hundred years away. The air is alive with a cleansing rain; it is smoothing away the nearby river's stench. The picture I have is far from clear, but I watch in expectation as the carriage's hirers – both men – strip themselves of cash and belongings, rather than getting their faces filled with gunpowder. And then Dreadnought peeps over the window frame; he wears a black mask, a heavy frown; his eyes glint.

'And I would also require that portmanteau, sir,' he says.

There is something familiar about the voice, the scene. I have been here before, in my dreams. Even in the dubious light I sense that I know the man wielding the weapon. My mind is cast back to the similarly dreadful evening in the waiting room.

The grey-haired but youthful man sitting hipside to the far window pales. 'You can't have this, sir,' he replies.

'It's entirely your choice.' This is Dreadnought. 'I would ask you to step down from the carriage, sir,' he continues.

'You don't understand.' The grey-haired man raises his right arm. There is an issue of chains tying his wrist to the portmanteau. 'I am merely a pawn in this game.'

Does Dreadnought smile beneath that mask? 'My dear sir,' he says. 'I regret to inform you that a pawn's life is verily a short one. Climb down,' Dreadnought orders.

'I do not carry the keys, sir,' the man complains.

'Then I will take your arm off, sir,' says Dreadnought, without a pause.

And I can see the skies – I can smell the lust of the river, and it must be the Thames. A vein is pulsing on the side of Dreadnought's neck. The courier has no way of knowing if Dreadnought is offering an idle threat, but down the man climbs; filthy water from a long-filled puddle soaks his shoes.

'Lift up your arm,' says Dreadnought.

Not a word of protest is offered – not from the courier, nor his travelling companion; and certainly not from the driver, who has set up the caper in the first place – and Dreadnought pokes his pistol into the armpit.

'Now lower it,' Dreadnought continues.

The weapon is sandwiched, and I am convinced that this pantomime of crime – will end with a sniff, a sigh, and with Dreadnought galloping off into the heather. It's inevitable.

Like the quivering courier (no doubt) I am awaiting the final warning – the snarled threat. But there is no last chance, not in Dreadnought's world. Instead there is a crack of thunder: Dreadnought has pulled the trigger and the gunpowder has ignited.

It's a phantasmagorical sight. Accompanied by its precious cargo, the arm leaps up into the air, like a circus dog. Having come away from its owner, it flips and ducks, with its trail of bloodspots like a comet's streak. I can smell the anguish, above the river's garlic breath. Spots of blood and spots of rain collide, midair.

Even before the pain is a fact, the man is screaming.

We all watch as his arm splashes down in a different puddle from the one that has ruined his footwear. Lopsided and unbalanced, the man falls over in the rain. Immediately his face takes on a patina of squelchy mud; for a second, as he writhes, it appears as though he is attempting to snort up the landscape.

Calmly, Dreadnought collects the portmanteau. Bizarre is the sight of him tucking the other man's arm beneath his own. With his free hand he orders the second traveller down from the carriage: a flick of the pistol. The other man shakes in his boots; he is crying. He believes that he will also die. Babbling something about having nothing else to hand over, he sets his feet on *terra firma*.

It occurs to me, not to query Dreadnought's morality or the fairness of the situation. It occurs to me to query where Dreadnought's horse might be. How on earth was he to make good his escape? Then I have it.

'Turn around, sir,' says Dreadnought.

Blubbing and lip-synching some muttered gobbledegook, the older man does as he has been instructed. I can feel the tension in his back.

Dreadnought does not shoot. He scales his way up into the carriage, and without another word being uttered, the horse's spine is clicked with the reins. The horse drags the carriage on. By way of farewell, Dreadnought pushes the severed arm out of the window and shakes it by the elbow so that the hand makes a kind of goodbye wave.

The driver and Dreadnought, I understand firmly: in cahoots. Rain like a falling river, a deadened percussion on the carriage's roof. And Dreadnought is about to tear down his mask. I want to see.

I woke up with the room spinning madly about me.

iv

Dreadnought took a toke on a cigar the size of a Labrador's foreleg. The smoke he exhaled was strangely pinkish in the light.

I squared my shoulders and finished my fourth brandy. Maintaining the guise of this being entirely off-the-cuff, I told him: 'I was betrayed at the earliest possible age. My parents died. They abandoned me, and I can't forgive 'em, even now.'

Dreadnought shrugged. 'That's a tough one for a nipper,' he conceded.

'You bet your arse it is. Which is why I know how badly betrayal can hurt,' I went on.

Me, the great betrayer.

Blowing smoke into my face, Dreadnought said, 'You know what I like about you, Rene? It's your confidence. Your spunk. You're not afraid to play, even if you get your balloon burst. He sniffed. 'Let's get some lunch,' he announced.

v

Do you know what Dreadnought's hobby is?

You may well believe that his timekillers are legion, what with all the thieving, extortion, fighting, joking and bad-egg-iness with which he decorates his day; but I'm referring to something that has no connection to earning a living.

Despite evidence to the contrary on the evening that Dreadnought and I dined together, Dreadnought likes to cook. More times than not he'll nuke a pizza or scratch open a tin of something, but when he has a few hours on his hands he actually cooks. Elaborately fulsome in his adjectives, he told me of the magisterial status of his farmhouse bake, and promised me that on my next visit he would prepare the same dish. 'As close as I like to get to the countryside,' he joked.

I stood in his kitchen, as if on guard, and I was eager to make conversation – or rather to appear un-cowed by the man's formidable presence. I said to him again: 'I grew up on a farm, you know.'

'Did it stink of cowshit the whole time?'

I smiled. 'Yeah it did, as a matter of fact.'

'You know what the only good thing about the country-side is, don't you, mate?' said Dreadnought.

'What's that?'

'It's the safest place to be when they drop the bomb.'

Later, he asked: 'Do you know why most criminals don't cook? Because most cookery books are a plate of *arse*, mate. What you want is a book that explains difficult meals in simple but entertaining language.'

I shrugged. 'It must exist – a book like that,' I replied.

He turned to face me. 'I been thinking of writing one myself.'

'A cookery book?'

'For *real* people, like.'

Dreadnought told me the proposed title. I had to sink ale to keep my wits about me.

'You don't like the title,' Dreadnought said sternly.

'No publisher will touch it, mate.'

'Why not?'

'Cooking for *Cunts*?' I repeated. 'You're joking, aren't you?'

But it was clear from the wounded expression on Dread-nought's face that he hadn't been joking at all. It occurred to me to wonder what the last book was that Dreadnought had read.

'It's just a bit strong, mate, that's all.'

'The "Cunts" bit?' he wanted to clarify.

I nodded. 'The "Cunts" Is where I see a possible obstacle.'

'I see.' He was pensive. 'What about "Arseholes"?' he enquired. His countenance was all robust professionalism. 'I'll settle for "Arseholes".'

'Cooking for Arseholes.'

He nodded. 'If I can't have a "cunt" I'll have an "arse-hole",' he told me.

'Yeah I've heard that rumour. It's a step in the right direction,' was all I could think of. Horror crawled across my skin.

'Let's *write* the little fucker, eh? Let's just write it.'

'I'm stunned,' I admitted.

'Yeah not bad is it.'

'But Dreadnought,' I said, 'I haven't got the faintest idea of how to write a cook book.'

He responded with a lazy sneer. 'You can type, can't you? Well let's make some cash then. What's your problem? Put our heads together.'

From an overhead cupboard Dreadnought took down a tubular tin of biscuits, an acquisition from Harrods. 'Have one,' he said, wrenching off the lid. Inside there were no biscuits: the tin was where Dreadnought kept his most expensive cigars.

'Special occasion, like.'

'True,' I agreed.

'You won't believe how much these didn't cost me, Rene.' Dreadnought found this droll. 'Life's so expensive these days.'

A presentiment of paranoia had wormed its way through the drink. What if I was being tested? What if Dreadnought was using the partnership as a way of getting into my apartment? What if he's already seen this manuscript?

'Do you know how to make a cheese sauce?' he asked me.

'Sure. A slab of cheese, a pint of milk, a microwave. It's physics.'

'Jesus. Talk about the slow boat to China,' said Dreadnought, irrelevantly (I think).

'Well how then?' I asked.

'No, do it your own way. We'll get these finer details later on. But don't get no ash in the effing mixture!' he warned.

Deciding to change the subject, I said, 'About my beard '

Dreadnought was content to embrace the novelty. Without further enticement he told me: 'I don't like it. They say it hides a guilty conscience or summing.'

'And what's wrong with that?' I wanted to know.

Dreadnought smiled. 'I take your point. But I still don't like it.'

vi

Flex is coming on like a gangster again – it's a full moon thing. Guy goes crazy. He goes around breaking beer bottles on football supporters' heads, giving it mental. Inciting violence, as they say on the box. *Fucking Flex*.

Take tonight. We're at Scottish Tony's, and Mujahid and me have got the headgear on; we're in the ring. We've set the receptors to max to show Scottish Tony what tough guys we are on the Bone that he sells us – just to keep him selling it, really. Guy likes the cabaret. So Mujahid cleans up in the first round, landing me a doozy on the chin. The receptors pick it up, twist it, pickle it, and turn it from pain to libido. Like, I'm already hard from a couple of lucky jabs he's got in – but this one knocks me over and I shudder and come in my jockstrap.

After that I'm weak – that's the idea – but I still manage to give the cunt a right seeing-to. A kick in the shins and we're diving for cover. He's shit himself. I lay in. By the time he's orgasmed, I'm a blob on the floor – and Flex calls, 'Wahid. Some business, mate.'

There's no time to shower, apparently. The three of us go out the back way and climb into Flex's car. We're used to quick getaways.

'What's the story?' asks Muji.

'It's Del. They've killed Del,' Flex replies.

Goose is waiting for us. Miniskirt, fit as fuck. 'It was brutal, man,' she says. 'He was just dancing.' She was in the Peapod, she tells us – a low-morale club. You get earplugs on the door, you get tuned in; it's supposed to make everyone act exactly the same, you go out of your skull, but some guys take it as a challenge and swallow some protective software before they go in, dodging the homogeneity. 'They laid into him with tyre-jacks.'

Well, we can all see what happened next.

Flex has gone silent. 'Get his head, Muji,' I say, but I don't have the weight.

'Get his head yourself,' I hear. '*I* ain't touching it.'

I pick up the head. Some red stuff's leaking down from the ragged towpath of the incision. Blood kisses me on the expensively-booted toe.

'No one else saw?' Flex pipes up.

Goose says no. 'One minute we're all slamdancing, the next there's four of 'em pushing Del out the door.'

'Did the management see?'

'Don't think so. Well, they haven't called no one if they did.' Goose is aggrieved. 'Flex, I didn't know these guys,' she goes on. 'But it didn't look random, man.'

Well, you don't say. Cutting off a guy's head in a public place is about as unrandom as it gets, wouldn't you agree?

'I'm gonna get who done this,' Flex mumbles – and you know with a guy like Flex, when he starts mumbling, when he starts giving out the gangster vibe and not concentrating on making himself look good, there's a lot of static in his head.

I wrap Del's head in my jacket and lay it carefully in the

boot of Flex's car. We're all waiting – even Goose – for Flex to pick up the baton. Biting the bullet I say, 'Back to mine.'

'No,' Flex replies, finally goaded. '*Mine*.'

Don't think any of us are looking forward to dissolving Del's body in the bath.

I can't resist one last attempt to look good in front of Goose. Or maybe I'm feeling a bit sorry for Flex. I volunteer to help move the body, even though I've already done my bit with the head. I get blood in my lap

Flex says to Goose, 'What did you see tonight?'

'I was in the Peapod, ripped to fuck.'

'Flex?' says Muji – but I've seen it too. As we're lifting Del's body into the boot, his shirt rides up and we see some thin flesh-coloured wires leading down to below his trouser line. Disrespectful to the dead or not, I lift the shirt higher. There's a small flat rectangle of opaque plastic, taped to Del's chest.

'He's been recording someone,' says Muji.

A receptor on his chest, a receptor in the groin – and of course, when we get him to Flex's we all know we'll find he's wearing software-encoded lenses.

He was recording someone and storing what he saw and felt in the central receptor – on his chest. 'We'll plug the fucker in when we get back,' Flex tells us.

This is what we watch.

There's a woman in a kitchen, peeling nicotine patches from her forearms with a look on her face that says *cured*. Never again will I need to smoke. Never again will the smell make me feel wistful. She sets fire to the cigarette box and watches the pyre with a brandy in her hand.

Then she springcleans with some music playing.

The kids come home from school. One's in the Sixth

Form and is not wearing a uniform; her mother calls her Sandra. The boy's younger and he tugs off a regulation tie.

'You're in a good mood,' Sandra says.

'I've quit,' their mother explains.

'Well I haven't. Look what Scottish Tony got me.' And Sandra fishes in her schoolbag for a rubber balloon. Very carefully she squeezes out some white powder. 'Want some?'

'Share with your brother.'

Though Sandra makes a face she calls out Tom's name.

The recording can just make out the boy shouting, 'What?'

'Do you want some Bone?'

'I'm watching cartoons!'

Sandra smiles and while the mother fills the kettle Sandra dips her head to the surface of the table and hoovers up.

'And that's your lot before dinner,' her mother tells her.

'What are we having?' Sandra asks.

'Chicken.'

Flex, Muji and I are looking at each other, having played the recording again. The girl got her gear from Scottish Tony. This means we have a place to start.

Del was a good guy, but I'm not cut up about his murder – not like Flex is. These things happen. What's the point of getting yourself lathered up about it? Del was a victim.

I go back to Tony's. By now it's nearly midnight, but there's a few late-nighters on the cycles, on the rowers. Tony's surprised to see me. He thinks I'm here for some more Bone. 'You know my rule, man,' he says, 'only one transaction per customer per day.'

'I'm here about a squaw. You supply Bone to her daughter. Her name's Sandra.'

'I could probably give you a number if you gave me a good reason.'

'How about a ton?'

To my surprise Scottish Tony shakes his head. 'Not talking about cash,' he replies. 'How about a real reason?'

'Flex wants to keep it quiet. Del's been killed. They sawed his head off.'

'It's impossible,' Scottish Tony replies. 'Guy was in here – twenty minutes ago.'

'I picked his head off a dustbin, Tony. It weren't connected to his body.'

'Del was in here, Wahid – I *spoke* to the cunt! We talked about horses.'

The three of us are at Flex's place.

Del is in the bath. It must've been Muji who wedged or balanced the head back on the shoulders – Flex is in a bit of a scramble – and it must've been Muji who cleaned the blood off the face.

What I was hoping was – I'd get to his place and Flex would go, 'You'll never guess the mistake we've made.' We'd have a giggle. We'd go over and give Goose a slap for being so dim and everyone's all right – apart from the poor bastard in the tub.

'Scottish Tony got it wrong,' Flex says. 'What else can it be?'

'But he talked to him!'

'He *says* he talked to him. Did you call the girl's number?'

'I thought *you* might want to.'

Flex nods and thanks me. 'In the morning. It's nearly two o'clock, she'll be asleep.'

'Is it a school day tomorrow?' asks Muji.

Nobody knows. No one can remember what day it is. We look at Del. He was the one who always kept the facts and figures straight; he was our glue – before he left us. I don't think Flex has ever forgiven his stepbrother for that.

Flex keeps chemicals in his larder, just in case. He never tires of telling us what work it is to mutilate a guy.

'We've got a choice,' he says now. 'We can dispose of the evidence or we can wait until we find his ex – if we find him – while the body's here.'

He makes it sound like no choice at all, really, but all the same I feel that Del deserves more than a protozolal acid bath.

'Listen, guys. Why don't I head over to Happy-Go-Lucky.' That's the club that Del liked best; it's where he met his partners, more often than not. Torture-cum-camp. 'I'll take Goose, to see if we might identify the cunts that did this.'

Muji said, 'Wahid, she ain't gonna give you one so forget about it.'

'Call her,' says Flex.

So it's me and Goose, in Goose's car, and it's a sunny day. This is about a year ago. She's a bit suspicious but she's agreed to come with me on a picnic. It's taken some pleading.

We're in a field and there's nothing to see. Just me and Goose on a blanket with the cool-box; we're eating lunch and I'm thinking about getting her clothes off, and suddenly up comes this guy, going on about private property. I'm losing face in front of Goose, big time, and so I tell him to piss off, we'll go when we're ready. To my surprise he walks away, up over a ridge – and I'm just tucking into a beer when I see him on his way back down again. Only this time he's carrying something.

A sword. One of them curvy ones, like pirates wield. A

cutlass, is it? 'Get up,' I say to Goose, not exactly bothered about looking like a flower. What's funny is, she doesn't resemble greased lightning as she rises to her feet, I can tell you that, and she goes, 'Fight him, Wahid. Sort him out!' Like she's well excited.

It's a stern test of my lust for Goose. I can stay and fight and risk getting myself hacked to pieces, or we can both make a run for Goose's car. The latter being a bit of a gamble in itself: if Goose is so keen to see me murdered, how can I be sure she'll bother to get the key in the ignition quickly? My third alternative is to wrestle the key away from Goose and drive away, with or without her. Not much of an alternative, of course – I never did learn to drive.

'All right, man, we're going,' I call, hoping that diplomacy will be enough. I don't care about letting Goose down.

He's getting closer and it occurs to me to wonder where on earth he got a sword from.

'I warned you, mate,' he answers. 'You can't say I didn't warn you.'

'Yeah, you warned me. I apologise. We're leaving. Come on, Goose.' I claim her hand.

Though she doesn't protest she does say, 'What about the picnic stuff?'

'I'll buy you a new cool-box. Come on.'

We get to the car, and Errol Flynn's just behind me. I manage to get the door locked as the cutlass clunks against the window. What I wouldn't have given for a gun!

'My car!' Goose complains.

'Well drive then!' I tell her.

As she moves forward along the dirt road we followed, our attacker tries to get in the way. The car clips his hip; he falls, screaming. And then Goose does a funny thing. She stops

– and I'm just about to start worrying about her developing a guilty conscience and checking that he's all right – when she engages reverse gear and we whine our way back towards him. This takes me by surprise.

So does the thump as we make contact – a thump that's surely not enough to represent having run over his entire body.

He's there, in the dust we've kicked up, rolling around. I'm not certain how I feel at seeing he's still alive. I think I indulged in a good deal of bad thoughts on his part.

'What should I do?' says Goose.

Now she asks me! 'Is he still holding the sword?'

'No, he dropped it.' She points.

Cautiously I exit the vehicle. At the very least I need to go over and kick him about a bit if I hope to stop Goose gossiping about what she'll call my cowardice. I approach him. It looks like his leg's fucked, his left leg. He's making some noise.

Private property, I keep thinking. What if his brothers of friends or security people turn up now? Or was it just a lie?

When I'm within range he risks hurting himself by rolling over to reach for the sword. I'm quicker than he can ever hope to be. I kick his arm away and stoop down for the weapon – and that's when things get confusing. As I catch hold of the sword, he catches hold of me. We wriggle. My footing slips; I fall – I fall not quite on top of him, but partly.

The sword trenches into his forehead.

Guy starts screaming. I'm struggling to get away from him but he's panicking and gripping hold, and there's blood all over my shirt – it's coming up like a garden sprinkler. And I just know – because that's the way things are – that someone's gonna turn up right now – but it doesn't happen. We're like two squaws in mud at clubs like Alpines. I lay into him. I lay into him with my free hand, but it isn't long before I'm using the sword. Instinct's taken over. He passes out. I roll away.

Breathing hard for a couple of moments, I look over to where Goose is now standing. She walks closer, her mouth covered by her hands, an expression both appeased and appalled on her face.

What worries me more than being thought of as a coward is the thought of how many people Goose might tell about what I've done. Start bragging of such things and just see how quickly the orderly queue forms – with men quite eager to disprove any notion of toughness.

'This is just between us, Goose,' I tell her.

'Okay.'

Wearily, expending great energy, I get to my feet. Between me and the attacker, we look like a butcher's dustbin. 'Get the picnic stuff. We were never here.'

I'm thinking about fingerprints when I talk about the picnic stuff, but I realise I'll have to take the sword as well. I don't want to go up over the hill in case there's someone waiting in the attacker's car, for whatever reason.

'I'll keep quiet on one condition,' says Goose.

'Which is?'

'I want a souvenir of our lovely day in the countryside,' she says.

Don't know why it's taken me something like three hours to acknowledge the similarities. But shock can slow things down for you, and perhaps I'm more shaken up than I imagined.

Del's been guillotined.

So was the guy on the day of the picnic. It was Goose's idea. 'A souvenir,' she called it – but we could both see that as a time-stalling tactic (and because I'd already damaged the neck quite badly and it'd be easypeasy to complete the mission) it wasn't a bad idea. It distanced me from the crime – by the time anyone managed to identify the body we'd be long away. And I never leave the city, so there'll be no way of tying me to the killing.

We took the head home in the cool-box.

But maybe they've found me, I realise now. Maybe Del was a warning.

Flex is gonna go spastic when he hears what happened a year ago. I don't see any choice in the matter – I'll have to tell him.

Goose is waiting in the Chaperone Zone, to the side of the Peapod. I honk the horn and one of the penguined bouncers gives me a *look*. The way I'm feeling now, I could go over there and glass the cunt – like Flex would – but there isn't time. Goose gets in.

'Did you take prophylactic software tonight?' I ask.

She's thought of this – it's clear in her *'Yeah, guy'* – she's thought of the question that someone was gonna ask: How did you get out of the Peapod to follow Del and the killers? The Peapod loops everyone together, via the plugs, and you're there as one for a slamdance. Usually – and I have to stress usually – you don't have the willpower to leave when you fancy – unless you've done the software. But why bother going in, Goose, I want to enquire, unless you're out to get ripped. I fail to pose the question.

I'm starting to wonder if Goose went into that building at all.

We arrive at Happy-Go-Lucky. We have to park four streets away because the area's rammed. There's an AI on the door: he gives me a sniff. And just above the din that's mushrooming out the doors I hear him say, 'Are you aware what kind of club this is?'

He means gay.

'She's my dominatrix,' I say.

'She doesn't *look* very domineering,' says the AI guy. 'And shouldn't *she* be speaking?'

'She told *me* to,' I answer.

We enter. Despite everything, Goose wants a drink. What's the time, Mr Wolf? It's half past four. I'm not as young as once I was and even the thought of alcohol makes me sleepy. I give Goose a twenty and I head off into the crowd. You don't need me to explain the sort of things I'm seeing, I'm sure.

There's Billy. In his basketball get-up, the five-three runt-of-the-litter bell-end; like he's ever gonna play basketball. I pull him aside. I say, 'I've got some bad news for you, Billy. Let's go somewhere quiet.'

He leans into my ear and says, 'I don't want to go somewhere quiet just to hear some bad news. What else you selling?'

'It's about Del. Come on.'

'We split up, Wahid. I've had enough of his bad news.'

'He's dead, Billy.'

A word about Del. A word about his stock

By the time his dad had finished running away from his first babymamma, Flex's mum, and his first child, Flex, then four months old, and by the time that she, the mother, in turn, had discovered the intricate pleasure of abandoning an unwanted child, the father had moved on to his next conquest and had impregnated her as a matter of course.

Flex was children-homed.

Del was smothered.

It doesn't take a genius to realise that if the three parents could have agreed to apportion affection with a bit of fairness, then things might've been different.

Del did okay at school, up to a point. What was it? Puberty? The full moon? What changed the cunt? Suddenly he's nutting his teachers and setting fire to shit. Dropping pills, negotiating deals.

Something happened, I understand now.

What if Flex knew what the guy was getting into? Where does that leave Muji and myself?

Billy's inconsolable. As he weeps I'm trying to assess what percentage is grief and what percentage crocodile. I don't know the guy well enough to do so.

If everyone was legally obliged to stick to one person all their life – like pandas, I think – then existence would be so much simpler. How many other partners of Del's will be crying soon? I wonder.

I also wonder: 'Did you give his housekey back?'

'No.'

'I need to borrow it. Look around.'

Billy nods. He is well aware of Del's connections with us. 'Just make sure someone pays, all right? Do what's necessary.'

We have a deal. Like I say, I'm not jigsawed, emotionally speaking, by Del's expiration – things happen for crying out loud – but I'm happy to engage with somebody's sense of ill-done-by justice.

At the bar, Goose is experiencing what it feels like to be ignored; for Goose this is something of a novelty – to be alone. She's sipping something purple through a straw and I go, 'We're leaving.'

'Mission accomplished?'

'Yeah, I broke the poor guy's heart. Mission accomplished.'

We're at the door and I turn, not looking for anything other than inspiration. Billy's approaching, dragging another guy behind him: it looks like a child abduction.

'Wahid!' Billy calls. 'This is Mazhar. Tell him what you just told me.'

I'm not sure who Billy's giving the order to but Mazhar speaks. 'I just saw Del,' he says.

'Where?' I'm leaning closer.

'The kebab shop. Buying food.'

'Are you sure it was Del?' I ask.

Goose looks ready to interrupt at any second. Understandably, she's confused.

Mazhar nods.

Billy is angry. 'So what are you saying to me, Wahid?' he wants to know.

'Left or right?' I say to Mazhar.

'Left or right what?'

'Out of the doors, I turn left or I turn right.' There must be a dozen places to get kebabs in the general locale, and I don't wanna fuck up the lead.

'Left.'

Goose can't keep up with me; she's wearing flats, not heels, but they're still no match for my trainers. Over my shoulder I call that I'll see her back at the car.

Man possessed, that's me. I must look like a right werewolf as I attack fast-food joint after fast-food joint, in search of Del. But I can't find him. A couple gets in my way and I headbutt the guy just for a way of releasing some steam. His girlfriend screams, I run away. It's five o'clock in the morning and I've seen enough trouble for one night as it is.

The light's good at this time of the year, and despite my lack of sleep I feel fine when the phone wakes me at ten o'clock, or just after. Unbelievably Goose is at my side. As usual, I didn't quite manage to give her one, but this time did successfully give her about three-quarters. I'm making progress.

It's Flex. I talk. 'You don't think Del has a twin, do you?' I say to conclude my piece.

'Wahid, it's got even weirder, mate,' he replies. 'Wake up this morning, yeah, and Del's not in the bathtub. He's nowhere.'

Flex phones Sandra – the number that Scottish Tony gave me. It goes straight to the message service and I say, 'She's probably in a lesson. Tell her to call you back.'

'It's regarding Scottish Tony – and a man named Del,' Flex finishes by saying.

That'll either be kill or cure.

'What next?' asks Muji. We're all at Flex's, obviously – examining the evidence. Specifically, we're in Flex's bathroom, with Flex now laying the mobile down on the cistern.

There's blood and gunk at the end of the tub opposite the taps. So it wasn't a dream: Del was here. Similarly, a breadcrumb trail of hardened splotches, leading to the door, out onto the landing and down the stairs – is one we've followed, the three of us, several times. The road is where the trail abruptly ceases. As if Del, balancing his head on his shoulders, was collected in a car.

Now's the time, I guess, to tell Flex about events at the picnic.

Flex doesn't take it like a man. Flex takes it like an ape. I'm a bit put out but nothing serious; when you hang around with guys like Flex you have to expect this sort of thing. When he cools down (about an hour later) he makes it clear that it's not the decapitation, it's the deception, he deplores.

The phone rings.

'Thanks for getting back to me,' Flex says. 'You're on a

mem-cam that Del shot. No, don't worry, it's not gonna get back to your mother. Where can we meet?'

The call ends and Flex goes, 'Well she's not involved, that's for sure.'

I didn't know she was in the frame in the first place, but I can't see that a denial she ever knew Del is enough to acquit her. I say so.

'No, mate,' says Flex. 'If she's involved she wouldn't give me the name of her school, would she? She just wants it over and done with quickly.'

'And not tell her mum.'

'And not tell her mum. But her mum knows she does Bone. It's on the recording. She tells her to share with her brother but he's watching cartoons.'

'It's not about Bone,' says Muji. It's the voice of common-sense, of course. 'I mean, who the fuck cares about Bone?'

'Is it worth meeting the girl?' I ask.

'Sure it is. How else are we gonna follow her home?' says Flex.

We follow her home. It's lunchtime.

She's walking with a further five friends. One by one they are jettisoned along the way.

The meeting Flex has with her is – as predicted – useless, so is not disappointing. The real purpose of this morning is to find out where Sandra lives; to chat to the mother.

There's a launderette and a gaggle of black boys, smoking; Sandra stops. Red herring, mate. She's soon moving on, past the toystore, the bike showroom, the Army sign-up place, and the blood bank. A large apartment block is her destination, it turns out. Muji and I hang back as Sandra starts to climb steps: an old-fashioned outside stairwell.

I get it into my head that one of us climbing the stairs will attract less attention than the two of us. 'Wait here,' I say to Muji. Routinely I wear trainers and I'm quiet as I ascend. I round a corner at the top. Along the landing to my left a door closes and I make my way towards it.

I've forgotten about Muji, I've forgotten about Flex; I'm thinking about Del – the walking talking Del.

With the palm of my hand I press the doorbell.

You never get used to the resulting shuffle within – to the waiting. Here is a household not used to receiving visitors.

Open Sesame.

'What the fucka you doing here?' asks Scottish Tony.

Flex is in Del's apartment. He makes himself coffee and toast.

He searches.

Del was not a fastidious organizer, but he was an efficient one. Flex shuffles through packets of photographs. Nothing unusual to see, although he doesn't recognize most of the people framed. He rifles through Del's drawers. Apart from a penchant for effeminate underwear – fuck all.

Then in the hall, just as he's about to exit, Flex looks up at the ceiling, following the upward progress of a spider he saw on his way in – the spider was dangling from one of them strings they make – and the spider's done the anti-abseil back to the top, and Flex sees a square door that will lead him up into an attic that he didn't know existed.

He reaches up and opens the hatch. The ladder descends like a spaceship gangplank, in a whisper of hydraulics, and Flex grits his teeth to climb. The light comes on automatically, triggered by the movement of the ladder.

Up he goes.

As Flex tells me the story I'm thinking – there was someone waiting for you; someone gave you a seeing-to.

Wrong on the second.

Half-right on the first.

Del is waiting for him. Asleep, yeah, but definitely waiting – waiting for someone. Or should I say 'the *Dels*' are waiting for him'?

Here a Del, there a Del.

And they are all asleep, erratically asleep – it looks like the remains of a boozeover slumber party. Variously attired, Del is slumped against the water tank, in a V-shape over wooden joists, embedded in bin bags of jumble.

Twenty-one of the cunts.

Including one who is sleeping with his head in his own lap. The Del we knew and loved, perhaps.

Then again, maybe not. Flex is not thinking too rationally – not checking.

As one they breathe, as one they lightly snore.

And then, as one, they open their eyes and start screaming.

'Scottish Tony,' I say. 'I could ask you the same question.'

'I live here. Now what's your excuse?'

'I was following Sandra.'

Tony crosses his arms; his forearms are as large as baby torsos. The tattoos re-establish their positions. 'What you do in your own time is your own business,' says he. 'But who the fuck is Sandra?'

'The girl we talked about last night. Connected to Del.'

'Oh yeah, of course. Sorry. My brain's not in a workzone. Well, what can I say? I'm sorry to disappoint you, Wahid – she ain't here.'

'Oh yes she is, Tone,' I dare to say. You don't contradict

the likes of Scottish Tony unless you're feeling confident.

'How about, if I'm right and you're wrong you volunteer to jump off this balcony? Cuz *nae* cunt calls me a liar.' He always gets more Scottish, does Scottish Tony, when he's vexed.

I hold up my hands. 'I'm sorry if I'm mistaken. All I know's, we followed that girl from the school and she came here, and when I saw your door closing I thought she…'

'Brenda!' calls Tony. 'Brenda, come here for a second will you?'

I'm confused.

'The only visitor I've had this early in the day,' – one p.m. or a sneeze shy – 'is my cleaner, Brenda.'

She sallies forth.

And *damn* she looks like Sandra. She looks like a sixth-former Sandra plus two or three years. *Is* it Sandra? I'm unwilling to accept the obvious. The clothes are different.

'Who are you?' I ask. 'Your name's *Brenda*?'

'What did I just say?' asks Tony.

'Yes,' says the woman.

'Not Sandra.'

'No.'

'I've made a mistake,' I have to say, but I'm not sure I have. The coincidence seems too remarkable. 'She looks exactly like you.' The hairstyle's a bit different, I note – and she didn't have time to change her clothes.

'So are you jumping or am I pushing, pal? The balcony.'

'Sorry, Tone, it was an honest mistake.'

Tony nods. 'Apology accepted. But that don't change the deal. Jump. Or I push you.'

'It weren't a *deal*.'

'Leave it, Tony,' says Brenda-not-Sandra. 'He's probably not all there.'

I can't believe what I'm hearing but evidently Tony is giving it some airplay, or whatever. His saying, 'Are you all Boned up, pal?' seems to point to a way out for me.

'I'm ripped to the tits,' I confess.

And I'm thinking, in another room, of what has happened, unable to deny the obvious. True, I was following Sandra from Sixth Form – but what if she was following someone – following Brenda – and using the schoolcrowd as a disguise?

Flex is gonna go mental about that, too.

Nodding his head Tony seems on the brink of agreeing – when he steps forward and hoys me the most terrific shove against the shoulders. I'm a Catherine Wheel: I tumble against the parapet, and my feet flip upwards.

There is nothing to cling to – and I fall.

Someone obliterates the intervening seconds; they're chopped out. And then the courtyard – children's swings and automated dogdirt collector – is looming like a ship from the fog.

More than one snap is heard. It's at moments like this that you long for the black curtain; you usher in, or wish you could, a period of self-disguise. Do I resemble a blob of guts and bile – or what do I resemble? I'm singing the pain tune.

The pain is *specific*, man.

And then darkness.

A touch to my shoulder brings me round again – but the journey is agonising.

'I thought as much,' says Scottish Tony. 'You're one of us, Wahid. Get up and stop being a cry-baby.'

I'm amazed to note that my limbs are fully functional. However, it's not the biggest shock of the day.

Who should pull up beside me but Flex. He's got a face

like a bulldog licking piss off a thistle.

'Get in,' he says, and I do.

'You won't believe what's going on,' I tell him, but before I can explain he goes:

'There's a lot of shit I don't believe today, Wahid.'

I'm apprehensive, to say the least. 'What you find?'

'A mem-cam. Of you and Goose.'

'Fuck. He was taping us?'

'Nah, it was a copy; Goose musta sold it on. But Wahid, you could be accused of missing the point right now. You and Goose, I said.'

'Sorry, Flex. A coupla times, that's all. And if it makes things any better I pickled early every time.'

'*Every* time?'

'Both times.'

'No. It doesn't make things much better, Wahid,' he says, although he sounds a bit calmer. 'I'm starting to wonder who the fuck you really are, mate.'

'Don't, Flex. You know who I am. What else you find?'

'Stuff. Unconnected images.' He pauses, and I'm aware there's something he's not telling me. 'As if Del was living a whole bunch of different lives. At the same time?'

The interrogative tone of voice is all I need. 'He was,' I tell Flex. 'There's more than one of him.'

'I know that, genius.'

'And there's more than one of me,' I conclude.

'Meaning?'

'Scottish Tony told me something incredible.'

Bone.

Every time you get ripped to the tits on Bone, what's going down? What's occurring? Not just chemically – but spiritually.

It's more than the sprinkle of good vibes or the sex accentuation. If Scottish Tony is correct – and I can't see many reasons to doubt him – then Boned-up out-of-your-head-ness is close to godliness – but only over a considerable period of time.

Says Tony: 'It's something I discovered about a year ago. When did you start using?'

'I was six. In the playground.'

Scottish Tony nods. 'A lifetime of Bone,' he says, 'you're ready. How's your leg?'

'I think it's broken.'

'Well I know that, genius – you just fell off a fourth storey balcony. But how *is* it?'

I consider. 'Not too bad, all things told.'

Again, he nods. 'From the evidence I've gathered,' says Scottish Tony, 'Bone also helps with the healing process. You'll probably be all right in a week's time.'

'All right enough to give you a decent kicking.'

'Watch it.'

'Why? What you gonna do – throw me off a balcony? What's going *on*?'

'The protracted use of Bone gives you access to a higher version of yourself,' I recite to Flex. We're still in his car and I can smell Del's blood from the boot.

'There are versions of yourself based on your most important life choices. Scottish Tony used the word *potentia*. But we can't see them with our minds the way they are; we're not strong enough. We need the Bone.'

It's quite a shock to learn that there are alternative versions of yourself, trying to seek your arse out: to be one again. If you've got your mind together, there isn't much that can happen to one *particular* draft to kill it off. Not even losing your head.

'Scottish Tony started his experiments,' I continue. 'Keeping tabs on people with his agents all over town.'

'One of 'em's Goose,' Flex offers.

This truth stings me. She set it up, at Scottish Tony's instigation – the picnic would-be massacre, and of course – Del. The picnic? We weren't on private property, so God knows what all the charades were about; but Tony was in a win-win situation. Even then I was ripped on Bone most of the time, and so was the cunt who attacked me. It appealed to Goose's sense of the macabre to take the guy's head – to give his spine draft a real challenge. It didn't work. It doesn't always, Tone told me. For some, dead means dead – and you have to learn to live with it.

Flex says, 'Did Del get wind of his other versions, Wahid? Did he know what was going on? Is that why he was recording all over town and taking photos?'

'Yeah.'

'Including one where he's a father of a girl called Sandra.' I say nothing. 'But why didn't she know his name when I called?'

'Your drafts can be called different names. Like Sandra and Brenda,' I explain. 'Sandra's started to work it out. She was following Brenda while I was following Sandra.'

We're at Scottish Tony's.

Flex makes the call to Muji: to pick up some protozolal acid from Flex's apartment on his way over. We all have keys to each other's places, and Muji's drawn the short straw this time. I can imagine him on the bus, with the timebomb in his lap.

It doesn't take long to clear the gym. Flex is carrying

Del's head by the hair, and even the big guy on reception offers only token resistance. I unlace his cheek with a razor that Del gave me in the car. 'It's a job, you silly cunt. Leave now. You've resigned.' He understands that you can get a new job faster'n you can get a new nose. Clutching his streaming face he scarpers.

Now it's a matter of waiting. I feel sick in the stomach.

Flex has gone gangster, even so early in the mid-afternoon. He's pacing up and down, talking to Del's head about what he's gonna do to Scottish Tony. Del's head is staring from the saddle of an exercise bike.

'See if his drafts come running,' Flex announces.

V. Spine Drafts

i

The vehicle is a masterpiece of malfunctioning decrepitude; the Bentley is a *right character*. In this shuddering jalopy, we burped and vibrated our way along to a venue in Ealing, where Dreadnought had an appointment with a Japaneseman. Illegally we parked: double yellows.

The window I rolled down was covered in a cataract of grime. To steady my nerves I lit a cigarette. Would Dreadnought approve of my smoking in his car?

Dreadnought made his return. The cockiness of his swagger suggested that something decent had occurred in the intervening – what was it? – seven or eight minutes. Well, he hadn't had time to get laid, so I assumed that one or both of his other energy-providers (money or violence) had been on show. Indeed, Dreadnought carried a small bag: had he just received protection money?

'Mission accomplished?'

He nodded. He had not completed his fidget for optimum comfort in the seat. Abruptly he did so. 'Tell you what, mate,' he said. 'Would you mind driving? From now on. I'm feeling a bit dicky as it goes.'

Dreadnought opened his bag. What he laid in his lap was a sliced black pudding, and what he wore on his face was the tender expression of unmitigated adoration.

'So what's wrong with you?'

'It's me stomach, Rene,' the man replied, and I knew I was in for something graphic. When it comes to descriptions that border on the hypochondriac – well, let's just say that Dreadnought doesn't do restrained. 'Me stomach's still giving me the arsehole. I had a ruby three days ago and I'm still suffering. I should sue the bastards, I really should.'

'It wasn't at Pekinese Pete's place, was it?'

'It was as a matter of fact.'

'No way. How can that place be open so quickly?'

'I didn't say it was open,' said Dreadnought. 'I said we ate there. With the smell of petrol in your nostrils the whole time. It was just a thank you meal, for doing the arson job. You should have been invited, I suppose.'

'It would have been nice,' I admitted. 'So you and Pete go back a bit, do you?'

'A bit. That's why I've given him some leeway this time around.'

On we drove, and Dreadnought sighed and crumpled up his breakfast wrappers. 'This place,' he said ruminatively, his eyes darting to the left and right (I checked). 'Do you ever feel that this whole city is full of maggots, Rene? This is Maggotville, mate.'

'I agree,' I told him. 'It's disgusting.'

'I bet Copenhagen's not this filthy. So what have you cunts got that we ain't?'

I shrugged. 'Respect,' I told him. 'Kids are taught to throw their litter in the bins, rather than it being assumed they'll understand the significance.'

Dreadnought allowed that this was not a bad idea at all, and then the conversation was curtailed. A school troop crossed at the lights.

It seemed like a long time, but eventually we pulled up to the Beef Encounter car park. I wondered what all of the other people of Dreadnought's acquaintance were doing today.

While making the tea I struggled to contemplate a standard nine-to-five with this man – which was what the day was beginning to look like. At any moment I expected him to tell me that I was off the hook until tomorrow, but the words wholly failed to arrive. Six sugars I spooned into Dreadnought's drink: he's a martyr to his sweet tooth. I was only dimly aware of the mobile – Dreadnought's mobile – giggling in the next room.

I carried the teas through. Dreadnought did not look happy. Nevertheless he did not forget his manners, and thanked me for the beverage. As I placed my rump in the chair he said: 'That was Brooker. You don't know nothing about engines do you?'

'Not much. What's up?'

'He's broken down,' he said in reply. 'Bound to happen, I suppose, but I bet he was thrashing the fucker from here to arseholes. You know what he's like – just a kid, really. But that don't help me. I need a van.'

'For what?' I asked.

Dreadnought regarded me coolly. 'That's for me to know,' he said, 'and you to find out.' He brightened. 'Finish the tea, then get on the blower. Call Dave Stroker, as he's your new mate. Tell him we need a van for a couple of days. Be convincing.'

With Stroker I drew a blank, but not until he'd put in a good deal of apologetic babbling and macho posturing.

'Dave? It's Rene. I was there for the money earlier on '

'There was nothing wrong with those notes, mate. And we counted them together.'

'That's not why I'm calling. Dreadnought needs to borrow a van for a coupla days.'

Stroker chuckled. 'What am I – a taxi service? Fuck off

out of it. You're having a laugh.'

'No, mate,' I told him slowly. 'We need a van. Don't ask me why.'

'I won't. But listen to this, Rene. My customers bring electrical equipment in for me to fix. What use do you think I have for a *van?*'

I don't know why this surprised me, but it did. 'You don't own one?'

'I don't own one. Try a rental agency. And fuck yourself.'

The line went dead.

'Who else do you know with a van?' I asked, having relayed the conversation to Dreadnought, who was sulking.

'Talk to Wrighty. Aquamarine Plumbing,' Dreadnought explained.

So it was that I travelled to Hangar Lane by Tube.

The only thing worth mentioning in relation to the pickup was Wrighty's obdurate nervousness. Tossing the keys from palm to palm, as though they were a weapon, I eventually asked, 'What do you think he's gonna do with it?'

'I wouldn't put anything past him,' Wrighty said – a thin man, pale, with straining limbs and dagger-sharp, monstrous lashes. 'But it's not insured.'

'No worries,' I attempted to convince him. 'In fact, Dreadnought has authorized me to waive your payment this month. As a gesture of thanks. Or call it what you will.'

'That man is all heart,' said Wrighty.

Driving away, I felt good – as if I'd just pulled off the blag of the century. I motored over to Beef Encounter. By now it was well into the afternoon and I was missing my stool at The Bloody Chamber. I was ready for a rest.

ii

They smoked him out of the house using a photograph of his daughter. She had an ashtray in her mouth and clothes pegs on her earlobes; she was wearing a blindfold, and Tanigawa gave up.

To a cool sunset drizzle the door whined open. On a neighbouring farm a cock mouthed off, and in the back of the car the watcher picked at his teeth with a front door key. He had the beginnings of a cold; he was not best pleased to be here. It always smelled of ordure in the countryside, and Dreadnought longed to get back to the Smoke. Enthusiastically coughing a mere second later, he watched as Tanigawa tested the air with an outstretched hand.

Charlie Peacock was up front, behind the wheel. 'The twat,' he said. 'Look at him, worried about getting a bit wet when his daughter's in a ditch, for all he knows.'

'The *size* of that cunt,' said Mickey, in the passenger seat. It took a lot to get Mickey excited, but Tanigawa's bulk was truly awesome. Tanigawa's bulk had been written about in the papers. The last time he'd been weighed, on scales that were used for gold bullion, the display had settled at forty-four stone, three pounds.

Tanigawa squeezed through the doorway. His arms – squidgy triangles of flesh – were held out, more or less, horizontally; they were unlowerable. Taking dainty, fussy steps in the mud and stones, he moved towards the second vehicle – the blue and white van.

Dreadnought got out of the car. His training shoes were inappropriate for the terrain but he wanted to be close enough to hear any dialogue that might occur. He squelched his way across the yard.

It was too much of an effort for Tanigawa to turn, but

at the van's side door – being opened by Brooker – he spoke. Projecting his voice over his left shoulder he said, 'Why?'

'She's safe. Get in the van.'

'No hurt no more. Okay.'

'I didn't hurt in the first place, mate. It was a trick. Charlie, get his phone, would you.'

'Eh?' said Tanigawa as Charlie Peacock fished his way through his jacket.

'A trick, mate. Computer?'

Tanigawa absorbed the lesson – it evidently struck him with the force of a physical blow. 'Computer?' he repeated. 'She okay?'

'She okay. She's with her mother.' Dreadnought had done his research; he knew that Tanigawa was estranged from his wife. 'Now get in.'

Booker helped load Tanigawa into the back. It was one of Dreadnought's axioms – that other people did the physical stuff – so he watched as the procedure was pantomimed out.

He's not gonna fit, Dreadnought thought.

They had got hold of the largest vehicle at Dreadnought's disposal – the van said Aquamarine Plumbing on the side – in return for a waiving of this month's protection money. And the fat bastard still couldn't get in. What next? A private jet? An airline carrier?

By wiggling a forefinger Dreadnought indicated that he requested the presence of the rest of his team. Gratifyingly he heard the car doors open straightaway. They came across to lend a hand – to lend a shoulder, lend an elbow.

The Japaneseman was wedged into the vehicle.

It was Charlie who noticed the resulting problem. The van tyres had sunk two inches into the mud, which led to a fraught conversation about having to heave the guy out again.

Brooker started the engine.

As first gear was engaged, the wheels started spinning. Mud spattered – and the van began to sashay. But it would not move forward more than an inch or two at a time.

'Keep trying,' said Dreadnought, and he ambled back over to the car. While shuffling through his options he had another cigarette, out of boredom and frustration as much as to satisfy any chemical need, and was pleased that it modified the stench of country ways. How can people live with that stink? he wondered. And what do you do all day anyway, once you've finished fucking about with the cows?

Dreadnought pulverized the cigarette butt. The van was getting stressed, and was starting to sound like a chainsaw. The guys were filthy; the air was blue – with fumes, with X-rated language. As Dreadnought rejoined them, Mickey opined that it would be better to wait for Tanigawa to slim down. 'Let nature take its course, like,' he said; 'pull him out when he's shed some of his load.'

'Just not feed him, you mean,' said Charlie.

'Exactly. Could live on what that cunt's got for ages.'

'No can do,' Dreadnought informed him casually.

'Why not?'

'Heartstrain, mate. New plan.'

Charlie knuckled the driver's window and drew his finger across his Adam's apple. Nodding his understanding, Brooker killed the engine.

'You know that thing about Mohamed and the mountain?' Dreadnought asked.

Mickey's eyebrows made contact in a crease above his nose. 'Mohamed Shabir?'

'No, not a Mohamed we know. *The* Mohamed. In the Bible, like. Why would I be telling you about a grocer?'

Mickey shrugged, a little wounded by Dreadnought's tone. 'Why you telling us about the *Bible*?'

'Watch it. The thing goes, if Mohamed won't go to the mountain, the mountain should go to Mohamed. Or summing like that.'

'So what you saying?' asked Charlie.

'Give me strength. We bring the stuff here,' Dreadnought replied.

'The food?'

'The cameras?'

Dreadnought nodded. 'The whole ball of wax. All right, boys?'

Charlie and Mickey nodded their heads, but Brooker was not so sure. 'And what about the van?' he wanted to know. 'Don't you have to give it back tonight? Wrighty's gonna go mental.'

Snorting his derision Dreadnought reached once more for his cigarettes.

'Wrighty? That little bogey, what's he gonna do, eh? Come round and mess with me taps? Stop me bog flushing? Do me a favour. He can wait for his van. If he starts to get a bit crisp, just give him a tickle, yeah? Set fire to something.' He paused. 'You look pained, Gaz.'

Brooker shrugged. 'Well he's given you what he needs for his work – and you're having a dump in his fridge.'

'Your point being?'

Both Charlie and Mickey tensed. They could see his tail rattling.

'Just don't seem fair, that's all.'

'Who said I'm fair, eh? Guy didn't pay his protection money this month.'

'But you told him not to!'

'Well there you go then, mate. Life's doubly unfair for some poor cunts.' Dreadnought peered at Tanigawa's slab-like buttocks. 'Has anyone checked he's still breathing?'

Mickey was accompanying Dreadnought, and he was less than comfortable about the idea. When Dreadnought needed an extra appendage there was every chance that matters were about to turn crisp – Dreadnought being essentially a solo worker.

'I'm ready,' Mickey nodded.

They left the fagsmoke-grey of the London street and a curlicue of hamburger aroma wafted with them up the stairs to the second floor. Opposite the door to the tanning salon was the door to the language school. It was into the latter establishment that they walked.

Shown through to Mr Rakishomo's office, they seated themselves before the great man. Mickey's hands, when he put them together, were wet with anticipation. Rakishomo was as impressive a bulk to behold as Tanigawa had been, the first time Mickey had clapped eyes on him. With Rakishomo the features were centralized raisins on a huge, lumpy cake of a face.

Suddenly the man smiled, the cheeks lifted. 'Success?' asked Rakishomo. And then repeated, on seeing Dreadnought's nod, 'Success.'

'But not everything went according to plan,' said Dreadnought, and then he explained what had happened.

Rakishomo made a series of offhand, carefree gesticulations, as the events were conveyed. When Dreadnought suggested the bit about moving a camera out into the sticks, the Japaneseman nodded. 'We have the equipment,' he said, 'and it won't be used until the students are sitting their Orals. It's locked in a cupboard upstairs. Take it.'

'Thanks. There's just one more thing,' said Dreadnought. 'When I say Tanigawa's stuck in the van, I mean he's only got his backside visible. We're gonna have to cut a hole in the side – to see his face.'

Rakishomo failed to grasp the point. 'I'm afraid my school doesn't have metal-cutters as well, Mr Dreadnought.'

'No, you don't understand. It's not my van, see.'

'Put whatever costs you incur on the bill. The equipment is upstairs.'

The two stood up. The interview was over, and Rakishomo was moving nowhere.

Even at the door Mickey could feel the weight of the man's breath on his back. Rakishomo impressed without needing recourse to anything as complex as a personality. His body did the talking.

Mickey had the impression that he was being ushered out on the flying carpet of one of the fatman's sighs.

Brooker realised that he'd been chosen to sit overnight guard in the front of the van for reasons other than his status as a rookie. He'd made Dreadnought vexed. And that was one thing he'd have to control – that lip of his. He was not here to offer his opinions.

Beside Brooker was Charlie, and in the back, of course, filling every available inch as surely as wet cement, was Tanigawa. He'd drifted off into a troubled doze about an hour earlier; he kept farting like an elephant. He'd asked if he could speak to his daughter, but Charlie, as the senior partner present, had told him no.

It was eight in the evening. Charlie turned on the radio and listened to the news.

'I wish we had some cards,' said Brooker.

'Why?'

The younger man turned to face the older. 'So we could play a game of course!'

'I don't play cards. Mug's game.'

'All right, I could play a game then.'

'But we haven't got any cards, so it's irrelevant, isn't it?' Charlie said.

'I suppose so. Just thinking of the long night ahead.'

Charlie shrugged. 'You'll get used to it,' he said. 'The first couple of all-nighters are horrible. You don't eat, you don't sleep, you need a piss, you need a bath; you start worrying about your b.o. and you can't wait to wash your hair. It's horrible. But by the time you've done as many as I have – well, just think of it as paid overtime in a nine-to-five job.'

'I've never had a nine-to-five job.'

'But you know what I mean.' Peacock sniffed. His good deed for the day had been done.

Brooker said, 'I'll bet you've done all-nighters in some strange places.'

'That's true. Outside a knicker factory once – the owner was down the tubes, and he let it slip that he was gonna burn the place down, for the insurance. Well, you know how people talk. The problem was, the insurance guy was also going down the tubes, and a fucking big payout like that was gonna hobble him. So the insurance guy pays Dreadnought to protect the owner's business from the owner.'

'Did it work?' Brooker asked.

'Well, the guy comes round one night with his blowtorch – and we're there. And we give the moose a right slap, and tell him to pull his socks up. Then Dreadnought's just getting into it, right, and to tell you the truth, I think it was gonna get a bit tasty – like he was gonna burn him or something – and another cunt turns up: the owner. The real owner. With his Swan Vestas and his paraffin. His paraffinalia.'

Ignoring or misunderstanding the silly pun, Brooker asked, 'So who was the first guy?'

'Well that's what we wanted to know. Turns out it was a random act of arson, like. So we give him a kick up the arse and tell him to bugger off. Take his torch, obviously. Then we had to start again, on the owner. I was knackered by the end.' Charlie chuckled.

Brooker said, 'I can't see anything that exciting happening tonight, can you?'

'No. Not unless Tiny Tim here is just faking it. Worse luck.'

'Do you think he did it?' asked Brooker. 'Did it deliberately, I mean.'

Charlie shrugged again. 'Probably not. Just a bad possibility if you're his size. He should've been more careful. But why don't you ask him when he wakes up. "Oi, matey, did you intend to squish your enemy's sister when you were giving her one, or what?" See what he says.'

'I thought they were friends.'

'Well they're enemies now,' said Charlie. 'Mind you, "friends" is pushing it a bit. Respectful colleagues. Acquaintances. Whatever. Similar ages, though. They had *The Guinness Book of Records* in common. And photoshoots, articles for health magazines: all that gubbins.'

Brooker knew that Tanigawa had usurped Rakishomo, their current employer, as the heaviest man in England. And he knew that Rakishomo had not been overjoyed with this development. Brooker took his cigarettes off the dashboard. 'Want one?'

'Trying to quit. Dreadnought reckons that Rakishomo wanted to give one to Tanigawa. Apparently in one of them articles he says he's gay. Maybe you could ask him about that as well, when he wakes up.'

Brooker exhaled. 'That's grim, that is. Can you imagine it? Those two fat arses eclipsing the moon. *Yuck*.'

'Come off it, mate,' Charlie replied. 'All that blubber? They'd be up half the night just searching for a cock between 'em. Would never work.'

They laughed. Then Brooker said, 'But he was giving Rakishomo's sister one.'

'Amazingly. God knows what was in it for *her*.'

'I reckon he did it deliberately,' Brooker opined. 'I mean, if you're fifteen tonnes, you don't go lying on top of a bird, do you?'

'Not unless she's into a bit of the kinky stuff. Suffocation.'

'Not she,' said Tanigawa, from the back. Brooker and Charlie started; the former's bottom even left his seat. The Japaneseman then said something that neither of them had expected, so late in the day. 'I no kill her,' he stated. 'Brother. Brother!'

Dreadnought had gambled on leaving Tanigawa in the van with two of the team (and he was not punishing Brooker for insubordination, despite what the other man suspected). A fidgety instinct informed him of his error of judgement throughout the night. He should *be* there, he was sure of it. As a result of this worrying he slept badly.

In the early hours Marilyn held his hand and, no stranger to insomnia herself, she whispered generic reassurances to a problem that she did not understand. She wasn't idle of mind; it was just that Dreadnought told her nothing about his business dealings. Come three o'clock and Dreadnought was tempted to drive out to the farm. He resisted. Was it a lack of faith – a lack of faith in his boys – that was hampering him so? Basically, what could go wrong? Dreadnought had thought long and hard about sleeping within easy reach of Tanigawa, but in the end what had kept him in London for the night was the dread of sleeping in the manurey air of the countryside. But standing with the razor in his hand the next morning, he couldn't wait to get out there. The boil-like bags beneath his eyes endeavoured to convince him to go back to bed – it was only five o'clock – but Dreadnought's system was starting to rev. Once spruced and shaved, he joined his wife in the narrow kitchen for a standing-up cup of coffee. He even accepted her offer of toast, not knowing when he'd next get a chance to eat. And he could hardly expect Mickey or Charlie to bring a picnic.

'So what you doing today?' Dreadnought asked.

'Nothing much. My step class tonight. Bit of shopping. Do you need anything?'

'No.' Dreadnought was increasingly of the opinion that he should ask her that same question with greater frequency. *Do you need anything, Mazza?* Is this enough for you? Christ alone knew why she hadn't left him years earlier. It wasn't much of an existence, after all, being a criminal's wife. Certainly, there was the gangster allure to which the halves of Mickey, of Charlie and maybe even of Brooker (it was too early to tell) strongly responded. But Mazza only received a watered-down version of that. She wasn't in it for the proximate buzz. She rarely met up with Mickey's missus, and her friends were few and far between. What did she *do* all day? The stock answer was shopping, but she never came back with much. Maybe there was a book he could buy – *The Secret Lives of Gangster Molls.*

Dreadnought stood still as Mazza combed his hair with her fingers. *Maybe she's having an affair,* he thought. 'Bye, darlin',' he said, stooping down to kiss her.

'Take care of yourself,' she replied. She did not question his sporting of rubber boots.

Maybe I'll have her followed.

The idea was out of his mind by the time he'd negotiated his way onto the pell-mell of the M25. True to form, his destination being the sticks, it started to rain before too long. And by the time he reached the farm it was lashing down – a real monsoon.

'Anything to report?' he asked Brooker, who had walked over to meet Dreadnought's car.

'He says he's hungry.'

'Tell him the cavalry's arrived. I'll give him *hungry* in a minute.'

'What you got?'

Dreadnought opened the boot. The boys gathered round and cooed, like old girls around a young mother's pram. In Dreadnought's boot was a scrum of supermarket bags, all of which were stuffed with produce. Even the most casual glance would have taken in pre-cooked chickens, tubs of ice-cream, sacks of apples and satsumas. There were dozens of tins; there was even a plate of sushi. There was Chinese, there was Indian; Italian, French and Greek. Pots of yoghurt, bricks of cheese and gallons of milk. Coke. Wine. Pizza. Cakes.

The food bill had come to ninety-three pounds of Rakishomo's money. And Tanigawa was going to eat all of it.

Today.

'And what was the other thing?' Dreadnought wanted to know.

'He said something funny: Rakishomo killed the woman,

he said.'

'Well he would, wouldn't he?' Dreadnought was cavalier. 'Get us on his side, like; I'm surprised he didn't try offering you a bribe.'

'Well he did, actually.'

'There you go then.'

'But Dreadnought – what if he's telling the truth? What if the other bloke's thinking: he won't fuck me but he'll fuck my sister. I'll splat him. But something goes wrong.'

'Gaz. Listen, mate,' said Dreadnought. 'What happened or didn't happen is none of your fucking business, to be blunt about it. Rakishomo's paying the bills so we do as he says; it's simple economics, or capitalism, or whatever you wanna call it. If Rakishomo wants us to forcefeed this cunt till he explodes, then that's what we'll do.'

He strolled over to the blue and white van. Charlie Peacock was there, drinking coffee from a flask that Mickey had thought to bring for them, Mickey having arrived twenty minutes earlier. 'All right, Charlie?'

'Sweet, boss. Brooker's brought you up to speed?'

'Yeah. And I'm not saying it's impossible either. What does Spare Ribs say?'

'Nothing much, boss. He understands a lot of English but can't say much. All we get is – Rakishomo did it.'

Dreadnought leaned into the van, intending to have a quiet word with the prisoner. What he said instead was: 'Christ, it stinks of piss around here.'

Charlie smirked. 'You forgot to get the *en suite* fitted.'

'Watch it.' As he retreated into the vile country air, Dreadnought was vexed and disappointed with himself: that he had failed to think of something so basic as bodily functions. What would happen when Tanigawa needed to move his bowel?

'Shall we have one more go at moving it?' Mickey asked, sharking in from the left and carrying the petrol-powered saw. 'It's just I'd rather be hidden.'

'Don't worry about it,' said Dreadnought. 'You can hide anything if the other cunt don't know what he's looking for. Get the cameras set up.'

As the boys got busy Dreadnought slipped and aqua-planed his way over to the farmhouse. (Behind him, the sound of the power saw cut open the morning with a long rasp.) He hadn't been interested in the house last night, but now, with nothing to do while the activities commenced in the rain, he was curious.

The place was a pigsty. It clearly hadn't been lived in for quite some time – unless you counted occupation by rodents and grubs. A cushion of dust covered most of the surfaces. And Tanigawa, Dreadnought deduced, had been living on tinned food and beer for the three days it had taken to find him. Empties were everywhere, lying around like spent cartridges, or stacked in the sink in a ragged pyramid.

Intending to cup his hands and bring water to his mouth, Dreadnought turned on the kitchen taps. Nothing came out. Unexpectedly, Dreadnought experienced a feeling of regret, of dolefulness. And just for a second he examined this feeling. 'How the mighty have fallen,' he was known to use as a catch-phrase, a summing-up, a précis of any given situation, and he used it, silently, now. He thought it sad, this come-down, the demotion.

Life's doubly unfair for some poor cunts, he remembered saying to Brooker the day before. He'd been talking about Wrighty the plumber, but the meaning was on-target if you were refer-ring to Tanigawa as well. Mutinous glands had made the man larger than a works vehicle – and because of these freakshow

properties he had lost the respect and the friendship of an hon-
ourable millionaire.

'Dreadnought?'

The man turned. Brooker was in the doorway, the appearance of a drowned rat upon him, with the mobile in an
outstretched hand. 'It's Wrighty.'

Dreadnought accepted the offering and said,
'Wrighty-mate.'

The connection wasn't great, and the squeal of metal being sliced was distracting, but it was straightforward enough to
hear Wrighty whining on about his van.

'Are you listening? Good. *Hire* a van for the next couple of
days. I don't care who from, just get me a receipt, all right? It's
on me. I need your van, what can I say?'

Dreadnought handed the mobile back to Brooker.
'Satisfied?'

'Surprised, boss.'

'But not a word to the boys, eh. Don't want 'em thinking
you've got me going soft. And call Barry, would you? Tell him
to go over to Wrighty's and give him a bruise.'

'Eh? Why?' Brooker asked.

'I've told him never to call me at the office,' said
Dreadnought.

In the next room, which would have been the lounge,
were the same spent cans, and also some hardening chunks
of bread. Dreadnought's attention was led to the photograph,
near the door. He stooped to pick it up: the girl in close-up,
with her mouth stretched wide by the installation of an ashtray; the look of terror that Dreadnought had not really noticed before; the earlobe pegs. Impressive things could be done
with computers, but Dreadnought wondered how Rakishomo
had conjured up the image. At the very least he would have

needed a picture to tinker with, and where had *that* come from?

Despite what he'd said to Brooker, the possibility that Rakishomo was lying had not occurred to Dreadnought. Re-examining the situation made him feel peculiar. If Rakishomo had killed his own sister because of a tiff over whom she was taking to bed, that was possible. Maybe the sister secretly wanted to give her *brother* one.

Dreadnought called up a guy called Wan – or Wan-no-Work, as he was sometimes known, the lazy arse. A pot-smoking restaurateur, with a decent chain of command of his own. 'And would you call me back when you've got something? Cheers, mate.' Connections in Chinatown, like. Different languages, different cultures, but Wan would be able to crawl closer than Dreadnought would.

Charlie Peacock had held a chainsaw before, but he was nervous. To save his eyeballs he wore the swimming goggles that Mickey had in his overnight bag. And as he got stuck in, his muscles felt numb.

The metal screamed, and before long the heat on Charlie's hands had become incredible. In his mind was the fear that he would decapitate Tanigawa, or gash his nose off or something.

Tanigawa was yelping.

The chainsaw teeth bit deep. The blade spat out iron filings as if they were fruit pips.

The yelps became louder.

Charlie wanted a new job.

Dreadnought waited until everything had gone quiet before going back into the bad weather. Not even the sloping rain could kill his spirits for the sight that met his eyes. He couldn't help it: he started to laugh. 'What does he think he *looks* like?' he went on. The great jowelly tit, Tanigawa, with his head hanging out of its metal carapace, resembled a giant snail, or a weird-arse tortoise – a dreamily strange vision to behold.

'All right,' said Dreadnought, 'when we turn the cameras on, I don't want no one getting starstruck, all right? I mean it, boys: no faces on film. Everyone got that?' He surveyed the nods. 'This ain't your fucking audition.'

Brooker chuckled, and Dreadnought was happy to get a reaction. He thought about doing the line about the casting couch, but decided that it might be a witticism too far.

'Take your rings off. Watches off. Roll your sleeves up,' said Dreadnought. Even as he was giving his orders, he wondered if any of them would be impressed by his foresight. Just in case, he elected to explain his motives. 'You have to think long-term when it comes to film. I don't want some copper coming up to me in a year's time and saying, "About that fat Jap." All right? Mickey, you're excluded: your tats.'

'Me what?'

'Your tattoos. Dead giveaway, mate.'

'Oh right. Sorry.'

'Nothing to be sorry about,' said Dreadnought. 'You can move the cameras, if they need moving. And remember – conversation to a minimum. Everyone ready?'

First up was a loaf of brown bread, and Charlie fed him: slice after slice, being masticated slowly and then swallowed. Everyone watched. For quite a long time Tanigawa seemed up to the task – but then again, Dreadnought had known that this would be the case: the lump hadn't eaten for ten hours.

Next came the first of the chickens. Brooker tore pieces off the bones and fed them to the Japaneseman, who had started to belch.

'Here, Dreadnought,' said Charlie, 'maybe we shouldn't be feeding him the skin.'

'Why not?'

'It's fattening, like.'

Breakfast lasted for nearly four hours. After the first of the chickens came some dessert – a six-pack of yoghurts. Tanigawa was sick five times.

He was allowed a rest for half an hour, then lunch commenced.

Dreadnought held the photograph six inches from Tanigawa's face. 'Who *is* she?' he asked.

No reply did Tanigawa make, save for a cavernous burp. A breeze blew the stench of Tanigawa's soiled trousers into Dreadnought's face, in a rainy clout. Dreadnought did not even acknowledge the smell.

'Who is she, you fat bastard?'

Dreadnought knelt down in the mud; although the rain was still falling, it was doing so with less enthusiasm than before. 'Answer me, Mr Tanigawa. Do it for yourself. Cuz I know you can understand me if I speak slowly. And I swear to God, if I don't get what I want I'm gonna set fire to this van. Forget the money.'

Dreadnought produced a cigarette. 'And I'll make you eat a packet of these, and I'll put some honey on your forehead and let the wasps have a pop, if it ever stops raining. Or you'll do me the courtesy of a response. *Who is she?*'

'Not girl,' said Tanigawa.

'Thank you. Not your girl, not your daughter.'

'No.'

'So did you do this to her, Mr Tanigawa?'

'No!'

'Did Rakishomo?'

'No.'

Becoming frustrated, Dreadnought said, 'Then who the fuck *is* she? Did you *find* her like this?'

This time his partner was Charlie, and this time Dreadnought carried a shiv, just in case. While holding the door open to a long line of Oriental students – a class had just concluded – he thought of what Wan had told him, over the phone. And he thought of the conversation that he'd shared with Tanigawa, via the shaky interpretative powers of Wan.

They climbed the stairs.

When they were shown through to Rakishomo, the Japaneseman was not shy to display his surprise at seeing the return of the cameras and tripods.

'So soon, Mr Dreadnought?'

Slowly Dreadnought replied, 'Mission accomplished, Mr Rakishomo. He went pop.' Absolutely no suggestion of humour was on Dreadnought's face. He and Charlie laid down the equipment as carefully as possible.

Charlie, in particular, was feeling sick.

'You can regard your sister's murder as avenged,' Dreadnought said, keeping his attention on the cheque that Rakishomo was writing.

'Mr Dreadnought, I am indebted to you,' said Rakishomo, 'but I will only be fully avenged once I have seen the film. I am sure you understand.'

'Of course. As surely as I'm sure you'll understand I hate being fucked about with.'

'Excuse me?'

Dreadnought took a step closer to the man's desk. 'A *game*,

Mr Rakishomo? You've had the gall to involve me in your silly little *game*?'

The fat man blinked, but he did not look scared. 'If you insist on adopting that tone, Mr Dreadnought, I will be obliged to ask you to leave.'

'You know what the worst bit is? I feel stupid because I didn't bother checking.' Carelessly Dreadnought tossed the photograph onto the desk.

'That's not Tanigawa's daughter, mate. He ain't *got* a daughter. Or a wife. Or an ex-wife, or a dairy business or any of that shit. I must've been mental, falling for that. I even started to believe that it was your sister – but that didn't work out because she's too young. The *girl* in that picture's not a *girl* at all. That's you, mate, and you owe me money.'

Wordlessly Rakishomo handed over the cheque, much to Charlie's astonishment.

'That would cover any damage to your colleague's van as well, I believe,' Rakishomo continued.

Back on the farm, Tanigawa's answer had made Dreadnought feel ignorant. 'So who the fuck is she?' Dreadnought had demanded.

'No girl!' Tanigawa had reiterated. 'Rakishomo!'

'You've done well, Mr Dreadnought,' said Rakishomo, now. 'And you're absolutely right – we've been playing what you call a silly game for the last twenty years, since that picture was taken along with some others.'

Christ, thought Dreadnought and Charlie. These mammoths aren't even *thirty* yet!

'You're into torture, aren't you?'

'Yes,' Rakishomo replied. 'Very much so, I'm afraid. We have been since we were children together in Osaka. Never sex: we were interested in pain. And we didn't always take photographs, of course. But they've been our signal for quite some time that a new game was about to begin. Even the way we've dared each other to get fatter all these years – even that's a form of torture, unless you think it's comfortable weighing over forty stone.'

Dreadnought pocketed his hands and said, 'Well you can start slimming now, can't you, Mr Rakishomo – because you've won. Or lost. Depending on the way you look at it. You can rent out your farm now: you won't be needing it again.'

Rakishomo looked perturbed. 'Where is he now?'

'Exactly where we left him,' said Dreadnought. 'If you get there tonight you'll be able to smell the charring instead of that horribly rural stink. Take a knife and fork. Tuck in. Really *punish* yourself.'

Long day, thought Dreadnought, going on to wonder what to eat for his dinner. Wednesday night was Mazza's step aerobics class, and she wouldn't be in until ten. If precedent was anything to go by, Dreadnought would be asleep on the couch when she arrived.

He had a lager and a pizza and he settled down to watch the soaps. Feeling stifled, he tried not to think about the day that drew to a close. He was too exhausted to shower.

Instead, he slept.

As he and Charlie had moved away from the language school, Dreadnought had thought of that foolish conundrum. How does a sadist hurt a masochist? By saying that he won't hurt him. Once in the safety of Mickey's car, Dreadnought had even told it, and Brooker alone had chuckled.

No one had been left to guard Tanigawa. In Dreadnought's opinion, no invigilation had been deemed necessary – although the Japaneseman, of course, had not been burnt to his death. Let Rakishomo sweat over that one, Dreadnought had thought: give him the extra thrill of anticipation. Tanigawa would starve until he was discovered.

When Dreadnought woke it was twenty past ten, and the telephone was ringing. Dreadnought reassembled his jigsawed brain and gave himself two slaps to either cheek.

'Hello?' he said, warily aware of a rat-in-a-cage feeling in his stomach.

'Is this the partner of Marilyn Jones?'

'It is.'

It was twenty past ten. Mazza's step class finished at half past nine. Even allowing for problems on the Tube she could have walked it by now, thought Dreadnought, his eyes picking out his jacket, his training shoes.

'This is the HeartLines Club, where your wife exercises. I'm afraid there's been a terrible accident,' the voice went on.

'What happened?' Dreadnought asked.

'She was run over by a van. The ambulance has just arrived.' It was a male voice, Dreadnought realised (it had taken him this long to be bothered to make the distinction), and like a lasso given insufficient wrist-flick, it was starting to wobble in its orbit.

'And you saw it, didn't you?'

'Yes,' the young man whined. 'I was putting the alarm on.'

'And the van didn't stop, did it?' Dreadnought's eyes leaked.

'No.'

'It's all right, son, it's all right,' said Dreadnought. 'Tell me one more thing, and then you can go home, all right?'

'Okay.'

'Did they reverse and do it again?'

'Yes.'

It was personal. He felt like a bomb. He felt like he was twenty-five stone.

Scarcely making it into the bathroom Dreadnought was sick.

Wrighty in his new hired van? Rakishomo?

Sighing wetly, snorkelly, Dreadnought pressed Speed-Dial 2, and Angie answered through a handkerchief of sleep.

'It's Dreadnought,' he told Charlie, although Angie had already passed on that information in the background. 'Get your clothes on, mate. I need a team. Pronto.'

VI. The Inspissation

i

Dreadnought sleeps. He seems calm.

His body churns with the unfinished.

My files corrupt and the time-lines slip. Things are happening in the wrong order.

Six months have passed. Summer has arrived (look what the cat dragged in) and the mood is lighter. Even Crisis Work is undertaken in a spirit of professional *joie de vivre* – with an eye on the weekend that has recently passed, or is to follow.

Dreadnought is about to locate a Pressure Point.

ii

We were in the back room at Beef Encounter. Like an eight year-old over his colouring book, endeavouring to keep his crayon-swipes within the lines, Dreadnought pored over his facts and figures. I had been called at six a.m. and it was now seven-thirty.

Now was as good a time as any.

'Theoretically, mate,' I said, 'if I needed to get something, and it was important that I got it, you'd help me, wouldn't you?'

Dreadnought sniffed. 'That would depend,' he said, 'on what sort of something we were talking about. *Theoretically*.'

Having expected such a response, I made a big deal of nodding my head and appearing humble. 'I need a gun,' I said.

If he was surprised, he made no show of it.

'I'd have to ask you why you wanted it.'

'And I'd have to tell you that I couldn't say.'

Dreadnought shrugged. 'Then I'd have to say *no*.'

iii

'Do you know when you've finished with the person you're with? It's when you start to use the same script when you're arguing. "Don't snap." "I'm not snapping." "Don't start." All that. And do you know what, Rene? Me and Mazza? We don't know each other's scripts. That's the beauty of the thing. That's love.'

Dreadnought has an allocated parking space, just outside his downstairs maisonette; but the privilege might as well have been cancelled. There was a Jeep parked inside my man's white lines. Needless to say, Dreadnought was not best pleased.

'Tell me what you want to do.'

Dreadnought shrugged. 'Nothing much. Put a 50p up the side, do the paintwork. Nothing serious.'

Eventually we found a space – sharking in on a motorbike that was pulling away, its rider a cube of black leathers and an obsidian visor.

We walked back to Dreadnought's place.

'You hungry, Rene?' Dreadnought asked. 'What do you have for breakfast?'

'Nothing. I've put on a stone since I came here,' I protested.

'And you'll put on two more before you leave,' Dreadnought replied.

'I'm not *leaving*.'

'You will,' Dreadnought told me, flapping his fingers at a fly. He had started walking, not in the direction of the maisonette. 'Everyone leaves me sooner or later, Rene.'

'You seem in a melancholy mood this morning. If you

don't mind my saying so.'

Hamfistedly egotistical as ever, Dreadnought regarded my observation as being unworthy of further comment, and he returned to the subject of food. He asked: 'What do you have for brekky in Denmark, Rene?'

'Oh you know. Wild birds, zebra, antelope, gnu. it's a European city, Dreadnought; it's really not that different. People have what people have.'

'So what you gonna have now?'

'Why? Where we going?'

The place was called John's Caff. It was near the Church of St Nathaniel the Decisive. There was a handwritten sign – black marker on blue paper – in the window. "Open 24 hours. Most of the time the food's okay." I didn't know if that was misplaced modesty or English humour. I decided I'd ask Dreadnought when we left, but I didn't. I needed to sleep.

Dreadnought and I sat near the counter, breathed on by coffee-urn aromas and bacon halitosis. With a weary sigh Dreadnought ordered. 'Two full English, mate,' he said, despite my protest that I wasn't too hungry.

The cholesterol arrived, and Dreadnought tucked in. He advised me to do the same, hinting merely that it might be the last meal for a little while.

'Been thinking,' said Dreadnought, suddenly. 'Your request.'

'The gun?'

Dreadnought's frown deepened. 'Yeah, a bit louder, eh, cunt?' he told me. 'Not sure if everyone got that. The *item*, all right? The *item*.'

'The item. Fine. What about it?'

'I got where I am by trusting in two things. One: my nose for a business deal. And two: my ability to judge the people around me.' The tines of his fork were loaded with bacon, sausage, egg yolk, black pudding and a solitary baked bean. Instead of shoving the parcel into his face, Dreadnought laid the fork down – a bridge over an slick of mushroom juice, fried bread fat and melted butter. 'The only thing I like to insist upon, Rene is loyalty. You give me that and I'll give you whatever you want. That's one of my abiding rules.'

Where was this heading?

'And I have to say, Rene, on both scores, you are something of an enigma.' With which he picked up the fork and loaded his jaws.

Somewhat shaken I answered, 'Have I done something wrong?'

The heavy mouth continued chewing; air that I imagined I could see puffed noisily from Dreadnought's hirsute nostrils. 'How about you tell me?'

'Tell you what?'

'You see, son, you're an enigma,' Dreadnought informed me again. 'You make enquiries to find me. You wanna work for me, you say…'

'I *do* wanna work for you,' I interrupted.

Dreadnought was slicing up some bacon, his eyes off me as he executed this task; a grid of worry lines gouged up his forehead. 'I know that, Rene: that's the bit 'at's confusing me. Alarm bells, mate.' He shovelled in the bacon and spoke as he chewed.

'What do you think I've done wrong?' I asked, placing down my knife and fork.

'What puzzles me is your obvious intelligence. So why, I'm asking myself, ain't this clever clogs assumed I'd check? Why ain't he thought – he'll check up on me so I better leave some decent droppings?' Dreadnought did not leave room for me to answer. 'I made some enquiries. Called in a couple of favours. Your breakfast is getting cold, Rene.'

'So am I. I don't get this.'

'No one's *heard* of you, mate: not in Copenhagen. Not in Denmark. Not as a pill pimp, that is,' said Dreadnought.

'Well, why should they have?' I asked him. 'I was small fry.'

'You were *no* fry, Rene. Now eat up.'

'I haven't done anything wrong.'

'You're a civil servant, Rene. You work in an office of public records. You've never pushed a drug; you push a pen. But what I don't understand, Rene – what niggles me – is this: How the fuck did you hear about me in the first place? Why you here?'

I pushed the plate to the side, longing for a drink stronger than that which half-filled the fat mug I raised to my lips. The coffee was lukewarm, with a trailer-park scent to its over-torched beans, a tiger-dung colour to its ripples.

iv

Every couple of days now, I swing past the Church of St Nathaniel the Decisive. It's difficult to say what draws me to the place, but the attraction is evidently mutual. The stonework shines on my approach. Call me what you will, but its eyes light up like those of a children's TV presenter. The church and I are in love. One of these days it's going to ask me to meet its parents.

This morning the graveyard was sighing gently. And I thought – as I always think when I'm here – this is a pressure point. Something will happen here.

And something did. Sitting down on the bench near to which I had received my ebullient and fruity kicking, I searched long and hard for the clues. The air was stewy. Birds overlooking my inertia gulped and chuckled. I gaped. Leaning back into the swing of my skull, I breathed like a diver with the Bends and waited for the light on sheet metal, the clash – the evidence.

v

Just home from an evening at Dreadnought's. So I'm drunk of course. We worked on a recipe. Earlier on in the week (could it only have been Tuesday?) he had sniffed, his eyes about four inches from my chin, and italically whispered, '*Rene, my son: got something for you.*' And he'd gripped my left wrist and shoved something small – a square of paper – into my palm. A bank note? I wondered with my nerves aflutter. Nodding my head, I'd squeezed tightly, then deposited whatever it was into my trouser pocket. This is what happened next.

Naturally I thought of drugs, maybe even of the elusive Bone, but I couldn't help but feel confused. I said, 'Cheers' as he sauntered away, the heels of his larrigans clicking. The scene being Beef Encounter, in the back room, alone, it was no big deal – or wouldn't have been, then – to open up the wrap to discover what powder was enveloped therein. Nervous, however, of discovery (by whom?), I jumped ship to the bathroom, which by the way is something to behold, and locked the door.

The unwrapping felt like a religious experience. I'm laughing as I type these words.

It was a shopping list. Good Lord, he had written me a shopping list, and at the bottom he had written:

My place. 7 o'clock. Thursday.

'Salad Niçoise with Hot Grilled Tuna' was apparently what Dreadnought intended to prepare (and I can now corroborate this plan); and among the ingredients were chicory leaves, anchovy fillets and 'capers'.

I stood beside that unbelievable toilet bowl for a good few minutes, genuinely uncertain of whether to weep or guffaw.

I read my instructions again – read the ruined tenements and council-rows of his wordage. And I should hardly be one to criticize other people's calligraphy. Personally, my hand-writing is as if a squirrel had dipped its paws in ink and then gone for a scamper across an acre of scattered sheets. I average about nine unrecognisable words on every piece of foolscap, which is why I type. But Dreadnought's hand shows a strong, laboured streak of perseverance: if at first you don't succeed, then try, try again. The note is littered with blotchings and crossings-out: and I can sense his effortful sweat, his conclusive full stops, the two a.m. squint and the pulse of a deadline to meet before retiring to bed.

If fresh tuna is NOT available, he informs me rigidly, *get halibut pieces or turbot.*

Will do, I thought.

Bring a Dictaphone, was a further directive. Sure, I said to myself, I'll get one when I'm on the high street in search of a dictionary. What are capers? The only capers I know of are the sort that Dreadnought and the boys get involved in: a robbery caper, an extortion caper, some violent capers…

So it came to be that tonight we made salad niçoise, and recorded our kitchen-bound antics on the Dictaphone. The food was far from onerous to put together, and delicious to the taste, but meal completed, I was more or less hoofed from the building with the instruction to 'make a start on that tape, Rene. I wanna see how it looks on paper.'

Well I can't do it now. I'm dog tired. I'm starting to worry about money. Today set me back £30 for the Dictaphone, £2 for the dictionary (Chambers Concise, from an Oxfam charity shop: a bargain) and around twenty quid for the shopping once I'd purchased some wine to accompany our meal. And now I'll have to fork out for a printer.

Capers turn out to be a sort of shrub with edible flowers. You live and learn.

vi

Memories I have yet to divulge.

Throwing knives into a tree – my aunt's best knives. Presumably I was longing to get caught, but it's impossible to tell from here. Presumably I was bored. I was often bored. Lonely, tired and bored.

So this is what I'd do.

Having moved on from torturing insects – an early proclivity – I would use my childish strength and inclination (not to mention my attention to detail) to strangle geese. Kick chickens. And then I would run away – I would hide in the hay barn.

Geese are stroppy. Territorial. Protective.

I enjoyed killing them most of all. If you take hold of the beak and spin the head quickly, as if you are stirring cake-mix in a bowl, you can break the bird's neck, but it fights you into the afterlife. It doesn't know it's dead. It's like a horror film, splashing and pecking as it shites away all that's in its bowels. At the moment of termination, it resembles a woodpecker, but the tree is imaginary – it's pecking space. So you kick it in the head.

Chickens? A lousy lay, ho ho. Don't expect me to know what the word is in English, but when I wasn't kicking chickens I was attempting to romance them. That sounds silly. But in my world at the time, there was no sense of predacity. It was love –

or at least lust. I would insert my erection into the egg-box and the chicken would die of a trauma.

You're joking if you believe that that was the extent of my cruelty. As far as tools were concerned, I had an adversary in the elemental form of fire.

I would steal fire and attempt to set light to cows' udders.

Dreadnought was wrong when he suggested that I have no connection to the world of crime. I'm in there. I'm with it.

vii

This evening I read through some of the early entries I had made since meeting Dreadnought. Here is one of them: an incident that I had almost forgotten.

Despite my initial reservations about *The Cookery Book*, I realise that this collaboration is working to my advantage. The very fact that we are in Dreadnought's kitchen means that he is not on duty: unfettered by the demands that are placed on the modern criminal, I find I talk to a subtly altered (for the better), more giving, more loquacious Dreadnought. We talk about a greater variety of subjects. What's more, under the guise of getting something down for the book, I am entitled to record everything on tape. It's win-win.

We were in the lounge ('parlour'), Dreadnought and I, discussing the book, when the phone rang. With no explanation necessary, I stood.

This had happened before, although rarely. Dreadnought does not get social calls. When I first used to go around, Dreadnought would flick me with a witheringly apologetic glance and say something like – *Sorry, mate. Would you mind just going into the kitchen for a few seconds?* And I would do so, uncomplainingly (because it was nice to get a breather from the man's intensity,

and besides, it was perfectly simple to hear what he was saying from the next room). So tonight, when the phone rang, I
collected the bottle and my half-finished glass and ambled into
that room.

I heard the following:

'Hello? Yes it is.' Pause. Then warily: 'Oh hello there. It's
nice to hear your voice again. Could you hold for a second,
please, Bernie?'

Bernie. I shuffled through my recent memories. The only
Bernie I was aware of was Bernie Acapulco, who principally
serviced Surrey Quays and New Cross Gate – the London that
simmered below the river.

'Rene-mate?'

With my alcoholic accoutrements still burdening my
hands (I had yet to place them down on the pristine kitchen
surfaces) I popped my head back round the doorframe. 'Yes,
boss,' I said, although I'd never said the B word before (and to
the best of my knowledge never would again).

'Could you fuck off into the bedroom for a minute, eh?'
said Dreadnought. 'This is a private one.'

'Sure.'

'And put some music on. There's a stereo next to the box.'

I had never been in Dreadnought's bedroom, so I'll en-
deavour to explain my shock at the niceness and normality of it
all. I closed the door, and then leaned against it. No sounds of
half a conversation could I hear: he'd been serious about the
music bit. So I took on board the simple CD-player and, as it
was already fit to go, I simply pressed PLAY.

Of all strange things, it was African music that emanat-
ed. I wouldn't have guessed that in a month of Sundays. The
volume was high. I didn't adjust it. The man wanted privacy.

The room was comprised of a nice large bed with a

white duvet. Pastel colours. A wardrobe that I doubted would conceal the rotting corpses of comedians and characters from Dreadnought's black book. The whole thing was a picture of calm and marital contentment – and it smelt nice. It smelt as though a woman ruled this roost.

I took a look at the CDs near the stereo. A catholic selection.

Did Dreadnought, I wondered, put on music when he made love?

I sat on the bed, and dug the throat of the bottle into my glass. In order to gain myself some space in that vessel, I hurriedly slurped and then topped the glass up again. The bottle I placed on the white-painted windowsill. Even though I am clinically unable to burp, I burped – and then took it as a sign.

But of what?

The call dragged on for a long time. I managed to fill the minutes by stretching myself drunker and drunker. There was nothing else to do.

Did I sleep? I'm not entirely sure, but I certainly tuned out for a couple of minutes – competently hypnotised by the music and drugged to a standstill by the brandy – and the only thing that kept my heart beating was when the door opened to a sudden noisy click.

It was Mazza who entered.

She closed the door and leaned on it, as I had, and said, 'Sorry. Same rules for me too. Who is it?'

'Bernie Acapulco, I think,' I told her.

Spruced and smelling good, she was dressed in casuals and carrying her well-upholstered sports bag. Her hair was damp. She had showered after her exercise class, I surmised, although I was still of the opinion that a regular session any-where was as decent an alibi as there was if you were indulging yourself in an affair. I said, 'How was the keep fit?'

She shrugged. 'I kept fit,' she replied. 'Do you mind if I change?'

'I'm not supposed to go out there till he's finished.'

'That's not what I asked. I need to change. I put the wrong bra in the gym bag and I need to throw it out: it's too old. Some of the wire's uncomfortable.'

I shook my head. 'I'm not brave enough,' I said.

'Ah, but *I* am,' she replied. 'Turn away. Get interested in that CD player.'

'I *am* interested in that CD player!' I deadpanned.

'Well there you are then. Follow your dream.'

I turned away. I stared at the machinery while behind me a woman whose husband enjoyed maiming people if the reason was right talked on, on the phone. To this minute I don't think I've ever felt more afraid.

'Okay,' Mazza said, eventually, 'you're safe.'

Still expecting a trap, I faced her warily. On her face was a wide and beautiful grin. The offending brassiere was dangling from her right index finger. 'You've surprised me,' Mazza said. 'You didn't peek.'

'I'm gay,' I lied.

'Even so. That takes a lot of gumption. Curiosity being what it is.'

I nodded. 'It being the thing that killed the cat,' I told her.

'And you're still alive,' said Mazza. 'Were you tempted?'

'Of course. Who wouldn't be?' I asked.

'My husband, for example?'

'I can't get involved in that,' I told her.

'You disappoint me. I'm joking. You're a good man, Rene.'

I was still sitting on the edge of the bed; Mazza was still standing, appearing exactly as she had when she entered, apart from the dangling bra.

'Would you kindly put that thing away?' I asked.

Mazza smiled. 'And you are very sweet,' she added. 'It must be something about our different cultures.'

Just as she was depositing the bra, with her bum in the air, Dreadnought knocked on his own bedroom door, and entered. Though his expression was stern, it would turn out that his discomfort had nothing to do with us.

'Evening, darling,' he said (no kiss). 'Rene, could you come out, mate? I have something to discuss with you.'

I was relieved to do so. As I stood up, being careful not to spill anything, I knew that the world of abstract blood and tears was a whole distance more pleasant than the real one that would have evolved if the man had witnessed or eavesdropped on anything that smacked of flirting.

We re-established our positions in the lounge.

'Pour me one, mate, would you?' said Dreadnought. 'I need it.'

'What's up?'

Before he would reveal as much he guzzled half a glass of brandy, and even then I thought he was going to keep going. But instead he said:

'I bet you can't guess who that was.'

'I can't,' I lied.

'Bernie Acapulco. Think coke. But there's a lot more to him than the drugs thing. As that phone call just proved.'

'Why, what did he want?'

'To hire one of my team,' said Dreadnought. 'Lease work.'

'And *you* said?'

'I'd have to sleep on it.'

Knowing full well that such a time-buyer could only in-dicate a dangerous proposition – or even an impossible one – I held my tongue until Dreadnought was ready to speak.

'It's not your run of the mill,' he went on, redundantly.

'But how much is he willing to pay?' I asked.

'Well, that's between me and him. You haven't heard the job.'

I decided to show a bit of initiative – show my mettle. 'Well it's hardly likely to be a bodyguard gig, a) if he's asking you to do it, and b) if you're struggling so hard to tell me about it. Am I right?'

Dreadnought sucked down the rest of his booze.

'Who said,' he asked, 'that I was struggling with anything?'

'Forgive me. This is your normal behaviour, right?'

'Fuck you, Rene,' said Dreadnought, quietly. 'Okay. It's a bit of terrorism he's after. He's having some bother with a cunt in the City. Someone owes him some dosh. Nothing petty. And so far nothing's worked. Not that he's gone the routes I normally would've, but there you go. He's chosen to go a more scenic route.'

'Which is?'

Dreadnought gulped. 'Here's the bag. What he wants is to fit one of my boys up with explosives. Get him to make an appointment with the cunt in question. Go up there and for him to say – it's *your choice, chief.* You either pay up right now or I pull the fucking pin. I got nothing to lose, mate. I got cancer – or summing.'

'Jesus.' I shook my head. 'And you're having doubts about this, eh?'

'But they ain't real explosives, of course. Or I woulda told the fucker to take a leap.'

'So what if they call his bluff?' I asked.

Dreadnought leaned forward to pour us each another. 'Think about it, Rene-mate. Cunt goes in with a pocket full of explosives. You're gonna do what? *Challenge* him? Fuck that. You're gonna give him what he wants and then say thank you.'

'So why can't he get one of his own men to do it?'

Dreadnought frowned. 'Do you have to ask?' he said. 'Because they know him, of course. They know the team. And so they'll know that Bernie ain't gonna sacrifice one of his own. It's not good business. What he wants this City cunt to realise is this: that he's got some fucking kamikaze wanker to do the dirty, and fuck 'em all. How are they to know it's all false? They'll be laying bricks, mate. *They'll* pay.'

I felt nauseous. 'So who have you got in the frame?' I asked. It was me. I damn well knew that it was going to be me.

But Dreadnought said, 'Brooker.'

'Is he ready?'

'For what? For entering a building and going up to the reception and saying he's arrived? Yeah, mate. I think he can handle that.'

'But he's twelve,' I protested. 'Give him a break.'

Dreadnought's voice had turned cold: 'I believe he needs the exposure.'

'It stinks. It's madness. Tell him to wash his own dishes.'

Dreadnought was struggling. I could tell. 'But the explosives will be *false*.'

'Says who?' I demanded. 'Bernie Acapulco?'

For the first time I wondered if Mazza was listening from the bedroom – in her soft new bra. Even though the African music was still a pulse, I could see her, with her ear against the door. And there was a fantasy on display. I almost, but not quite, got the one out that Mazza was standing there with nothing to conceal her top half. She was naked.

'I want to do it,' I said.

Dreadnought regarded me with a fresh sense of wonder.

The drink that he'd only just poured – he waited until he'd finished that one before he presented himself as being in a fit state to continue.

'I always thought of you as a loyal cunt, Rene. You know that. '

'I know that, Dreadnought.' And at exactly that same point I understood that I had just been scammed. Oh, woe is me. Whether or not Brooker had ever been in the frame was a different matter; Dreadnought had got me to commit to this lunatic scheme.

Mazza came out of the bedroom and wondered if either of us wished for a cup of tea. Unsurprisingly, we both refused. Not more than twenty minutes later, we tasted the late evening air. We were on a mission – to obtain more brandy, more smokes.

It was while on this mission that Dreadnought let me have it. He said, 'No, Rene. Thanks all the same. I want Brooker to field this one.'

'Come on, Dreadnought,' I protested. 'You said it was mine.'

'I said nothing of the sort.'

A silence grew. Dreadnought paid the man in the off-licence.

Two thoughts have occurred to me since. The first – and most flattering – is that Dreadnought doesn't believe the mission to be as risk-free as he was letting on, and he would rather see Brooker get injured (or worse) than he would me.

The second is that he is testing – really *testing* – the younger recruit.

I don't know which I prefer.

It's now just after four. It's time to pretend to go to sleep.

viii

Five-thirty a.m. and I've just had my first call of the day.

It was Brooker, sounding drunk and worried. I had a very good (and accurate) feeling of what was about to follow.

'I hope I didn't wake you, Rene.'

'You didn't,' I answered truthfully.

'I just need a word. About something Dreadnought's asked me to do.'

He elucidated the point.

Going along with his sense of consternation I asked, 'Well what are you going to do?'

'That's what I'm ringing about. What do you think?'

It was a pressure point, I realised, now that it was all but on top of me.

For a long time now I have known that Brooker and Dreadnought fall out, that something happens to sever the bond. What I don't know is why I took me so long to realise that I personally might be the cause of the rift.

'I wouldn't touch the job with a ten-foot barge-pole. Leave it to another sap.'

The phone line throbbed with silence. When he could speak again, having examined his emotions, no doubt, at the thought of being unfaithful to Dreadnought, Brooker sounded like he was shivering. 'Cheers, mate,' was all he said, and I was certain that I could feel him plotting against our boss.

I grinned as I made the morning coffee.

ix

Dreadnought considered my request for a good few seconds. 'I have to ask you why, Rene.'

'Of course. He embarrassed me.'

'Not as much as you did him.' Dreadnought frowned. 'Is

there something between the two of you I don't know about?'

'He jilted me at the altar.'

'Seriously.'

'I don't appreciate being made to look stupid.'

'I can relate to that.' Dreadnought sniffed. 'You sure that's all.'

'On my life.'

'I trust you, Rene Okay. You can do what you will for thirty minutes. If you want to use tools – fine. But I want him alive and well, or well-ish, when I get him back. Understand? You can cut him if you want, but I want the major arteries left untouched. They're mine. Deal?'

'Deal. You're assuming I know where they are, though,' I said.

'The arteries? Course you do, mate. If you didn't you wouldn't be on my team.'

With a grimace I took his face in my hands. He made no sound; all the same a slurping noise could be heard. A gruesome slick of perspiration was on his jowls.

'Frank.' I said it kindly. 'Frank, you know you're going to die, don't you? Let me hear you say it.'

Voice croaking but without a pause – 'I'm going to die,' said Frank. His flesh was slack, but it suddenly tightened: he was aiming for a smile. Eyes like polished stones. 'But you know what keeps me happy, Rene? The thought that it was Dreadnought, and not you, who did this damage. Just tell me one thing. Did you engineer all this?'

'Of course I did.'

Frank nodded. 'Now tell me one more thing,' he said. 'How are you going to stop me telling Dreadnought that?'

'I'm not. In fact, I'm going to watch you as you try to convince him. Call me curious.'

'But what makes you think you're safe?'

I opened his smile a little wider – either side – with the handsaw. When I'd done what I'd done, the room still rang – was heavy – with unfinished screams and the man before my waist resembled a clown, downtrodden and dirty.

Then it was Dreadnought's turn.

But that was later.

Making certain there were a good few metres between us, I turned, as if hearing his appellation a fraction of a second before it came.

'Rene!'

I was already facing his cheesy grin. 'It's possible you might be needing this, you soft bastard,' he brayed. He was holding up my watch by the buckle.

'Not as much as you'll be needing this,' I replied, displaying no emotion whatever. I held up his tatty brown wallet, good and long, so that plenty of people could see me.

He called me a name.

'Yeah yeah,' I croaked back. The wallet described a couple of rotations on its way back to its owner. 'And while you're there, Frank, check your credit cards. You've got so fucking lazy and useless, I might've done anything in those couple of seconds.'

'You're a cunt, Rene,' Frank repeated.

'Sure. But a cleverer cunt'n *you'll* ever be. Look.' I shot my jacket sleeve, revealing a watch on my right wrist. 'You're so predictable I even knew you'd steal from me. You're pathetic.'

'And you're dead, Rene,' Frank replied.

The jeers, the jokes, were swelling and multiplying.

'I mean it. You're dead.'

'Sure. Do you want to keep that?' I asked, referring with

an outstretched finger to the watch that Frank the Ferret still pinched aloft. 'I have another one.'

x

'Mazza, I have to ask you a question,' I said.

'I've been waiting,' she told me. 'It'll be something about what he's like to live with.'

It felt strange to be so diligently wrongfooted, so out-classed. 'He's a violent man, after all,' I tried to explain.

'And he also makes you laugh, Rene: I've heard you, like a pair of schoolgirls talking about boys and makeup. You bring out something positive in each other,' Mazza finished.

'Well that's good to know,' I told her, 'but so what?'

'So why not assume that he'll be funny with me at home?' Mazza's voice was calm but she was clearly peeved. 'Your assumption, Rene, is – he uses me as his punchbag.'

I protested. 'I didn't say anything like that, Mazza!'

'Not with words, maybe. Well, allow me to defend the honour of my husband, Rene. He's not once so much as lifted a finger to me, all right?'

'Fine.' I don't know who was more upset at this point, but I certainly felt like a louse for posing the question. Nor could I really deny that I'd anticipated an alternative response; perhaps my imagination had bled dry before getting to the 'punchbag' scene, but I'd be lying if I said that I had failed to conjure up the occasional slap or place-keeping prod. At the very least I'd longed for a deposition on some of Dreadnought's favourite and more urgent antics in bed.

Nothing.

'We trust each other. Not just because I could cause him grief with one call, but because I knew what he was when I married him. He didn't just become what he is now.'

This intrigued me. 'And what did he become? And please don't say "a businessman".'

'I wouldn't. An immortal,' Mazza replied.

'As in: his spirit'll live on and on?'

Mazza shrugged. 'If you'd prefer,' she said.

'No, that's not good enough. You can't just leave it at that.' I paused. A gamble always hinges on being able to afford what you might lose. There being only one thing that I could ill-afford to lose – Dreadnought's respect – you might say that I took one hell of a gamble at this point. I said: 'Do you know something, Mazza?'

Again, she shrugged. 'I know lots of things, Rene.'

My voice was chisel on granite. 'Please let me in.'

With an unexpected, confidence-belying click in her throat, Mazza nodded her head. It was not what I had expected.

BOOK TWO:
INSPECTIONS OF THE WOUNDED

I. Maggotville

IN THE SPACE OF TEN DAYS, Dreadnought bid farewell to his mother and to Mazza.

I cannot posit a thought as to how the man coped. When *my* mother died, I was seven years old. Elvis Presley had died the previous week. And Dad had already left: he'd escaped four years earlier. What I best recall is the day of my mother's funeral. Throughout, I was treated with the blushed respect awarded to a visiting dignitary – a boy king, perhaps, or the son of a megalomaniacal billionaire. I was dressed in black. Mum was lowered into the ground.

I was offered the choice of whether or not to attend the funeral of Dreadnought's mother. As Dreadnought had said: 'It's up to you, mate. You didn't know her, after all.' And I'd said: 'I'd like to show my support, if I may.' To this Dreadnought had lowered his head and muttered: 'Good man.'

The day was windy; the air was a chisel. Accompanied by Gary Brooker and Fat Gina, I took my place, three quarters of the way to the back of the Church of St Nathaniel the Decisive, on a long hard bench. I trembled and sweated inside my new suit. Frank the Ferret was behind me, flanked by two beautiful teenaged daughters. (Where was their mother? Did they have one? Or had Frank stolen the girls, as he stole everything else?) For the length of the service – from the opening bars of 'The Green, Green Grass of Home' by Tom Jones, with the coffin being carried in by four pallbearers, through the eulogies, the hymns ('Our Father, Who Art in Heaven' in English was a trial: I stayed silent), to the closing notes of 'Delilah' – I kept my sweating palm on my wallet.

In front of me (unexpectedly) was Dave Stroker. To the disapproval of those around us, Stroker read the day's edition of *The Sport*. He judged tits at the funeral of Dreadnought's old girl. Who, by the way, had not died from the lump in her left breast (though it hadn't done her any favours); she had died of a random, unfair heart attack.

The appearance of who gave me the hives? Go on, guess. Who was three rows in front of me? Go on.

Des Lewis.

Bells rang during 'The Green, Green Grass of Home', during 'Our Father', during Dreadnought's spunky tribute, and then during 'Delilah'.

'Why why WHY…'

BONG.

'…Delilah '

BONG.

To my surprise – and to my gutfelt consternation – Charlie Peacock read from T.S. Eliot. Not *The Waste Lands*. None of the biggies. Peacock read the bit about the father's children, the relevance of which skated past my consciousness. And then he sat down.

Thank God I hadn't been asked to read.

Then Des Lewis read. Des! The man who's been in conflict with Dreadnought since the year dot. Des read a poem from an anonymous author. 'I'd like your memory of me to be a happy one…' Des wore Armani. The suit made him look like an upper-class otter. And I thought: They *want* this history between them. Dreadnought asking Des to read was a way of acknowledging his counterpart, but it was also solidarity through contempt. Des read beautifully. Would I be totally out of order to suggest that on Dreadnought's behalf I fell in love with Des Lewis for the duration of his recital?

Outside, in the corrosive wind, the committal was conducted.

I don't know if pubs keep any sort of records of how many people attend their paid-for functions, but I would hazard a guess that the number of mourners in The Bloody Chamber for Dreadnought's Mum's wake was at the upper end of the scale. The place was packed. A hundred people? More? The saloon bar was three-deep with drinkers by the time I had chauffeured Brooker, Wrighty and Denim Jackie over in Dreadnought's Bentley. We entered. Paul Anka sang from the jukebox. The noise inside that place – the noise was suffocating. How the English love to laugh once the funeral has been and gone!

In the Bentley, there had been no such din Well, let me rephrase that. The engine, that day, was in a particularly playful mood: tattoo-gun buzzings; an alarming (new) noise of a whipcrack (ride 'em, cowboy!) and the customary sounds of hydraulic winches, a building site in full post-tabloid-and-cuppa throttle; the watery clicks, dripping taps, submarine pulses, snake hisses and baboon shrieks. What I meant was: there was no conversation between us. Not once I'd uttered what had turned out to be a highly sensitive question. If I'd had any idea of what I'd been about to cause, I would have kept my mouth shut.

Attempting levity I had said: 'What's the story with Dreadnought and Des Lewis?' To my left, on the passenger seat, Mickey had visibly tensed; Mickey had resembled his pre-violence self. Just for a second I'd assumed that I was about to receive a slap – or, even worse, a tickle. I think I must have tensed, too.

'Don't go there, Rene,' was all that Mickey seemed to have to say on the matter. Putting my query, perhaps, down to the puppyish zeal with which I had entered my first few weeks in Dreadnought's employ, Mickey seemed to relax. But I could feel that the atmosphere had changed: I had killed off sadness, I had strangulated sobriety. And replaced it with what? My question had introduced our old friend, guilt.

'Guys, I'm sorry,' I added. 'If it's a sore point.'

'Just leave it, Rene.' This came, scarcely believably, from Wrighty, in the back. It had crossed my mind that Wrighty's presence might have been the reason why Mickey did not wish to speak about Des Lewis; but it seemed as though Wrighty knew the full SP as well. Who else? Brooker? Brooker had joined the fold at the same time that I had: did even Gary Brooker know the story?

After a jolting half-mile of non-communication, I was mildly pleased to be nearly broadsided by a juggernaut emerging from the slip road that leads to the swimming baths. Cursing the driver gave me something to do for a few more agonizing seconds. I put on the radio.

By the time I'd finished my third pint at the wake, my earlier contention that it wouldn't be the time or place to make further enquiries was looking shaky. The non-argument in the Bentley had deep-sixed my confidence. What I wanted to do, I suppose, was get Des Lewis in a headlock and force the guy to confess.

I angled up to him instead. He was standing at the buffet table (on top of the pool table), patiently cherry-picking for his plate. He was temporarily alone. I said:

'Des? Des Lewis?'

'Yes, mate. You must be Rene.'

'That's right,' I answered, absurdly flattered that he would know this. 'Does my reputation precede me?'

'No.' Des Lewis was deadpan. He placed some chicken bollocks onto his plate. He has the most impossibly hairy knuckles that humankind has seen this side of the Missing Link. 'I make it my business to know the new faces,' he said. 'How you settling in, son?'

'Not bad. Well, in fact. Do you mean you know everyone here?' I asked.

Lewis looked at the buffet spread; he contemplated a Scotch egg that appeared too undertanned – it was practically grey – to be healthy. 'Couple of the birds are unfamiliar, but I know the faces. Does that expression translate okay?' he asked, warily.

'Yeah. I know what a face is,' I told him.

'And you have plans?' Des asked me. 'Plans in that direction.'

'To be a face? Not really.'

'He's still got it then,' Des said.

'Got what?' I asked. 'Who?'

'The Dreadnought.' Des smiled. It was the first time I'd heard anyone use the definite article before Dreadnought's name. 'Still got the ability to pick from his fair share of bullshitters.'

I frowned. 'I'm not *lying*, Des.'

'Sure you ain't. Do you recommend the salmonella or the Mad Cow Disease?' he asked.

'I haven't touched anything,' I replied, and I decided to take the plunge. 'You go back a bit, then, do you? You and Dreadnought?'

'Oh yes. The salmonella, I think,' said Des, ruminatively,

now picking up a plump Scotch egg. The plate that he was loading was five inches deep. It made me feel queasy. From a resident of a country in which herrings are eaten for breakfast, I suppose this might sound a bit rich: but what the hell is England's obsession with *coleslaw* all about?

Des Lewis paused. Briefly – and not at all pleasantly – he reminded me of an animal: he reminded me, in fact, of a mammoth. Something about the singleminded attention to one task at a time. He turned to face me. 'I suppose I owe you an apology,' he said.

'For what?'

'It was me. It was my idea.'

'To do what?'

'Break into your room at the Dolphin Hotel. Soz.'

'You did what?' I asked.

'Well I didn't do it, obviously. What do *I* know about B and E?' said Des, smiling. 'But Dreadnought's on the dog and he's like "Des-mate? I need a spot of advice." So I've told him: "You're a cheeky monkey and no fucky mistake, D." And he's told me: "I got a new boy, right? He's from Denmark, of all places. What do you suggest?" So it's me who says, "Check his passport. Where's he live?" Dreadnought paid someone to have a look through your belongings.'

I was furious. 'Who?'

'I shouldna told you, mate. Sorry. Day's got me 'ead messed up.'

'Frank the Ferret by any chance?' I ventured. 'That fucking bastard: I'll brain the twat, given the chance.'

'Spoken like a true Londoner.'

'Des. I've been thinking about this for a while,' I said.

'Frank? He's not worth it, mate.'

'Not Frank. You. You and Dreadnought: what's the story?

No one'll tell me. What you did. What he did.'

'What *I* did?' said Des. 'Son, you'll be choosing your words more carefully than that in the future, I trust.'

'I don't know,' I told him.

'Well you won't. It's personal.'

'It's not business?'

'I just told you: it's personal.' Des was becoming antsy. 'So. If you'll excuse me, I'd like to eat my weight in pub diseases.' He left.

'Yeah. Your bones are showing,' I said to his back.

ii

Mazza's funeral was something else.

I was there at the Church of St Nathaniel the Decisive. Where else would I have been? Miss that and you'd better have a decent excuse. Chronic malaria. Terminal stupidity.

I was there: black suit, black tie. I had shaved my face to the bone (not literally). In my left trouser pocket I had a small bottle of smelling salts, just in case anyone passed out.

No one did: the emotional pitch of the day was too high. Only us dogs (*we* dogs?) could hear it. Dogs of Crime. Crime Canines. Although I often think that the humble alligator – predacity, sleepy digestion – would be a more suitable comparison. Only those who knew Mazza knew what she'd left us with, which was bottomless yearning. I loved her more than words could say. I hadn't even known that myself, until then.

It's personal, I kept thinking of Des Lewis saying. Yeah, no joke. What isn't? And what am I going to tell Dreadnought about why I'm here – why I'm *really* here – if he should ask?

This was the question breakdancing at the back of my head as the pallbearers lowered Mazza's coffin onto the hurdles at the front of the church. The vicar's name was Margaret (the same vicar who had conducted the service for Dolly, Dreadnought's Mum), and she looked long and hard at the settled teak. A tear was in her eye. Mine, too. I was six rows from the front. Dreadnought was sitting next to Mazza's father, in the first.

'We are gathered here today,' Margaret started to say.

FLASH.

Dreadnought and Mazza, nose to nose, sharing an ice-cream cone. Anvil sun; bonnets of foam on the chesty waves in the background.

FLASH.

My first glimpse (my one and only) of Mazza's nether regions, the vagina dilated not in lust but in childbirth. The bottom raised off the hospital's once-white sheets: a perfect shot of her cosmetically bleached anus. (Eat your dinner off that.) But the child is not well. The child – a boy – the child resembles a kitten.

FLASH.

I am there, on a four-poster bed. An earlier spine draft of Mazza (ringlets and rouge, a painted birthmark above her right nipple) eats grapes from the soft bowl of my pubic triangle. I have always longed to adore you, I tell her as she dribbles small grape pips and spittle into my erection.

FLASH.

Do you want this?

FLASH.

Do it, Muji.

FLASH.

'God, I can't,' I whispered aloud into the hymn ('Jerusalem').

FLASH.

Blurred voices; slurred voices. Altered voices: altered by

their passage through time, like a poorly transported bottle of vintage claret. Like a poorly transported monkey. I don't know who's speaking. At first I assume it's me – me to Mazza.

But that's not my erection: not in this life and not in any of my four other directions of lives. I'm smaller; I'm wider. Two centuries in the past a prostitute informed me that I had, and I quote, 'a beautiful cock, like a broom handle; smooth'. *This* man (Dreadnought?) had one of those chickens that looks like the helmet was an afterthought: an extra bit bolted on. it's as swollen as a lamb's heart, and it's angling in for an un-bleached anus

Their first vodka-sodden, booze-delayed attempt at anal sex. It's almost sweet. Young love. And my, what a terrific gross of meat you have on you, Dreadnought sir.

I take a step back from the memory. Not Dreadnought but Des Lewis is wielding the hard-on.

It's personal, Des had told me. Des had slipped a length to Dreadnought's wife: the balloon knot.

No.

The recipient's arse is too wide; it's too hairy.

It's personal.

God help us all, I thought as I attempted to convince those around me in the pews (with a Brooker to my left, a Pea-cock to my right; there a Gina, there a Jackie, everywhere a Dave Dave) that my tears had all to do with the ceremony: a reading from Deuteronomy. That I was fully and uncomplicat-edly of the moment.

FLASH.

'Never forget me, son,' Des whispers. And true to his words at the time – 'I won't – Dreadnought never has.

iii

Work went on. No rest for the wicked.

Dreadnought had given me a tinkle on the mobile. 'Come round to Beef Encounter, would you? And pick the boy up on the way. Got a tickle for you.'

We had arrived at the shop by the front door. I'd acknowledged that there might be trouble ahead. The air had smelled different: not beefy, exactly, but lightly zoo-related.

I think it's fair to say that neither of us – me or Brooker – could have foreseen a monkey in a cage, on Dreadnought's desk.

'Primate?' I asked.

'Gold star. Waiting for you, mate,' Dreadnought answered. 'That's the job.' The monkey had recommenced the consumption of its snack. The sound was akin to a slippered frogman flapping his way from the crime scene. 'To take this little sod across town. You ever heard of Bernie Acapulco?'

Brooker shook his head.

'So named because of his fondness for Colombian marching powder, if nothing else. Phew know what I mean. The ole clip round the nostrils.'

Brooker frowned. 'But Dreadnought, that don't even *work*. Acapulco's not in Colombia. It's in Mexico, innit.'

Dreadnought was displeased. He rallied quickly. 'All right then, smartarse,' he went on. 'So named because he's a *cunt*. That better?'

'Much,' I added.

'Now. You wanna argue about a two-bit gangster's surname or do you wanna talk about the job in hand? Your choice.'

'The job. Sorry, Dreadnought.'

'Should think so.'

The monkey turned its back: it was slim, merrily muscled

– grey and tan were the colours of its fur. It farted astonishingly.

'Lord.'

We vacated the backroom and took a step outside for a querulous puff on our eagerly torched cigarettes.

'So what's the game?' asked Brooker. He sounded like a man who had just crawled across the desert. 'Why don't he come and get it himself?'

Dreadnought shrugged. 'Ours ain't to reason why. You up for it?'

'Yeah. What's the cream?'

'Two and a half. Successful completion, like. One snag.'

I'd been waiting for this clause. Evidently so had Brooker, who now said 'Go on' in a wary voice.

'You gotta do it in less than an hour.'

'Eh?'

'Just remembered. Need some shopping.' Dreadnought was distracted. 'Follow me, if you'd be so. Follow me.'

We entered through the back way of the next shop along. It was Mohamed Shabir's tiny supermarket. Not a word was said as we strolled past frozen pizzas, beef pies, fish fingers. Dreadnought leaned into a tomb-like freezer for a satchel of stillborn chips.

Brooker had been with Dreadnought for much less than a year, and I happened to know, having shared the occasional conversation on the subject, that he remained in awe of the older man: the tactical insights, the business *nous*, the canny prescience of delegation. That said (and again, Brooker had been at pains to ensure that I took his point completely: he'd been drunk) Brooker was no effing spud. No chance. He had learned to stick up for himself a bit. 'You have to, don't you?'

'He's only allowing an hour,' Dreadnought explained. 'From here to Ealing Broadway. In the rush hour.'

The idea grazed against Brooker's notion of logical fair play. 'But what's the fucking point?' he demanded. 'Why bother?'

'Gary.' Dreadnought – I could see – was spading away for that elusive inner calm. 'Tell me summing. Do you understand when a twat wiggles his fingers and makes half a mill?'

'No.'

'Or you understand when a computer four-eyes invents summing and a bagga twats pay him a king's ransom?'

'No.'

'Well then. Move the fucking monkey,' said Dreadnought.

iv

Dave Stroker did another runner.

It was a lip-flap after Christmas. The geese had stopped getting fat: the geese were dead. (Goose was dead.) And Dave absconded.

Owing the monthly.

In the back room at Beef Encounter, Dreadnought had taken the news with an ambassadorial nod of the head. 'I see.' And then he had gone back to perusing his fingernails, searching for answers. 'You know summing, Rene?'

'What's that, boss?'

'I'm too old for the Dave Strokers of this world. Fly solo. Fly solo, Rene,' he decided. 'Fly being the operative. Melbourne, I presume.'

'Yes.' But it had taken an unmentioned number of connections between my booted toes and the backside of Stroker's mother before I'd landed upon this piece of information. Maggotville protects its own. And for the record? Kicking a woman in her mid-sixties should be no cunt's idea of fun. I felt travestied and self-betrayed throughout.

'When?' Dreadnought asked.

'Tomorrow.'

'So where's he now?'

'Brother. Northampton.'

Dreadnought sniffed. 'Too obvious,' he declared. 'Not if Mickey getting ticklish with his Mum ain't currency enough.'

'Good.'

'Why? You not like Northampton?'

'It's a place I never visited, Dreadnought,' I told him. 'I was banking on a trip abroad.'

'I want you, Rene, on that fucking bird that Stroker's on. Watch the films. Read your Oompa-Loompa '

'Danish.'

'And shadow the cunt. Arseholes to breakfast-time,' said Dreadnought. 'He take a bogey moment, you're telling me the colour, the size, the consistency. Wallop? He's on the throne? I want a report on how many splashes. You're his guardian angel, Rene: expenses paid. Every move he makes. Like that song. By Bruce Springsteen.'

'Sting,' I corrected him (dangerously).

'Fuck it, Rene. Bruce Springsting, then. Allow yourself a moment off your pedestal, if you would.' Dreadnought sighed.

'The idea being what?'

'You shut him up,' said Dreadnought. 'Make him wriggle like a fat boy at a dance Follow him silly.'

v

Terminal Three of London's Heathrow Airport.

I caught up with Stroker in the Outward Bound Lounge. 'Nain't done nothing wrong,' he said immediately and defiantly.

'Monthly.'

'I left it with me mum!' he raised his voice to protest.

'Keep your voice down, Dave,' I said, taking the seat beside him. Ignoring the stares of a few holidaymakers around us, I went on: 'It's time for you and your mum to have a nice heart-to-heart, Dave. She's of a different opinion.'

'But I left it with her!'

'Then she's spent it, mate,' I told him. 'Anyway, it's irrelevant now; the money's not the issue.

'It is to me!' said Stroker. He leaned forward, his elbows on his knees, his fingertips on his temples. 'But I *left* it with her,' he repeated. 'Devious fucking bitch.'

'Oi. Not your mum, son,' I warned him. 'You don't show your mother disrespect.'

'Not even when she gets you beaten up?' Stroker sounded incredulous.

'I haven't laid a finger on you, Dave.'

'But I'm sort of assuming that you're not going over to watch the cricket.'

'I've already told you: I'm going over to watch you,' I said. 'Do you fancy a pint?'

'We haven't got time, Rene.'

'Nonsense. There's always time for a pint, Dave.'

'Christ. Well, it's your round.'

'Deal.'

Having repaired to the little bar, I ordered two brimming glasses of Worrying Brown and four double whiskies. I had plenty of cash in my pocket. And besides, I had the shakes: I needed the hair of the dog that bit me.

'They won't let you on if you're drunk,' said Stroker. I might have thought that a sensible strategy on his part would be to get me oiled: specifically to get me barred from boarding. Still, maybe he'd thought this and then reconsidered. Disallowed access to the plane, what other pranks might I indulge myself in?

'Well, they won't let me off once I'm on, will they?' I answered, equably enough. 'Once we're on, it's the long haul. I might even sleep.'

I'm not entirely certain what Dave was referring to when he asked, mildly, quietly, 'Is it worth it, Rene?' but I shrugged in an understanding manner and downed my first double. An eerie thought hit home. What if Stroker got too drunk to travel? At Mazza's wake he had been insensible by mid-afternoon; at closing time that evening he'd been found unconscious in the goldfish pond in the pub's back yard. Dave Peacock had not been amused.

The flight left on time.

Roughly two-thirds of the way to Kuala Lumpur, Dave Stroker returned from one of his frequent visits to the plane's lavatory, this time with half a roll of toilet paper attached to his upper lip like a limpet. As he passed me – his seat was five rows in front of mine – I asked him what was wrong. 'Another nosebleed,' was the (obvious) answer. I had slept through much of the flight so far, and through Stroker's two earlier nosebleeds.

I had other things to worry about. Specifically, two other things: the first – that the air-hostess had made it known, in no uncertain terms, that I was not to be served any alcohol; and two – the conversation, the lesson I'd learned from Stroker an hour earlier.

'Been thinking.'

'I'll notify the tabloids.'

'What about this?' said Stroker. 'You and me: together. This is no life for an educated man like you '

'Who told you I was educated?' I asked, attempting sarcasm – and failing.

'Dreadnought did. Who else? You and me: together. You join my team.'

'You serious?'

'As a heart-attack, mate,' said Stroker. 'I'm building, see? Little apples and all that. He's been cock of the walk for too long. Let's hit him where it hurts. Make him feel bad. What do you say?'

'Why would I want to make Dreadnought feel bad?' I asked.

'Because I'd be paying you to.'

'But you don't have any money,' I told him, trying to make my voice twinkle.

'I pay you to beat me up,' he began.

'Don't worry, it won't cost you a penny. Or a dime, by the time we're there. Go back to your seat, Dave. Watch a film.'

'Listen. You sort me out and we take some pictures – but we say that someone else did it. Then I can get all high and mighty about Dreadnought not taking my contract seriously: the protection. Then he'll have to lower the rates because he won't be able to find the culprits. Then I give you the difference. Monthly.'

'I like the word culprits,' I said, 'but I don't see what's in it for you.'

'It's all about not putting your eggs in one basket,' said Stroker.

'A good idea, in theory.' But then he would own me; then my blood would have his antibodies in it. 'I think I'll stick to Plan A. You know why?'

'Why?'

'Two reasons, Dave. One: you can't be trusted. And two: you don't want to underestimate a guy like Dreadnought. To go back to the obvious – who do you think is paying for this trip?'

'Me.'

'In the long run, yes, but Dreadnought in the short.' I smiled. 'I'm curious. What do you really think is going to happen?'

'You're going to kick my teeth out.'

'I didn't say that explicitly,' I told him, 'but that's about the size of it. Not literally your teeth, mind.'

This conversation: on a crowded plane.

'Why don't you just pay the cunt? Monthly. I don't understand you, Dave. None of this would be necessary.'

'I'm broke.'

'Sure. So broke you can pay for a ticket to Melbourne.'

Dave was stoic. 'It's credit card money,' he explained.

'This is the twenty-first century, babe,' I answered, making a mental note never to use the word *babe* in the company of a man ever again. 'Dreadnought takes credit cards.'

There was a pause. Then Stroker said, 'So tell me. What else do you have in mind? It can't be just following me.'

'That's what I was asking *you*!' I coughed. 'Have a think about it,' I advised. 'I'm going to watch the film for a bit. When it finishes, I'll ask you again. Bearing in mind I have no relatives in Australia.'

The film was called *Glass Bowl*. Don't bother. I was actually relieved when Stroker touched my shoulder again, two hours later. By this point we were both clinically strafed on hangovers. 'I've worked it out,' he told me, adopting his kneeling position.

'Go on.'

'Your presence here is designed to keep me scared. And then you're going to follow me to where I'm headed – to worry me about the safety of my loved ones. If I have any loved ones.'

'Oh you do,' I said. 'You've made two escape attempts to the same place. *Of course* you know people there.'

'So you're going to frighten me. Cool.'

'I didn't say that was all, but you've got the right idea – finally.'

'Unless I disappear,' said Stroker, weirdly.

'From the plane? Good luck.'

'Stranger things have been known.'

'No they haven't. Where you gonna go?' I asked. 'The lav? Fine. Have a nosebleed on me. I'll wait till you come out. The pilot's cabin? Also fine: if you can get in in the first place. The cargo hold? Cool. It fucking *will* be cool, mate. You'll freeze your arse off down there.'

For the first time Stroker regarded me with an almost theatrical disdain. 'I didn't say hide,' he said; 'I said *disappear*.'

'Go on. I'm intrigued,' I told him honestly.

vi

What tears me from Flex is betrayal.

His.

It is Flex's betrayal of his mother. He lets her down, and that makes him a cunt: because you don't do that. You don't get your mum in a headlock, and you don't charge rent, and you don't let her down when she needs you.

'But you don't understand,' he says.

'I understand enough.'

'No you don't.'

We've been on the Bone since breakfast. It is now nineteen hundred hours, and come to think of it – Bone *was* our breakfast.

That's the thing about it: you don't remember to eat, and you don't remember what you ate if by some chance you do recall the need.

Flex is sturdy.

We're in a mock-1950s, mock-American diner, and I'm astonished. The desire for food-food is retro enough as it is, but this is just the living end. However, from time to time Flex will appoint himself the arbiter of taste in such regards. It is called Leonardo's. But where are we?

There was no flash to get here.

'You're not serious, are you?' I ask.

'About what?'

'The subject of food.'

'When did you last eat something solid, Wahid?' Flex wants to know. 'Eat a steak.'

'I can't, man. Eat a cow?'

'Yeah! It's better than fucking one!'

'In what way?'

Flex shrugs. 'Basic rights, is it. Correct me if I'm wrong but I do not believe there's yet been an established practice for halal bovine sodomy.'

'Well, you might have me there,' I admit.

'Where's Goose?'

vii

We are leaving. Flex has consumed a steak the size of a briefcase, and I have taken down a bowl of cigarette soup. (Quite yum.) We have already discussed the option of a round or two at Scottish Tony's place: the gloves, the sensors. But my bruises haven't healed from last time. He is telling me about his latest purchase – an implant called Cloacal Clits – when Goose arrives outside Leonardo's. 'The values,' he is saying, 'are sparkling. I could feel her shit on my balls, man.' But Goose's features change the subject.

'What?'

'Flex.'

'What, man?' he asks her.

'Babe. It's your mum.' says Goose.

'Oh no.'

'I'm so sorry.' Goose is crying. 'She's come alive again.'

'No.'

'Darly-babe,' Goose continues, while I maintain a flaw-less silence. 'Apparently, they did everything they could.'

For a little while Flex is even too upset to hit Goose or to hit me. When eventually he cleans the fork he has stolen on my throat, I feel relieved. I feel happy. I vow to send him a condolence implant in the morning.

viii

Live with animals and sooner or later you start to think like an animal. You start to appreciate the humdrum, too. You start to wonder if this is what you've been searching for, your entire life.

'Fucking hell,' said Dreadnought. He was shaking his head, in disbelief. He referred to an unamused waitress at The Balti Drum one evening. All he'd done was ask, for a laugh like, if the finger-bowl water was supposed to taste like soap. 'I couldn't taste no meat or nothing,' he added. 'And honestly, the face on her, Rene! You'd've thought I'd just slapped her arse.'

Dreadnought had made the self-same comment to the self-same waitress a week or so earlier. I might well have been tired of the gag, too.

'Some people,' I said with a rueful tilt of the head.

I found myself thinking of Mazza. I wish I had seen her even semi-naked. I wondered if she was listening from the bed-room – in her soft new bra. Even though the African music was still a pulse, I could see her, curious, not knowing where to listen. I almost formed the fantasy that Mazza was standing there with nothing to conceal her top half.

'I've always thought of you as a loyal cunt, Rene,' said Dreadnought.

'Thanks.'

Mazza came out of the bedroom and wondered if either of us wished for a cup of tea. Unsurprisingly, we both refused. Not more than twenty minutes later, we tasted the late evening air. We were on a mission: to obtain more brandy, more smokes, more diversionary tactics.

'Tell me more about Denmark, would you, Rene?'

'What would you like to know?' I asked.

Dreadnought didn't answer my question. 'Sometimes, mate, I just get fucking sick of this place. Do you know what I mean?'

'I don't blame you. It stinks.'

Dreadnought chuckled. 'You think this smells bad. Wait until we have to do some more work in the country. Which I'll avoid as long as possible.'

'I was born in the country,' I reminded him.

'Yeah, but not in *our* country.'

'Right. We put a different perfume on our cows' arses in Denmark.'

'You're being sarcastic,' Dreadnought said.

'You're learning,' I answered and I took a moment to wonder how many others — Brooker included — would have been allowed to get away with a bit of point-scoring like that. Was it simple gratitude or relief at finding someone who wanted to share his free time that had saved my Danish bacon on this occasion? My thoughts were in a late-night mash.

ix

It is difficult to say into which division of mourning Dreadnought threw his fullest, purest energy: his mother's or Mazza's. But it's fair to say that neither death went unpunished. Not in the timeline that is closest to my heart, at any rate. Make no mistake about it: Dreadnought's world is a man's, man's world. And yet it is the loss of two women in his life that pole-axes – briefly – his confidence and psychopathic sensibilities.

Although Dreadnought's campaign of questioning any-one, medical, religious and bureaucratic alike (come one, come all) who had held in their hands any aspect of Dolly's life, health or death remained civil and polite, there would be no sense in denying that it was conducted in any way other than a paramilitary style. Eventually he was satisfied that all that could have been done had been done. With a generalised sniff and a day-long rattle of coughs, he settled up the undertaker's bill (four grand!) and set to work finding Mazza's killer singular or killers plural.

Needless to say, this was not simple terrain to tramp through: not for any of us. Never the most patient man when it came to the indiscretions and general sauce of others, Dread-nought almost seemed to start a new life in the weeks following Mazza's murder. It was the all-new Dreadnought Show for a while there. (On occasions I wondered where I was in time.) The new and improved Dreadnought: improved in all his fine-tuned unimprovements. He became his cherished Bent-ley: large and noisy, perplexingly unreliable. One time he even picked Charlie Peacock up on his *swearing*. He flicked Brooker's nose on hearing from the younger man a joke of admittedly dubious taste, citing me as the reason for the reaction.

'Don't forget,' Dreadnought said, 'our friend Rene is from overseas as well.'

I don't know how we coped. If the aftermath of Dolly's death was paramilitary, then the aftermath of Mazza's was *military*. Foot soldiers – me and the lads – awaited instructions at the bottom of the chain of command. And it was brutal. Menace – the corporations, control and strategic administrations of menace – became our abiding concept. Menace had evolved into our god.

So who was Dreadnought? A god's god.

One good thing that happened during the run-up to what must have been a fiercely lugubrious Christmas for Flex was that I met the woman who had literally been the woman of my dreams: Monelle. She's a very nice thing: she is dark-skinned, chubbily pretty with the adolescent puppy fat that I happen to know will shrink away, and dark-eyed with horizontal ringlets sprouting from her temples and scalp. She is currently fourteen years old, and a big girl for her age, and she is Denim Jackie's first and only daughter.

Should I have seen this latter fact coming? This relationship with Denim Jackie? Ah! Let me not be hard on myself: it wasn't easy to discern – and besides, mate, these times are *well* confusing. Most of my information about Monelle arrives while I am in the presence of Denim Jackie. *Physical* presence, that is. But wait: in what condition do I happen to be in on most occasions when I encounter Denim Jackie? That's right. Thoroughly wankered. So let me not be too hard on myself. Let me, instead, be hard on Monelle Montfagian.

What age will I be – what age am I? – when I lose my virginity to Monelle? My first woman. At the time of typing I am already thirty-three (my birthday went unnoticed and un-remarked-upon), and Monelle is a twee fourteen. Some age difference. Some age. At how-old have I arrived when I open those thick legs wide? At how-old have I arrived when I spray myself inside her?

Curiously enough, my reaction on meeting Denim Jackie's daughter for the first time was entirely dissimilar to that of meeting Mazza. I had never met Dolly, but oh, these women in my life! It's a man's world – built by women. With Mazza? The closest I know to love; a schoolboy and his notebook, to be filled with poetry about stars and flowers and all things bright and beautiful. But with Monelle? I don't know. Something tribal. Something prequisitive: elemental fear.

The searches for Mazza's killer(s) drew blanks.

II. The Laughter of Crocodiles

i

'I was on a bus once,' said Stroker. 'I think I was about ten, maybe twelve. Young, anyway. And there were these boys from school, they got on the bus. They were bullies.'

These were among the last words that Dave Stroker ever said to me.

'We should really ask someone to swap positions,' I told him. 'I could sell tickets to that spot you're kneeling on.'

'So I says to myself – I say Dave? Why you put up with this malarkey. Losing your lunch money. Your dignity. Just disappear, fuck's sake.'

'Nice work if you can get it,' I said.

'But you *have* got it, Rene,' said Stroker. 'Like attracts like. You been places from your armchair or I'm a Dutchman.'

He paused and I waited. Kwala Lumpur was still half an hour away. The films had been discontinued. I had nothing to read or to write with.

'Tell me, Rene,' said Stroker, leaning closer to my crotch. 'What you call 'em? Me? I call 'em the Impediments.'

'Who?' I asked.

'The forces.' Stroker smiled. 'The ones that take you *outside time*, mate,' he answered.

'And you know what precisely?'

'I just told you: I know the Impediments.'

'Right. And in what way are they impeding anything?' I said. 'Seems to me, Dave, they're giving you everything you want.'

'Except my life back. Sure. Where do you go?' Stroker asked.

It was a twenty-hour flight to Melbourne, Victoria. To be frank? There seemed no point in not speaking the truth. It felt like a revelation.

'The past. And the future.'

Stroker scowled. 'Well no shit,' he answered. 'Would you care to be more specific?'

'You first,' I said cautiously.

'Neanderthal, I think. I live in a cave with my two wives. The full bit: I drag 'em around by the hair; get them up the duff. It's brill. Then I go forward two million years in a space-ship made of diamonds,' Stroker finished.

I waited two seconds. 'Bugger off, Dave,' I said. 'Go back to your seat.'

Stroker laughed. 'Alternative timestreams indeed!' he said. 'Oh, Rene, you sad man. We did have a laugh about that one. Dear oh dear. What do you do for an encore? Anyway. I suppose I'm just saying goodbye, Rene.'

'Goodbye?'

'Yeah. I've had a long think about it and I've decided I don't much care for your plan.'

'You don't *care* for it?'

'No.'

'Oh this is good. Where are you going?'

'Somewhere you'll never find me.'

'But we've been through this, Dave. I'll say it slowly. *We're on a plane.* So unless you're planning on jumping there's no-where to go.'

Stroker smiled. 'So limited,' he told me, giving me cause for concern: perhaps he did intend to jump. 'I'll be seeing you again, like *not*.' With which he headed back for the lavatories, raising a blood-spattered tissue to his freshly-leaking nose.

ii

He resembled a slightly upper-class scarecrow as he weaved his way to Denim Jackie's. He resembled a freshly assembled bonfire guy: an amalgam of earlier, and well-used, parts: Gary Brooker. Gary Brooker on his way to attempt a scam. Which would crumble.

Through the double doors he scrambled – getting the whole push-pull thing arse-about-face. Juggling coins and paper, he paid his entrance fee in cash (band on) and then blurted his way in with the elegance and charm of an unexpected twin's arrival. He spent a few seconds reclaiming his balance and securing his bearings. With a thorough stare he scoured the room. Brooker was anchored down by drink. Brooker was *wankered*.

Denim Jackie was not on duty: fortunately for Brooker, if for nobody else. The word had gone around that Jackie had ventured abroad to Benidorm for her annual holiday. As Brooker clambered, as if up a scree, towards the bar, the attendant barman (his name-badge said 'Dave') marked him out of ten. A one. Even wall-eyed pissheads gave elaborate shakes of the head and the occasional frown-and-tut as Brooker attempted to find harbour at the mahogany sally-port. Brooker said, 'A pie-na whisky-chase, yeah?'

'Ain't you had enough, mate?' Dave asked.

To give the man his credit, Brooker did at least plump the query for a moment, as if it were a flattened pillow. Then he said, in his slowest voice, 'But why would I ask for more if I've already had enough?'

'All right, mate. Say it again what you want.'

The drinks arrived. Causing a greedy neck-warming sensation, Brooker downed the whisky in one go. Then he used the lager to put the fire out. To a sigh that would be heard from one end of the bar to the other, Brooker slumped down on his stool. His upper body, more or less, described a sphere.

'What time's the show?'

Dave appeared surprised. The band – a tribute act called The Roaring Stones – had arrived and were being pampered backstage; but Dave failed to comprehend how a man like this would ever have been privy to such information. 'About nine. Any second now.'

Brooker gargled lager with the enthusiasm of a drowned man newly flushed by oxygen. Brooker coughed. 'I'll stay for twenty minutes,' he said, 'and then I'll take the list and try to make a night of it.'

Dave waited and whitened and Brooker gave him his full attention: the university-fresh face; the cooked-fat blanched forehead skin. 'Do you or do you not know who I am, my friend?' Brooker asked.

'Who are you?'

Mention of the list had thrown him. Only a few people knew about the list. 'I work for Dreadnought,' Brooker fibbed. 'Sent me to collect the list.'

Dave's eyes grew piggy with suspicion. 'I'll have to check this,' he warned but Brooker just shrugged.

'Check away. Got this to finish and I wanna hear 'Angie' anyway. It's me bird's name. My ex-bird, I should say.'

What clinched it for Dave was the way that Brooker now rotated away and turned his back: a gesture seeped in carefree insouciance. While moving to the other end of the bar, under the pretence of collecting a few dirty glasses, the barman made his decision. Denim Jackie had left him in charge while she holidayed; he didn't wish to be regarded as the sort of wimp who could not make his own mind up. Barring a negligible mistake over the ordering of tonic water, Dave had handled the pub with aplomb.

He would hand over the list with a moonish, half-cowed expression and something like 'Sorry, mate: you can't be too careful.' The matter, all being well, would be resolved in an instant. Five stars for the golden boy.

Brooker applauded as the Roaring Stones arrived on stage, packeted, primped and pimped – all faux-1970s glitter and glam. There was fake-Jagger, there was fake-Keith. This being an East End pub gig, the band carried its own instruments onto the dinky podium. Leaving your instruments unattended in a place like this was flirting with fate.

Tune-ups. Dave watched Brooker and Brooker regarded the band. The pint was finished and Brooker yodelled for another.

The lead singer's elasticated one-word greeting suggested that he might have taken his impersonation of Jagger a step too far. It sounded like 'Ull-o-ow.' Then three voices at two microphones a cappella'd the opening words in an eerie extension to the actual.

'She's a *how*-a-wow-wownky tarnk woman!'

Breathe. Breathe. Breathe.

'Gimme, gimme, gimme the harnky tarnk blue-oooz.'

Brooker set to on his new pint. Many a lisp and slurp, a fart and burp ensued. The Roaring Stones did their thing, and fake-Jagger strangled his vowels through the repertoire.

The list to which Brooker had referred was a burglar's tool, and little more. It was simple. When there was a band or a comedian on, some people chose to pre-book their tickets and make a special evening of it. Such people would often use credit cards. As part of the booking process, Denim Jackie would ask for an address to send the tickets to. This meant that on the night in question there was a fair to middling chance that a property would be unoccupied, temporarily. Dreadnought would send in Frank the Ferret or Chemo-Sebby – with the ten-gallon holdall and the skeleton key. A three-way split would be resolved: the thief, Dreadnought, and of course Denim Jackie.

'Here you go, mate,' bellowed Dave as he handed over the list. 'Just a few this time.'

Brooker accepted the piece of paper. He wrapped lager around his tongue and hollered, 'Cheers!' His heart was aflame; his blood rinsed powerfully. Brooker forced himself to endure the rest of 'Ruby Tuesday' before completing his pint. Then he stood and performed a dumb salute.

'Later, potater,' he said to Dave the barman.

Dave stabbed a small glass at an optic.

Brooker had not heard the band play 'Angie' and would never know if it had been part of the evening's selection. Other matters were more important. What was on his mind were the addresses – which he now scanned with his liquid vision, attempting to determine which was closest and which the furthest away. Panic rumbled inside his torso. It had started to rain. Brooker knew that he had come a greater distance than ever before: he had cheated on Dreadnought. Somewhere down the line there'd be hell to pay.

He got into his car. In truth, Brooker could scarcely focus further than the windshield glass, but he prodded the engine into life anyway. The nearest address was near Walthamstow Station. Brooker had grown up here.

The journey, nevertheless, was frantic; parking was simple: the block had underground spaces. Brooker chose to leave his vehicle near the children's play area: the area which no child would be seen dead in. Vandalised swings, wood chippings, a rash of graffiti, some dogdirt and the remains, it seemed, of an early bonfire. Rain drizzled. Swaying in the earthy breeze, Brooker regarded the area with discomfort. All it needed for utter infant impracticality was an abandoned syringe, some soiled dressings, a dead pet or two, a knot of condoms, a co-matose junkie. Sad.

'Mind your car for you, mister?' said a youthful voice: a girl's. She was nine or ten, sitting on top of a wall by the slope down to the parking lot – sitting with her twin sister, and dressed in identical clothes to the other girl.

'Mind your car for you?' she repeated.

'How much?'

'Tenner.'

'I'll give you two quid. I'll only be in there five minutes.'

The girl shrugged. 'You know where you can stick your two quid, mate. I ain't gonna be responsible for nothing for two quid.'

'Jesus. What are you doing outside at this time anyway?' Brooker wanted to know.

'Minding cars,' the twins said simultaneously.

'A fiver if the car's hunky dory when I get back. Deal?'

The girls checked with one another. As one they nodded. 'Deal.'

'Good. This place got security locks or what?'

'Hasn't everywhere?'

'She'll have to buzz you in.'

'She?'

'Your bird.'

'Your bit of minge.'

'Can't you talk nicely?'

'Why?'

'Why not? Fuck's sake! Get me in, could you? You live here?'

'Yeah.'

'A tenner should do it.'

'Fiver.'

'You can't love her very much.'

'Do we have a deal?' Brooker was starting to feel, an entire twelve hours too soon, the rum effects of his overburdened kidney: he wanted to vomit; he wanted to hit someone. What if these two brats, so idly content to execute a scam of their own in the piddling rain, lived in the very flat that he was all set to ransack? Embarrassing: Brooker would even be ten pounds down on the deal.

'Up front,' said one of the girls.

'You're on.' Brooker approached the pair and sliced his right hand into the right pocket of his pants. Not for the first time that evening he juggled change. 'Here.'

'You wankered intcha, mate.'

The girls laughed.

'Yeah I am a bit. Do you want this fiver?'

One of the girls held out her hand – the girl who had spoken originally. Into it Brooker tipped a waterfall of loose coins and lint.

The girls propelled themselves off the wall. Soaked to the skin. Brooker started off towards the front door of the building. The girls were close behind him, and Brooker turned sharply to face them. 'And where do you think you two are going?' he demanded.

'To let you in, man.'

'Who's looking after my car? We had a deal. One of you: one of you comes with me. The other one watches my motor.'

'No way.'

'Or give me my money back. We had an arrangement.' It shamed Gary Brooker to acknowledge the sense of superiority. Was this the best that he could do? – to outwit pre-teenagers in the gathering murk? But he could not deny it: Brooker felt better for having swift-footed these sisters – and he enjoyed the idea of separating and scaring them.

'What's your name, darling?' Brooker asked the girl who accompanied him all the way to the heavy front door.

'Gwyneth.'

'And your sister?'

'Tina.'

Tina had dropped back. Almost touching, Gwyneth and Brooker approached the entrance. The girl fished in her tight front pockets for a key. It was the tiny purse in which it was en-cased that saddened Brooker so. Nothing so childish, he found himself opining, than a miniscule purse in a miniscule palm.

They entered. The lobby was square, small and atmo-spherically clogged with disinfectant: the cleaner had splashed it around like aftershave.

'You're on your own now,' Gwyneth said, and Brooker nodded.

'Fine.'

'When you come out we get the other five, right?'

'You could get a whole load more than that,' Brooker re-plied. 'But it means you have to keep your mouth shut. Can you do that?'

'I don't know.'

The lift arrived. Without a beat Brooker entered. 'See you in a bit.'

'Wait! What you doing?'

'Thieving. What you think I'm doing?'

Gwyneth stepped into the car. Brooker could tell that she

was as nervous as hell.

The doors wrinkled shut.

Brooker bubbled with undiluted loathing. It was clear that his life and the life of this child were immiscible. A wild burp rose up Brooker's alimentary canal. His arm shot out to an accompanying growl: the heel of his hand connected with Gwyneth's temple. The shock of the blow sent her head to the wall of the elevator car.

She whimpered. Stepping closer Brooker managed to find an outlet for the frustration in which he'd bathed for so long. Although Gwyneth scarcely made it up to his Adam's apple, Brooker leaned in with a left and then a right to Gwyneth's face.

The girl began to squeak. The noise angered Brooker even more, and as much out of triumph as anything else, he laid in with a few digs to her undeveloped body.

The conflict was short-lived. Gwyneth slumped down. She found a corner of the car and curled into a ball. Brooker stepped out, feeling bad, feeling the worst. The girl was crying as Brooker ambled away. The flat he was after was 399. He found it and rang the bell.

No one answered. To make certain he rang again. This time the bell was so strident that it resembled the building's pulse. The bad tooth in Brooker's mouth reverberated.

Brooker removed the chisel and the hammer from two different pockets, and caring not a jot for the noise he made, set to on the rust-pocked lock. The corridor was bald and bare, and the blows ricocheted up and down: a terrible din. Brooker knew that he might have only a few seconds before somebody complained.

A door opened. A brown face in a headscarf peered around the frame. Brooker sighed. With a haughty look of compromised privacy Brooker turned.

'I call police.'

'Yeah you do that, darling,' Brooker replied and recommenced knocking five bells of shit out of the flat's front door. He was sweating. His frustration drew spittle, which effervesced in the miniscule splinter between his lips. Brooker put his back into it.

The lock fell to pieces like pastry.

iii

There was only time to drop his suitcase of goodies before the man's two palms made contact with his chest. The case fell. Brooker toppled back into the elevator car, insistent on keeping balanced.

The other man – shortish, brutish-looking, resplendent in a lugubrious 'tache and iron filing teeth – followed him into the cave. 'Do you wanna know what we called cunts like you in the Navy?' he asked.

'What are you talking about?'

'Slapping kiddies around, eh, you bully. Is what I'm talking about.'

Brooker was perfunctorily jabbed: cheek and chin.

'What do you have to say for yourself, cunt? She's my neighbour's girl.'

'I didn't slap her,' said Brooker, and received a blow to the side of the head. 'Leave it out, mate,' he slurred. Not that the poke had hurt, or caused much discomfort: it was more the truth that this imbecilic altercation was eating time.

'Or you'll do what, you *bully*?'

The gauche antagonism scythed efficiently through Brooker's stratum of inebriation. He stood up for himself. Snot puddled on the isosceles above his top lip. 'Leave it *out*,' he shouted.

Brooker stepped towards him and aimed a volley of fist-blows into his face and neck.

The little girl had started screaming. Bothered little by the resulting din, Brooker maintained his assault on the aggrieved resident. Both men swore as they went at it hammer and tongs.

In time, Brooker allowed his victim to lie at Gwyneth's feet, unmolested. Behind his back the elevator doors closed. Pointing a finger he said to the girl, 'Shut your mouth. Shut up now.' Then to his opponent: 'What's the matter with you, eh? – picking fights with total strangers: you thick or summing? I coulda mangled you, you worthless turd. And you were in the *Navy?* You should be ashamed of yourself, fighting like a woman like that. You're a disgrace. Take some lessons.'

With which, breathing heavily, raggedly, Brooker made for the heavy metal door. Outside, the air was cold and rain lanced down; Brooker felt the chill of perspiration beneath his shirt. Not bad, he thought, but it would be ill-advised to dilly-dally. To the car! Brooker marched across to the children's play area, and heard the door swing closed with a thorough click at precisely the same instant that he remembered where he'd left the suitcase.

Too drunk for this nonsense, he thought.

'Where is she?' asked a girl's voice. 'Where's me sister?'

Information came lurching. 'Oh God,' Brooker whispered, recalling that he'd dropped the case in the lift, and had left his hammer and chisel in the burgled flat. Two metres from the car Brooker wondered if what he was experiencing qualified as a panic attack.

The other girl approached. She sounded displeased as she reminded Brooker of the money he owed. 'For keeping your car safe,' she said.

'It's Tina, isn't it?' Brooker asked. 'I'll make it ten if you do me a favour. I've left my case in the lift.'

'You weren't carrying no case,' Tina answered.

'It's my girlfriend's,' said Brooker. 'I'll give you another fiver if you go and get it.'

'All right. Up front though,' Tina told him sternly.

This was going too slowly, and Brooker was starting to feel the rub. Everyone knew that you had to speculate to accumulate, but how much was he already down on the night? He fished for the requisite five pounds, pausing only to consider asking if this girl would take a cheque. He handed her the coins; she rough-housed them into her jeans pocket. 'And now a fiver for the case,' she told him.

It was a lose-lose situation, Brooker clarified suddenly. If he gave her the money, she would go in and meet Gwyneth and the vigilante, and stay put. But if he insisted on seeing the case before he issued the payment, she would still enter the building and not return.

'Give me my money back,' Brooker demanded.

The elfish smile that Tina now drew suggested that she understood the fun to be at an end. She ran from the children's play area.

'Up your arse, mate,' she called, but the tone of voice was warm and friendly.

For Brooker, there was nothing to do but leave. The burn of booze in his chest felt waspish, like a sting. His tooth took this moment to remind him that it had not finished playing up. Everything had gone wrong. For a split second Brooker even believed that he'd dropped his car keys. If this had been the case he might as well have phoned the law himself: *come and get me.*

The engine gunned. Brooker reversed out, his tail-lights changing the rain to drops of blood. He would motor on over to The Bottom of the Barrel and get last orders. Maybe a snack, too; had he eaten today? Brooker couldn't remember anything but beer and spirits passing his lips. Oh no, there'd been that bacon sarnie at The Graveside: with all that gristle it had been like eating a Rubik's Cube.

Traffic lights up ahead. Fortunately the driver in front was having the same idea as Brooker: to race forwards before the light could turn red. You had to admire such common sense and good grace. Brooker was half a metre behind, nothing more, and was indulgently reprimanding himself for his lack of planning this evening – when the driver of the car ahead changed his mind and slammed on the brakes.

There was not even a second to swear. There was less than a second to acknowledge why the driver had decided not to jump the lights: a police car was parked across the junction, outside the kebab shop.

And then there was noise.

So much noise.

iv

On paper, probably, provoking a spontaneous reaction might sound good, but do we really want to do it in our lives? We're happy provoking something gentle – a fond smile of reminiscence, a flicker of befuddlement at a question posed – but do we want to provoke extreme reactions in our daily existences? *I* don't. But I did it anyway – I provoked an extreme reaction – on the morning that I kangarooed the Bentley to Bible Street Cars. A guy named Roy had said that he'd have a look at it on Dreadnought's behalf. And when I arrived I provoked the extreme reaction of *maniacal laughter*.

Mechanics must poke their thermometers, of course, into the sickest of vehicles; but there was something about the Bentley's appearance – appearance or demeanour – that changed the mood at the garage that day. I had honestly never seen anything quite like it. Rotund, ill-shaven and fashionably dirty for his profession, Roy had already been on the outside courtyard, having a smoke. At the first glimpse of the Bentley he had built his way up to a laughing jag of imbecilic, disturbing proportions. A full five minutes later, Roy now leaning against the wall to the reception area, and with tears springing out of his face he called, 'Lads! Lads, come out here! Quick! Oh my word.' And he was off again.

Roy's team – a similarly shaped but much younger man named Dennis, and a beanpole called Chris – emerged from the cave. There was nothing to discuss. Immediately they started snorting and bellowing their mirth. No doubt wearing a concerned expression, I allowed this to continue for yet another five minutes. I even popped the hood, the better to expedite some sort of examination. The hint remained untaken. The very sight of the Bentley had catapulted the men into a world made only of humour.

'Where's Gaz?' asked Roy, briefly gaining his composure. 'He should see this, too. Where is he?'

'Making the brews,' Dennis answered.

'Gaz! Gazza, get out here, mate!'

They waited. Chris had taken to holding his crotch, unsure of whether or not he could keep the urine in his bladder. Dennis managed to climb back off his knees, having previously collapsed from a momentary lack of oxygen. Roy dried his eyes.

'What?' I asked. '*What?*'

'Oh Lordy,' was how Roy answered. 'Where did you

beam that one down from?'

'What?'

'Hang on. Here's Gaz. Gazza-mate,' said Roy, the skin around his eyes crinkling and deepening. 'You ever seen something like this?'

Gazza was provoked into a spontaneous reaction of his own, but it wasn't laughter. So was I. But I wasn't laughing either. Our eyes met; my heart sank.

It was Brooker.

v

A spontaneous reaction: another one that I provoked; another one that I inspired.

It was of course Dreadnought's.

'Rene? Run that past me again.'

'I can't explain it!' I shouted.

'Run that past me again.'

I waited. 'He got away,' I repeated.

What had happened?

Stroker had not returned from the plane's toilet, bloody-nosed or otherwise. An increasingly surreal series of minutes had elapsed.

In quiet desperation, quite frankly, I had eventually notified the very same hostess who had issued the no-booze dictum. I explained. But not before I'd lumbered the length and not inconsiderable breadth of the British Airways flight, in search of the quixotic Stroker. No dice. He had to have sat somewhere else, I had reasoned. Moon-faced and moon-eyed passengers, some of them liquid on airline moonshine had returned my gaze with expressions borrowed from the bureau of disbelief. My cheek. My sauce. My nerve. I couldn't find him. I couldn't find the character.

Toilets: empty. Staff kitchen preparation area: empty. Disobeying the pilot's announcement, the admonitory light above my head, and the assertion of the hostesses themselves, I had prowled and patrolled the bird, looking for Dave. And he wasn't there. He wasn't there. The cockpit was the only possibility: not even the disgusted yelps of First Class had offered up anything more, from me, than a disconnected moan of frustration.

Kuala Lumpur, I decided. Get him there: airport toilets. However, my heart had refused to settle down and rest. Every couple of seconds, I had leaned my body out into the aisle, the better to view the seat that had once belonged to the escaped. Good and ready for the challenge, I had even ensured that I was first, or among them, to disembark.

'Rene? You can find him – choice is yours,' said Dreadnought, 'you can find him or you can suffer the consequences on your return. Your decision.' He hardly paused for breath. 'Mav-fact: *don't* find him and don't bother. Coming back. Won't be nothing worth twenty-odd hours of travelling for you here, cunt. Go back to your tax returns.'

'I'm not an accountant,' I said.

'You're not a shadow either!'

'I apologise.'

'Rene. I don't give, if I'm honest, a monkey's toss what you used to do,' said Dreadnought. 'But I give you one thing to do. He's found. Okay? Or don't darken my cliffs. He's found.' He paused. 'He's found.'

vi

'What do you think you're doing?' I ask.

'Need the money.' He shrugs.

'The *money?* He'll slap you the length of Tuesday, man! You signed a contract!'

Indignantly Brooker pipes up. 'I did no such thing!'

'Well you should have. Christ.'

There is a long pause.

'I need to work, Rene,' Gary informs me.

When Dreadnought finds out that Brooker has been moonlighting, he will use the younger man's eyelashes for rectum-ticklers. He'll spank him silly.

Wouldn't blame him either.

Part of the initial interview: you don't do it. You don't floozy around with another job, willy nilly (whatever that means). It's simple. *You don't do it.*

vii

To my astonishment, it is Mickey – surly, caveman Mickey, the same man who, one gets the impression, doesn't much care for speaking – it is Mickey, post-Dolly and post-Mazza, who is nudged to a rare moment of confession by a catastrophic intake of alcohol, even by *his* standards, and by the magic ingredient of a litmus paper wrap of amphetamine.

'Tell you summing,' I deciphered him saying. Me, I'd only had eight or nine pints. 'Shunt be saying this but it ain't the first time.'

'What ain't?'

'Summon poked her.'

'Who?'

'Mazza.'

'Someone *poked* her?'

'Keep your voice down!'

'Who, Charlie?' I asked, not even attempting to keep the jealousy out of my voice.

'You. If the rumours are true,' he replied.

'They're not. I'm horrified,' I added, in genuine terror. 'Are you winding me up, Mickey?'

'Rumours '

'Mickey, nothing ever happened between me and Mazza.'

'So you say,' Mickey conceded, shrugging, the three syllables uttered, for some reason, in a rising scale of singsong. 'Then Frank. Then Des.'

'Frank the Ferret? Des Lewis? You're *wrong*, Mick. As if!' It was all too ridiculous to be true. 'Dreadnought doesn't think I shagged his wife, does he? Because I didn't.' By repeating the refutation I was praying that Mickey would remember our conversation when he sobered up.

Mickey started giggling.

viii

'You've changed genres, mate.'

A conversation with Dreadnought, but a far from conventional, entertaining or even simple one. And things up to then had gone relatively swimmingly. Now I couldn't hear him very well: I was in the next room – in the bedroom. Not long into our evening of preparing lobster thermidore – me with my Dictaphone, my notepad, my poised biro, and Dreadnought at the stove, testing temperatures with his thumb – he had taken a business call, and of course I had been banished to the boudoir. Shamefaced, almost, I had closed the door and prepared myself to eavesdrop. I had sat on Mazza's side of the bed, but of course there would be no Mazza to fill it again.

No Mazza. At which unavoidable conclusion, I confess, a tear had formed. The room still wore her presence. Lightly tanned though the ceiling was from a generation of Dreadnought's cigarette smoke (post-coital? lazy breakfast?), the bedroom had Mazza's stamp. Do all bedrooms of married couples lean eventually towards the woman's tastes? Seriously, I'd like to know. Uncle Hektor's and Aunt Else's bedroom had been a masterpiece nightmare of chintz, pink, frills, florals and lace. And *he* had butchered livestock for a living. Correlation? The harder — the needier, the bloodier — the man's job, the more vibrantly feminine their marital room? Possibly. But what if the wife is the thug? How butch would the room have to be then? Football posters? Flesh mags? Socks rotting in piles on the upturned maws of discarded pizza boxes?

Has Dreadnought even been in here since Mazza died? I wondered. The bed was made, for one thing, and I can't imagine my manager as a bed-making kind of guy. A glisten of perfume was in the air. Some of Mazza's laundry was in a tidy pile on the dresser, telling the story of a woman who was interrupted during the process of filing away her things. Interrupted permanently.

What made me do it?

What compelled me to rise from my space on the Flex bed, run my eyes across the vast array of possible objects of Mazza's to steal — a lipstick that had touched her mouth, a canister of fragrant spray, the former being simple to conceal — and to let my eyes roam back again to that tidy stack of laundry? Did the Devil make me do it? Did market forces make me do it? I took a pair of Mazza's briefs and stuffed them into the pocket of my slacks.

'You've changed genres, mate,' Dreadnought called. I jolted. Having misheard him, my first inclination was that I was being accused of changing jumpers. Getting out of my clothes in Dreadnought's bedroom? Incriminating evidence, that, I could imagine him saying; like in a sex farce.

I returned to the kitchen. For a snack while he prepared

dinner, Dreadnought was spooning cottage cheese from the pot. The pint of brandy and coke (equal measures) that he had only sipped before the phone rang, no more than three minutes earlier, was now empty. An aperitif often gave Dreadnought the munchies.

'That was Peephole Pete,' he said. 'Tell me, Rene: what's your views on the porn industry?'

'There's something for everyone,' I told him.

'Very diplomatic. Seriously.'

'You said I'd changed genres,' I said. 'I have nothing to do with pornography.'

'I didn't say you did. That's something different,' said Dreadnought. 'What I was referring to there is you've gone from mainstream to crime – and now science fiction. You've changed genres.'

'Science fiction,' I repeated. 'I knew you wouldn't believe me.' He had promised, my having told him why I had first come to London to find him, to think about what I'd said – credit due that he didn't laugh it out of John's Caff outright – and now he was passing on his verdict. I was science fiction, pure and simple. And what could I show him as proof?

Dreadnought reached for the Dictaphone, which was on top of the bread bin. He thumbed the STOP button: don't want no one hearing this, do we? I read into the action. 'Let's sit down. I didn't say I didn't believe you.'

As I started work on my pint of vodka and orange – the brandies of the previous occasions having done my digestive system no favours – I waited for more information. The brow curdled: Dreadnought was composing his thoughts. I continued to work on my drink.

'It's a wild tale, I'll give you that.'

'I've known about you since I was a child,' I told him

again, and he nodded.

'I was your imaginary friend.'

'Sort of.'

'Then you became involved in genealogy. You had a feel for it.'

I nodded. 'I often knew more about people than they thought I knew.' I shrugged. 'It seemed like an obvious career choice.'

'Right. I want to read your notes, Rene.'

Did my face give me away? Was I fast enough? I said, 'What notes, Dreadnought?' in as calm a voice as I could muster.

'You're not telling me you're not writing this down,' Dreadnought said. 'What's your laptop for?'

'Downloading porn.'

'Well, obviously. But what else?'

'You can't read them,' I told him.

'Pardon me?'

'You can't. They're not finished,' I said quickly.

Dreadnought laughed. Leaning forward (he's gaining weight) he picked up the bottle of brandy and filled his pint glass to the halfway mark. 'And what's to say Frank the Ferret ain't round your flat right now, Rene.'

'It's password protected.'

Dreadnought poured in the Coca-Cola. 'We have ways of getting passwords, Rene. Technology's nuffing when you happen to embody the quality of perseverance. Like I do.'

'Then I'll ask you politely,' I said. For Dutch courage I took a good long swig. 'Please let me finish what I've started.'

'What *I* started, you mean,' Dreadnought countered. In three long swallows he drank half a pint. 'Besides. Surely you know how it all ends if you're so gifted.'

'You don't believe me, then,' I wanted to clarify.

'Who killed Mazza, Rene?'

'I don't know.'

'Then what's the *point* of your knack?' he demanded.

'I didn't say it had a point! It's just *there*. But it's not an exact science, Dreadnought. I wish it was. I see drafts of you in the future and in the past.'

'You told me.'

'Well I'm telling you again!' I said. 'Sometimes slightly to the side, where things are the same but only more so. Where a virus – a normal computer virus – can fuck up an entire house's electricity system. It can't happen, can it? But it *does*, Dreadnought.'

The alcohol or the relief of finally shedding my load was making me emotional. With the heel of my hand I wiped clean my nostrils. I took a large swallow. And I listened to the one sentence that I hadn't ever considered him uttering. The shock made me drop my pint glass, spilling the contents on the ghastly Persian rug.

He said: 'Yes, I've had that vision myself.' And then he added: 'You can lick that mess up for a start, Rene. Who knows? Things are so whacked-out, she might be coming home in a minute.'

III. Invisible Pills

i

When I look back, it's with an acknowledging sigh that I realise my behaviour at Kuala Lumpur Airport would not have gone unnoticed. Among the police staff I made lots of new friends. My interpreter was a sterling figure of a man as well. They held me for nigh-on two hours, after one of KL's Finest had roughhoused me to the floor outside a holding-bay trattoria. The office was cool, smelt vaguely of a photographic darkroom. I was allowed to smoke.

The fact that the BA staff corroborated my story of there having been a passenger in Dave Stroker's seat when the plane took off was more of a hindrance than a help. It opened up a new feast of worms, never mind a can. Where had he gone? How did I know him? No longer could I be regarded as a simple-minded nuisance, kicking in the stall doors of every toilet at Kuala Lumpur Airport, having drunk heavily before the flight. This was more serious. I finished my cigarettes, and my interpreter kindly offered to fetch me more.

Upon my release, I checked at the desk if I could get on the next flight back to London. No dice. The ticket was good but the flight was full. So my choices were: to go out into the language barriers of Kuala Lumpur, if I could, and try to find Stroker; or to continue my onward journey to Melbourne. I opted, in the end – and the decision cost me sweat and a hardy battering on the credit card for airport coffees – for the third alternative: I would sit it out in the departure lounge. After all, Stroker had a decent record of allowing himself to be captured in airport lounges.

Having calmed down a smidge, I used my card again, this time in the bookshop – figuring that I might as well get some research work done: research on Brooker. If our Gary was the one who would betray our Dreadnought, it made sense to keep tabs on his hobbies, on Gary's hobbies, the better to stay part of his life once he'd been outcast. I coughed up for a broadsheet, a tabloid, *The Racing Post, What Car?, Gone to the Dogs* (a scruffy edition for the greyhound-racing lover) and *Jazz to the Max* (to keep up with Brooker's ululations of proud respect for the likes of Miles Davis). I settled down in the smoking section, keeping half an eye open for the Strokemeister.

When I got back to London, I was ready. For taunts, threats, dismissal. It wasn't much to hold my esteem together, but I could go this far: I had done my best. The Bloody Chamber had opened early to show the England game (England versus Denmark: define 'irony') in Japan on the big screen. Eight forty-five in the morning, and I was ordering my first pint. This had to stop. But some of the staff had been in since dawn, watching the pre-match footage, and Dave Peacock in particular was uncharacteristically wankered. I sat down and said, 'Morning, lads.'

'Christ,' said Charlie Peacock, turning to me with an expression of feigned horror on his face. 'He can see us!'

'Yeah yeah '

'The invisible pills ain't working, boys! New batch, new batch! Abort!'

'Yeah yeah.'

The laughter of crocodiles.

As Gary suggested a game of hide and seek, Mickey launched into his caterwauled rendition of 'When Will I See You Again?'

You take the piss-takes. It's the only thing you can do: take the piss-takes. 'Yeah yeah.'

'Beam me up, Scotty!' shouted Dreadnought himself (to my relief).

'Yeah yeah.'

We passed, altogether, an easy enough seventy minutes of jibes along similar lines – Strawberry Jeff, a rare appearance, putting Queen's 'The Invisible Man' on the jukebox; Brooker playing I Spy With My Little Eye game, something beginning with D (the answer was dick) – when Dreadnought sat up straight, had a spit, announced he was forgoing the hilarities for a moment in favour of a wet, groaned up to his feet, leaned in to my ear and said, 'Words, Rene. Later.'

Words.

It wasn't until Dreadnought dropped his bombshell – as his mother had forty-two years earlier, detonating the fat baby after whose own girth he had been named upon the world – about having what he called 'visions' of his own that I would seriously doubt that I, and I alone among the world's citizens, could possess such as gift as I do. But as soon as he told me that, I knew one thing. Stroker could do it, too.

Stroker knew timelines as well. And more. The stroker had learned how to use them. He had taken his invisible pills.

ii

Greed is Brooker's downfall unless you factor in women. Which, I guess, points to the same failing in his psychological make-up. I see it clearly. Having wooed, for example, the girl of his dreams – Angie – he remains unsatisfied. His relationship with Trudi, his sister, is a disaster. I can't see his mother anywhere. Perhaps I should ask Dreadnought.

Greed is also apparent in Brooker's attitude to eating,

drinking, gambling and drugs. He blows himself out, the throat of a bullfrog. He loses everything. Everything but his watch, possibly, his hair, his cock and the glasses that he will soon need to wear.

Greed is Gary's friend. Greed tells Gary to forsake Dreadnought's condition of employment which states that no other manager may share a staff member. But Greed didn't kill Mazza Flex. Neither did Gary Brooker.

I did.

Only joking! Man! Am I in a funny mood or what. For the prying eyes of Dreadnought who may be reading this, or Frank the Ferret, Conscience or God, I am only joking. I need to lie down. I need to get up. I need to float in-between.

I need a drink.

iii

If the word belatedly means anything in context, I will belatedly explain how I managed to steal Frank the Ferret's wallet that time. Granted, it took some practice, but on the whole, I was disappointed in Frank that a man of his profession should have allowed the theft to be made so easily. All it had taken was the purchase of a book and an idea of Pekinese Pete's.

We're at his restaurant: it's me, Dreadnought, Brooker, Mickey, Denim Jackie, Charlie Peacock and Monelle. And Frank the Ferret. To the internal moans and strainings of my digestive system, I spoon in a curry of atom-splitting intensity. I've already visited the lavatory four times, and this is only the starter. I return to the table and Monelle replaces her hand on my penis, under the table, with a vacant expression on her face. I let it lie there.

Up to his old and categorically boring tricks, Frank the

Ferret is fattening up a no-doubt truthful tale of a blag he has recently pulled off in Paddington. 'So she thinks I've stole her watch, but I say to her "Darlin. It's on your other wrist." She's so busy apologising for what I done and what she's said, she ain't noticed I've got the necklace from her throat and her diamond stud from her belly button. It's a sin! Them halter tops! *Right* invitation.'

We laugh unconvincingly. That Frank can switch your own watch from one wrist to the other, in order to perpetrate a better scam, is beyond perusal; he's even done better than that. He once stole a car, specifically to park it elsewhere and steal a man's tie in the aftermath. It was Sunday and he'd been bored and gone out for a walk.

As Monelle fakes a yawn, leans a bit closer and takes a good cupped hold on my scrotum, it is Charlie Peacock who says, 'You should write some of this down, Frank.'

'Can't.' Smoke spirals from Ferret's nostrils as he adds: 'Don't know one end of the pen from the other.'

'You're illiterate?' I ask.

'Yeah.' He regards me with irrefutable hostility.

'Leave it, Rene,' says ringmaster Dreadnought. 'Frank. He used a bad word. Cunt can't help it he's Danish. He's working in his second tongue.'

No one minds when Monelle is sick on my lap. She has done well to finish thirteen alcopops.

iv

Last night Mazza arrived at my headside in a dream.

'Think more laterally,' she implored me.

I must have spine drafts of my own. Dave vanished. He knew how to manipulate something I'd never learned the colour of, the nature of.

Stroker was the key to everything. I'd led myself miles off the mark with Gary Brooker. Brooker had always been a waste of time, but I hadn't been able to see that. Of all the strange problems I had had in that direction, the one that floored me was this: Gary Brooker had always been *too visible*.

On a scale of betrayal from one to ten, Brooker is a three. He's a no fry, in Dreadnought's terminology. He's a rookie. Big deal: he took a moonlight here, a kickback there, here a bung, there a bunse, everywhere a backhand. He's farmyard corn. He is *nothing*.

His sacking was perfunctory but tearful. The meeting was scheduled for five in the morning at John's Caff, ominously enough: John's Caff, that bullseye of bad news. That hotbed of difficult info-transfer. As tabloid establishments went, John's Caff was bad news.

The hardcore was present. Charlie Peacock had the sort of cold that results in a moustache of sores and blisters. Mickey was grumpily hungover. I was nervous.

In walked Dreadnought. Spruced and efficient-looking, he approached the counter and ordered five Full Englishes. I had come to learn what it was – what it is – that so repulsed me about the Full English breakfast: the mixture of egg yolk, undercooked beans and black pudding. A second term abortion of food. Why do you put yourselves through this? I would rather have raw herrings, and that's saying something.

While tucking into our food, or in my case nibbling nauseously on a sailor's rope sausage, Dreadnought called for an update of our individual projects. Personally, I gave mine while napkinning a facepack of fried bread grease from the webbing between my thumb and forefinger. I told him that everything was fine and he told me that that was delicious. Which was more than our breakfast was. Midway through, I took a break to light a cigarette and open the can of lager that John is not licensed to sell but sells anyway. No one minded. And no one told Mickey that he had a shoestring of bacon rind on his chin for a full seven minutes.

Dreadnought downed his sixth forkload of chips and pork fat and then laid down his utensils. 'I also wanted to talk to you, Gary,' he said, 'about your extracurricular.'

'Sorry, boss?' Gary asked.

Dreadnought smiled: always a worrying sign. 'Perplexing as it is to my constitution, Gary, I find myself needing to de-code the fact that you've been balling me. You been giving me one up the balloon knot.'

'Boss?' asked Gary, reasonably enough.

We had all stopped eating. Dreadnought arched his not inconsiderable body in Brooker's direction. The reptile grin. The lantern forehead, as wrinkled as crenellated iron.

Brooker had turned to me. 'You cunt,' he said. 'What you say?'

'Gary.' This was Dreadnought.

'What you say?'

'Nothing!'

'Gary.' Dreadnought? Being ignored?

'Can't *believe* you, Rene!'

It was a disaster in potentia. It mugged my heart; it beat my heart silly. Brooker had just signed my own death warrant. And yet I love that little fucker.

Dreadnought rotated in my direction. 'You *knew*, Rene?'

The solidity of silence from Charlie and Mickey was overwhelming. It was chicken fat in my gullet. Oh Gary, I wanted to say, why these lies?

But I didn't.

'He's doing some work for Roy at Bible Street Cars,' I

said. 'I don't know anything else,' I lied, deciding not to mention Brooker's solo flights. 'Sorry, Gary.'

Dreadnought nodded. He balanced out our betrayals, ounce by ounce, the scales shifting millimetres at a time. One of us was about to receive a tickle.

Astonishing all present, not to mention alarming John in his grease-bedoodled waistcoat at the counter, and to the baffled consternation of fellow eaters and tabloid-readers, Dreadnought did what I should have learnt to expect from the man: the unexpected.

He started to cry.

Ignorance being bliss in some quarters, both Charlie and Mickey resumed their consumption of their heart-threatening breakfasts. No glance at Dreadnought's façade did they make. It was me. Or it was Brooker. The thought of food was disulfiram in my gut. I settled on my can and lit a cigarette.

Dreadnought recovered. By the time I had returned from the toilet, Gary Brooker had gone. Gary Brooker had left the establishment. He was no more than a footnote.

I vowed at that moment that come rain or come shine I would learn what Dave Stroker had learned to do.

v

The ages are right.

Dreadnought Dad; Brooker Son. It would work, logically speaking. The ages sync, the lifestyles sync.

We have to talk. But do we? Thursday evenings, working on *Cooking for Cunts* (or for whoever), and I'm wondering how best to put it. *Dreadnought? Is Gary Brooker your son?* I don't say it. I can never say it. Instead, we work; I record and I write. Dreadnought cooks up one anatomy or another. We get drunk on brandy or vodka and we ignore the issue like experts.

We are the Ignorers.

vi

The early signs were favourable.

Not only did the Bentley start on my fourteenth attempt, but we managed to pull away from Dreadnought's allocated parking space without stalling, kangarooing, spontaneously combusting or exploding. We even arrived at the end of the street before the first of the engine's noises started up. Sadly, things weren't going to stay so rosy. Indignantly, the thought crossed my mind that whoever had killed Mazza needn't have gone to the bother of getting a van to run her down: they had only needed to hand her the keys to the Bentley. She would have been dead before she was halfway to Hammersmith.

Neither Dreadnought nor I took too seriously the subject of the left windscreen wiper disconnecting itself and flying off. With an audible *ping* it cartwheeled over the roof of the car, a dead bird. We let it go; we were silently reluctant to stop the Bentley in case I couldn't make it start again. Meanwhile, the engine banged its pots and pans together; the engine was a one-man band. As with the wiper, we maintained a discreet silence on the topic. The exhaust pipe farted and the brakes squealed in outrage when I had the audacity to use them, in deference to a red light's sullen stare. We paid these impediments no mind. Where matters started to become alarming was when the heater blew out an aroma of Camembert.

'You parped, Rene?' asked Dreadnought, conversationally, thereby teaching me a new word.

'I thought it was *you*.'

Dreadnought rolled down his window, sticking out a buxom elbow, and then lit a cigarette, to rid our rattling rat-cage of the cheesy odour. 'How much did Roy charge you for this cunt?'

My wallet still smarted from the recent extraction. 'Two hundred and fifty.' The car had been at Bible Street for two days: unfortunately Dennis had been hospitalised with internal injuries resulting from laughing too much, and as a precaution Roy would only allow Chris to work on the engine for half an hour at a time.

'I'll have a word with that character,' Dreadnought told me.

The car agreed to take us to the Church of St Nathaniel the Decisive. Peppery cobbles cackled and a salty sky stank: the condiments, the condiments of our lives. We got out of the Bentley and slammed the doors. A hubcap popped off like the cork from a bottle of champagne. It rolled on its axis; it spun and shivered and died, there on the bleached stones.

It was mid-morning. Somewhere around dawn I had received a call from Gary Brooker. It had taken me aback. Via rumours and the gossip-mill, I had kept tabs on Gary's progress around town. Unedifying and not very pretty viewing, that was; it is hard to watch a man drown and dissolve, knowing that no lifeline, jacket or coagulant will help him. Brooker was going to the dogs – and not in the sense of gambling. The gambling itself was worse; but then so was everything else. If one per cent of the rumour was true, Brooker was doing his liver and lungs irreparable harm. I had been convinced for several days that his first taste of the drug called Bone would be as a gift from yours truly, although how this was to happen remained beyond me.

Anyway, the phone call.

'I need some money, Rene.'

'I know.'

He waited. Then he added: 'Well, do you have any?'

'I'm not giving you money, Gary.'

'You owe me.'

'Do I?' Cuddling the phone between my right shoulder and my cheek, I returned to the bathroom, where I'd remembered I'd left a tumbler of vodka. I hadn't fancied it the night before, in the bath (or *it* hadn't fancied *me*) but I had fancied the two bottles I'd drunk before it. Waking up in the cold bathwater an hour or so later had been enough to convince me that it was time for bed. But I knew this was going to be a busy day, even if I hadn't banked on Brooker's call. I had my first sip of the day.

'You lost me my fucking job!'

'No, Gary; you did that with no help from me.'

We had made up our differences a week earlier. It would be fair to say that Gary and I were not on best speaking terms after I ensured that he got the boot from Dreadnought's camp. This was made, in fact, abundantly clear as soon as I saw him approach, with the heavy sock of coins in this right hand. Have-a-go surgeon, Dr Flex, nursed the gash to my temple himself, personally applying pressure to the frozen pork chop on top of the wound, there in the back office at Beef Encounter. Flex had offered to send Charlie and Mickey around to teach Brooker a few home truths. I declined. Apart from anything else, I had reasoned, the lads would still be worn out after the hiding they'd given *me*. Dreadnought saw the pathos, and duly snorted. It had been a bit special, that kicking from Charlie and Mickey. On the day that I took Dreadnought to church, I was still hobbling slightly and passing blood in my water. But it was business, the lads had explained. *No secrets*.

Brooker said into my ear, 'Oh Rene. Warm I gonna do?' The anger had passed – or at least had taken a break. 'Me Dole's gone in thirty minutes; Angie's creating about leaving me again; the bailiffs have taken all the good stuff; and Roy ain't got no more hours for me.'

'Get another job,' I said. 'Stop gambling, stop drinking and stop smoking.'

'And do what all day?' he asked me in a confused and cornered voice.

'Get a *job*.'

'No can do, Rene. Not the nine-to-five.'

'Be a night-watchman.' Vodka was curdling my stomach lining and I seriously needed a dump. I sat down on the toilet, if you need to know.

'A nightwatchman, eh?' said Brooker. 'How do you become one of them?'

'Ask at your next signing-on. Listen, Gary, I've got to go.'

Dreadnought regarded the ejected hubcap with scorn, and I could see his point. It was another in a line of a bad comedian's bad jokes. He did not stoop to pick up the disc. He spat on it. Then he kicked the Bentley in its rear. We walked to the crosses that would serve as headstones until the ground settled. Dorothy Flex and Marilyn Flex: side by side. Pot plants on the plots. It was Dreadnought who started crying first, but I was not far behind him. As much for personal support as to comfort him, I put my left arm over Dreadnought's shoulders and said something blandly reassuring.

'They're looking down, D. They know how much they're loved.'

'I hope so, Rene. I'd like to believe that.'

vii

We waited there in silence for ten minutes. There was something crystalline about the morning, which served to encourage me that anything might happen. The air felt new, not the reconstituted, recycled rubbish that we're used to in London. The air felt washed. Laundered. We were Adam and Eve; it was the Day of Creation. Just us, and the rest of the lucky dead, down there in Maggotville. Dreadnought cracked his knuckles.

'Well? When do the horses come crashing in from thin air?' he enquired. 'We could do with a cavalry around here.'

'Talk to me about Mazza.'

'I've done nothing *but* since she died.'

'Not here you haven't.'

'Okay. What do you want to know?'

'What's she like,' I said carefully, 'in her other versions? What do you see?'

We stared at Mazza's cross: at four directions of Mazza. Up, down and to the left and to the right. I had an image of her smiling in her coffin. I had an image of her kneeling on the bed, butt naked. I want to watch her eating her dinner, picking spinach from between her teeth.

'She's beautiful,' Dreadnought whispered as I pocketed my right hand and began affectionately to fondle the underwear that I'd stolen from their bedroom. 'She's an angel.'

After we'd both finished crying again I said, 'I need to sit down, Dreadnought. I'm not feeling very well.'

'Did you have any breakfast?'

'Just a vodka to settle my nerves. And guess who called. Gary Brooker.'

'Whoop-de-doo. That bench there?'

'Yeah, that'll do. He's really sorry, Dreadnought,' I persisted. 'He'd love to come back.'

'Too late,' Dreadnought told me. 'And eat some toast in the morning.'

'Okay.'

'It's a one-shot life, Rene,' he went on. 'Brooker blew it. I don't blame Roy. But I loved that boy. *Loved* him.'

My caution was thrown to the wind. 'He's your son, isn't he?' I said.

The buxom frown. 'What makes you think that? Summing you seen?'

'No. Just a feeling.'

Dreadnought had taken my query better than I'd anticipated. While I hadn't exactly expected a headbutt, a furious denial or a full-scale nervous breakdown, I had pretty much banked on a less subtle reaction than the shrug that I now received.

'Who knows? My life's got so crazy and crisp, Rene, that I wouldn't put anything past it.' He sighed. 'Do you believe in God?' he asked me.

'Not as a Supreme Being, no. But someone or something is looking over us, Dreadnought. How else do you explain what you and I see? And Dave Stroker.'

'Do *not* mention that cunt's name in a holy place, Renemate,' said Dreadnought.

'Sorry.'

'But it's more than a holy place, innit?'

'I think so,' I said. 'I call them Pressure Points.'

'Nice.'

'I want to do what Stroker's learned to do. It feels like my logical next step,' I recited from what I'd rehearsed while shaving. 'To go to one of our other draft-lines.'

'Did you bring a passport?' he asked.

'My head is my passport,' I told him, framing my next sentences cautiously. 'Boss? Boss, I want you to do something for me. A favour.'

He turned in my direction.

'I want you, as hard as you can, to punch me in the face,' I said.

viii

I heeled away a lather of blood from my chin.

'Again,' I said. 'Knock me silly, you fat poof!'

'No, I can't. It's not right.'

'I dare you,' I said.

'*Dare* me?'

'Go on!'

'It's embarrassing, Rene. You ain't done nothing,' said Dreadnought.

I stood face to face with the man and I looked him in the eye. 'Des Lewis told me all about it, Dreadnought. Told me he laughed as he was doing it an' all.'

'Doing what?'

'Giving you one. One up the pipe.'

Dreadnought chuckled. 'He never has!'

'*Oh* yes.'

'I think I'd remember!'

I shrugged. 'Maybe he drugged you,' I suggested.

'Yes. And maybe he didn't. Look, Rene, it's nonsense, okay? Let's go for a drink; you look like you could do with cheering up. Buy you a pint.'

'I saw it, Dreadnought.'

'I don't care what you saw, son. Des Lewis is my half-brother. And that's all there is, okay? Cunt's always despised me because our dad left his first wife and married me mum. There. I said it,' said Dreadnought. 'Let's go.'

'Dread?'

'Don't call me Dread.'

'Dread? You know that Mazza had a fling or two, don't you?' I asked.

Dreadnought looked pained. 'Why do it, Rene? She's in the ground.'

'One of them was me,' I said.

'Don't, Rene '

'Mazza and Monelle: together. With me.'

His punch caught me squarely on the jaw. I stepped backwards. You know you're in trouble when Dreadnought gets fervent but does not say a word. He moved in on me like a wasp. I tried not to protect myself, but have you any idea of how difficult that is?

I closed my eyes when Dreadnought reached into his inside pocket for his cigar cutter. It was at that moment that I knew I'd just lost a finger. Bye bye, finger. Digit: toodle-oo. I'll miss you. That moment was when I knew the term *pressure point* can have a host of different meanings.

His next punch closed my eyes harder.

IV. Cooking the Anatomy

i

A word about my neighbours, twenty floors up, there in the block on Fellows Road, Swiss Cottage. There's a guy called Price who lives next door: Alan Price. He's a librarian and a writer. He's fiftyish, lean and balding. I'm thirtyish, once-lean and balding. He's in a lot better shape than I am. But what can I do? The three pub meals a day, largely uneaten, but all the same; the tides of beer, storms of brandy and streams of whisky; the sixty-a-day habit: this life is killing me. Life's supposed to do the other thing, isn't it? Make you live? But no; my life is definitely taking me in the other direction – a one-way ticket, and going fast in cattle class. How does Price do it? How do Londoners stay slim? When we meet in the lift, he is affable but cautious; he's a child confronted by a first ice-cream – he doesn't know what to do about me. Can it be that I sweat out violence from my pores? Can he smell it on me? The thought occurred to me the other day – it's nice to be loved – that he might be sizing me up as a character for something he's writing. One day, if we get close, I'll offer to share notes and experiences. No, I won't. There won't be time.

It's not Price but my neighbour on the other side – an elderly, stately and longsuffering guy from Cambodia, called Apple Steven – who meets me by chance as I enter the building. He is exiting the lift. As I've yet to be in receipt of my drubbing from Dreadnought, there is nothing about my appearance to make the man frightened, but frightened he most certainly is.

'Oh man,' Apple says. 'Mortal news. They break into you

flat, Rene-man. See 'em me own two peepers. They nick you sound system, you TV.'

'My laptop?' I demand as I stride towards the elevator.

'All gone, man,' says Apple. 'I say – what you doing? I call the snouts. They say – no aggro, granddad, or you next. I go inside.'

The door is unfolding shut. I press the button for the twentieth, vowing to kill that Frank the Ferret.

Thank God, I think in retrospect, for the infrequent but terrifying power cuts that this building endures: the ones that convinced me in the first place to back up all my work, just in case. And thank God for the generalised sense of panic and awareness that comes as a by-product of living in any city that whispers: that which you cherish, you hide.

So high-pitched is Dreadnought's voice when I call him to demand an explanation that for a fraction of a second I think it's Mazza.

'Was just about to call you but I broke a glass by accident. Speared me thumb. Can we do some work on *Cooking?*'

'Never mind that. I'm furious.' I explain.

He listens. 'I can assure I've authorized no such thing. What makes you think it's Frank the Ferret?'

'Well who the fuck else would it be?'

'Calm down,' says Dreadnought. 'Does it have Frank's badge?'

'Meaning what?'

Dreadnought sighs. 'Can you tell some cunt's been there for a start?'

'Yeah. Half my shit's missing.'

'I'm alluding to damage, Rene.'

'The door's a bit bashed,' I answer.

'Then it weren't Frank. Frank don't do damage. This'll

come as a surprise, no doubt, but there are other burglars in London aside from Frank the Ferret.'

'Name them. I'll track 'em down one by one.'

Dreadnought exhales. 'I would rate that,' he informs me, 'among one of your poorer decisions.'

'Well, I can't just sit here and do nothing at all. My stuff's gone.' I listed the inventory of missing goods. 'And the laptop, Dreadnought. Our book's gone.'

'Bugger. I'll meet you at Frank's.'

It is only on the platform, waiting for the train for the short Jubilee Line journey to West Hampstead, there to change for my connection to Acton Central, that there is another possibility. But it's too late to return to the block to bang on Apple Steven's door for a description of the thief. Maybe I will do that later. And Price's, too.

I can see him. The sandy hair and mongrel's smile; the needing to be loved – to be feared, to be copied; the one man who keeps cropping up and creeping up.

It was Gary Brooker who burgled my flat.

ii

'There *once* was an ugly duckling,' a man sang to anybody who would listen. 'His fevvers all diddle and dumb!'

I walked past him, thinking: yes mate, it was you. But you never did make it to the swan stage, did you? The fat lips, outjutted like a beak; the hollow chest, the gut; the definitive waddle as he patrolled and marched past, repeatedly, the door leading into a cacophonous club called The Anatomy, all the while cleaning out his right ear with the nib of a fountain pen.

'You can't come in. Private function.' His voice was hormone-led, surely. No one talks in that fat-guy pipe-and-whistle anymore: unless, of course, he happens to be fat. The Ugly

Duckling was certainly ugly – he was a Frankenstein's mon-
ster of razor cuts, bottle scars, *acne vulgaris* and all with the ba-
nana-yellow pallor to his skin that shrieks loudly and competently of liver damage. 'So fuck off.'

'Nice bedside manner you got there,' I replied. 'Listen.
Would it surprise you to hear that I have a track record of
arson? I could be cooking The Anatomy in thirty seconds flat.'

'Just try it.'

'I might do that,' I said. 'But listen, beautiful, I didn't
come here for a fight. I didn't even come here for a drink,' I
lied, although I'd yet to encounter how much anything cost
here and if I had the simple wherewithal to pay.

'A bird?' asked the Ugly Duckling.

'Her name is Goose. Goes out with…'

'Flex. Yeah man, I know.'

'Well?'

'You from outside of town?'

'Could say that.'

'Know what you're getting your ass into?' he asked me.

'Possibly not.'

'Well check, man. You a friend?'

'I'm his brother. So where do I find him?' I pressed.

The Ugly Duckling flinched and mimed with his hand a
fish's chaotic strokes and zig-zags through the ebbs. 'He's here
and there, guy. Wherever he lays his hat.'

'And what about Bone?'

'Excuse me?'

'Where can I buy some Bone?'

Duckling ducked slightly, saying 'Shit, man' – he ducked
the invisible arrows, the pulses of sonars. 'You're losing me my
job.'

'You're losing me my time,' I told him.

iii

'Why would *I*, a respectable goods-navigator, deem it worthy of my skills and professional status,' said Frank the Ferret, indignantly, 'to lower myself to the point of pinching items from this bumboy?' He pointed a pencil-thin index finger at my increasingly doubling chin.

Goods-navigator? I thought in protest.

It was Brooker. Always Brooker. Yet here I was, finding myself saying: 'Frank? I know it was you. And if I don't get my stuff back, in particular one item the identity of which I will not reveal, me and Dreadnought are going to set fire to you in your car. Understand?'

Insult good old Bluff as much as you desire, but you can't whack it for a decent kick in the thorax. From its original – or recent at least – yellow appearance, Frank the Ferret's face skin now went back to white.

'I didn't do it!'

'Well, Frank,' said Dreadnought, in his heaviest voice. 'Find out who the fuck did. This is out of order. Rene happens to be a friend of mine. And you cunts gossip like fishwives.'

iv

The protracted use of Bone gives you access to a higher version of yourself.

There are versions of yourself based on your most important life choices.

I found the entrance to Scottish Tony's gym in a short parade of shops, near a tube station that does not exist in home reality: the station of Nathaniel Square. I don't know why I was surprised. Nor why I was surprised that the façade of the establishment resembled Beef Encounter. However, there were differences. Having walked through the open doorway, I imagined that what I saw – largely unused treadmills, rowing machines, bikes and weights – would have looked in place in any training centre in the twenty-first. It was only while descending the stairs to the fight ring, punchbags and medicine balls did I get a sense that I was moving into more unfamiliar territory.

The door was opened for me. Impeccable manners, these hoodlums, hardnuts and hooligans of the future. With a migrained nod I entered. I saw hydraulic muscles; I saw piston-pump biceps and dog-rutt backsides. An orgy of exercise. In the ring, two fighters with headgear donned slugged it out like bare-knucklers. Supporting their efforts was a clutch of screaming middle-aged men.

I asked after the whereabouts of either Scottish Tony or Flex. 'Check the office,' I was told, and I headed in that direction. I knocked.

'Are you Scottish Tony?' I asked.

'Depends on who wants to know.'

This is always a character's way of saying yes. 'You know Flex,' I stated. 'And I'm one of the drafts of Wahid, his mate.'

Scottish Tony wriggled closer while remaining chairbound. 'The fucky you tarkin boot?' was how it sounded.

'You ain't deaf,' I told him. 'Now here's the thing, Scottish Tony.' I approached his desk. 'The protracted use of Bone makes you close to a perusal of your other selves. You remember,' I added, 'or *think* you remember telling Flex and Wahid about alternative personal versions. Well, here I am: proof.'

For the first time since I arrived, Scottish Tony regarded me as something other than a madman fresh from Bedlam. 'Your name?'

'Rene.'

'And where do you think you are now, I asked.'

'Further on from where I started,' I replied.

Scottish Tony circumnavigated the heavy and peri-od-piece desk. He shook my hand; it was an eye-to-eye mo-ment. 'It's two thousand and six, son,' he said, appearing to give up the pretence of ignorance. 'It's not just people who have drafts: it's the time-frames themselves. Tell me, please, how you made the transition.'

'I don't know how long I'm here. I need some Bone.'

'Son? No explanations, no Bone. We *both* need to know. It's cycles, man. It's an everlasting loop: you, me and the rest.'

As briefly and succinctly as I could, I rabbited through what I knew. While doing so, the Gordian knot of needing to transport myself back to Blighty – *my* Blighty, my grey, my faithless – hung over my head. If Stroker had been able to move his body between frames, and now so had I, there was no reason to assume that the cargoing of physical possessions was *verboten*. I would take back a measure of Bone, to introduce it to our system. But also to use it as proof.

Scottish Tony listened with full attention. As distinct from Dreadnought himself, he required no alcoholic pep-breaks to punctuate my recital. There was love, I would swear, on his face, in his eyes, as he perched his considerable rump on the corner of the desk, and as he angles his barnacled face my way. I spoke swiftly. Scottish Tony lent me his ear. The skylarking wriggle of amusement of his nose; the slumlord sneer of ap-proval, of approbation But Tony listened. It was something to behold, I tell you frankly, to be listened to so avidly. And then he said:

'It's time for Bone.'

Beautiful. I nodded, and we exited the office.

Referring not to any timepiece on his wrist but rather to intuition, Tony said, 'It's around noon. Too early for an ap-pearance from Flex, by a mile. But you might get to see Muji and Wahid.'

    'That would do.'

    Scottish Tony was pointing at the fight ring.

    The feeling – the imploring sensation – of not wanting to locate what you're seeking now crept up on me. A crazed captain, I raised my eyes. I saw what I'd ignored: the gladiatorial nonsense that was all the rage inside the ropes It was Muji and Wahid, headgear on. To my befuddlement, I hadn't noticed them on the way in. Other things on my mind, but even so

    Scottish Tony said, 'You recognise these cunts?'

    'Yeah, I recognise them,' I answered. It felt like this: it was a fluttering in my chest, far worse than any dose of heartburn I'd ever been subject to.

v

    Though it was smaller-scale than many of my revelations, I experienced, this very day, the revelation that I can be a very jealous man on the subject of a woman. I was really quite astounded. I hadn't liked learning the various whispers of Mazza's affairs against Dreadnought: these stories, while I guess they must be true, are unverifiable on the grounds that no one actually knows anyone who did the deed with Mrs Flex. Or if they do, they're not telling. High on speed that time in the pub, Mickey had taken an unqualified risky gamble by favouring me with the slur on Mazza's sexual behaviour. The following day he'd called me early: I'd been in the shower, but you don't go far without your phone. I killed the jets, and Mickey, who rarely called anyone for fun, started bawling like a baby into my ear about how I couldn't tell anyone of what he'd said, not anyone, it was his life and his livelihood on the line for Christ's sake, and couldn't I see that? I could. I told him that I could but he wasn't listening. After ten or so minutes he quietened down, asking if I gave my word. Spit shake? Spit shake, I told him somewhat grandly. Then he added (out of character): 'You have the soul of a poet, Rene.' I thanked him, disconnected the call, restarted the shower and resumed my ruminations on Mazza. My money was, and still is, on Des Lewis.

But it's not Mazza who has caused me jealousy today. It's Monelle.

A routine morning visit to the newsagent for cigarettes, The Racing Post, and a pint bottle of vodka. Nothing unusual: a low sky of flat-chested cloud; a torrential downpour and who should be returning from her paper round but Monelle! I admit, the sight cheered me – the sight of Monelle on her bicycle, the wide beige strip of her luminous yellow bag athwart the chest that I had yet to see (although God knows I've had my chances!). 'Hi.'

Sheepishly Monelle replied, 'Oh hi, Rene.'

'You okay?'

'I think so.'

'Well, are you or aren't you?' I asked in a mellifluous – is that the word? – singsong. Trying, as ever, to keep it light – light.

'No, then,' she answered.

'Go on then,' I told her. School problems? I wondered, and then reflected: Does she go to school?

'I'm sorry, Rene, it's over. I've been sleeping with someone else.'

This news achieved its detonation on a day when I was feeling particularly under the foul weather. You don't get used to kickings, you know. You don't. So added to the recent pummellings to which I'd been privileged, this fait accompli served me an ace, right into the thicket and the balls.

'You've been doing what?' I asked.

'Sorry, Rene.'

It's human to ask, it's the universal to ask, but I hated myself for asking, 'Why? Who?'

Let's back up a step here, I thought. Let's wait. Catch our breaths. Apart from fondling and fumbling her way through a succession of concussive but incomplete handjobs – at dinner, in the pub, on a much-regretted visit to a dancefloor – we had not, little Monelle and I, done anything intimate. Perhaps this was my problem. Perhaps she wanted wrong done to her but I hadn't been able to be a wrongdoer. Politely but unchangeably, I had turned down her offers of trips to the pub toilets, to the trashcans in the alley, and even to the freezer room at Beef En- counter, which I have no idea how she knows about. Monelle? A class act, no doubt about it; but I had rather thought, on this occasion, that I might be able to succeed with a half-mad fourteen year-old of dubious sexual principles. Call me naïve. But I had expected this one to go my way. Was I too gallant? Even medium-range-intelligence teenaged slags don't want a thirty-ish bald bloke running to fat.

'I'm in love,' she informed me. The adverb that follows could be wistfully.

'Ah, fuck off,' I mumbled.

'No, you fuck off.'

I entered the shop – ding-a-ling! – and approached the counter. Monelle followed. Oversensitive as I might be to the omens of bad fortune, I really couldn't help thinking that this one had the very real chance of going diabolically wrong.

'What's going on?' asked the shopkeeper, from beneath a deadweight of leaden brow.

'He just tell me na fuck off!'

'What?'

'You tell her na fuck off?'

'No.'

'Yeah did!' said Monelle.

'You tell her na fuck off!'

'Yes,' I answered wearily, already preparing to leave.

'Well '

Well you fuck off, I predicted. It would not be the worst event of the week: being barred from a newsagent's shop, having been dumped by a fourteen year-old lunatic.

'Well, good on you, son,' said the shopkeeper. 'She's a lazy girl at the best of times, mate '

'Aw, Dad.'

'Shut it. If she forgot your paper this morning, sir, I take full responsibility. Eighty Marlboro Lights and a bottle of Chekhov, is it, sir?'

'Yes, please,' I answered. And The Racing Post,' I added. If the owner wanted to mistake me for someone who took regular delivery of a daily, that was that cunt's lookout. But why was I feeling so down at the loss of the girl whose wanks would reduce me to tears? And even then I would have to finish off on my own, once I'd got back to Swiss Cottage. Was it love?

Was it fuck.

It was, I think, nothing more than the animal intensity of having been replaced and bettered. My stock had shrunk, my value had withered – like a useless limb, deteriorating and wasting away.

'Aw Dad,' repeated Monelle.

vi

I am in no doubt that it was Brooker's money worries that led him to what, as far as I know or can tell, was his first solo-flight burglary. Presumably he sold the gear afterwards at Gadgets.

'Gary.' I delineate the nature of my call and conclude by

saying, as a compromise: 'I want half of what you earned.'

'I've spent it.' He doesn't even bother to deny it.

'Then expect your pounding,' I say.

'Rene '

'Just the laptop. I need the computer,' I tell him. 'I've been working on a cooking project with Dreadnought. He's not happy.'

'Cooking?'

'For Cunts,' I add.

'Sorry?'

'Give it back, Gaz.'

'I sold it.'

'Well un-fucking-sell it!'

Some silence sounds like bliss, and some silence sounds like panic. Gary Brooker's, at this stage, veers towards the latter's scale. Gary is browning his shorts.

'Rene, what you want me to do?' he asks. 'I punted it down Gadgets. He ain't gonna just give it to me!'

So it is, with heavy and jellied heart, that I make the journey – the loops, hesitations and barmy nature of the tube – to Dreadnought's co-owned Gadgets.

The work experience, her name is Sarah, carefully explains that in the absence of Metal Mickey, her manager, she is not authorized to make such a decision. I sympathize, I do, and in the absence of Metal Mickey, her manager, I explain, using the hammer that I've brought along for the occasion, that I'm not authorized to take no for an answer. Having assumed that a meagre showing of the weapon would be enough to state my case, I am disappointed to learn that I need to use the implement: on two TV screens.

Happy with the re-acquisition of my laptop, I am almost instantaneously obliged to defend my possession when a seven-foot cidered-up cowboy has no choice but to bump into me on the pavement outside. He is launching into a foam-mouthed, quick-blinking tirade about civil liberties as I lay the laptop on the boot of a dinosaur Cortina and shoe the dick confidently in the gonads. He goes down. Of course he does. What else is he going to do? He goes down. But it's random; it's nothing personal; it's simply a case of like attracting like. He's just in the wrong place at the wrong time.

vii

I'd seen him, of course: I'd seen Gary Brooker in the cemetery of the Church of St Nathaniel the Decisive. That spiritual lump in the distance. That dollup of dungy sandy hair. And I'd seen him getting closer as soon as Dreadnought had broken my nose. I saw him – as you should see all guardian angels – through a squit of noseblood.

Gary approached. Brooker strode in our direction: my saviour, appearing as a lugubriously rolled bogey. Gary Brooker had a head full of steam and a pair of eyes doused in red mist. Brooker was going to fuck Dreadnought in the face.

Near the bench on which we'd sat, Dreadnought and I, a disappearance occurred: the vanishing lady of my conscious-ness. While I might have slipped back and forth to reality – and certainly enough to note with alarm the cigar-cutter clamping my flaccid penis – I was slowly melting and dissolving.

It was only the worry of Brooker stroking Dreadnought that kept me, I'm sure, from an easy egress from this life. Brooker's presence was contributory, but I didn't want Gary to save me from the pain: the pain was crucial. The stress was necessary.

And then I left.

When I returned, it was to find both Dreadnought and Brooker on the self-same bench, sitting close together – a first date. They were not exactly embracing or snogging (good word), but there was an inevitable hint of camaraderie there: they had witnessed the spontaneous vanishing of Rene.

I awoke, face down, on the fresh soil of the grave of Mazza Flex. Like an insect I wriggled around, soiling my shabby shabware, and with agony a constant I got to my feet.

'Did I go?' I asked, unnecessarily: the expressions on their faces told me everything.

I held out my hand. Between my thumb and forefinger I was dangling a balloon; and in the balloon was a cake-making quantity of white powder. 'I got it.' It was proof. 'I got the Bone.'

Then the pain effectively strapped me in the face and heart. My knees didn't want to know; I dropped back down to the turf When was the last time I cried? I cried then Oh yeah, a few minutes earlier, while contemplating the life of Marilyn F.

Effing and jeffing, Brooker made a wonky-stride walk over to where I had knelt. 'What the fuck's going on?' he asked. But asked like a lamb asking if he really did have to be throat-slashed.

My nose was broken. My voice, when it came, came out strange. By zipping up my fly I pocketed my pork sword. I said, 'I'm going to give you some of this. Free.'

'Lead me on!'

viii

'Des? I'm trying to tie up a couple of loose ends.'

'Who's this?'

'You know who this is, Des. Now. I'm pretty sure you had sex with Dreadnought Flex, against his will. I don't think he knows about it. I believe that,' I said.

'Rene?'

'Yes. You buggered him, Des, because you were jealous of him and because you could.'

Des's voice took on the full featherweight of imminent amusement. Into the bracket he croaked, 'Tell me more.'

'I will. Shall we meet?'

'No, tell me now.'

Invisible to Des, I shrugged. 'Okay. You supplied him with a quantity of a substance called Bone. Obtained either personally or via a traveller to an alternative way of life, Des.'

Des paused. 'You been drinking, Rene?' he asked with acidic need-to-know.

'Yes.' I took another gulp, in fact. 'Do you deny any of the above?'

'Keep going.'

'Either you or one of your scumbag associates,' I said, re-specting the invitation, 'have been somewhere only few can go. And either you or one of you scumbag associates has worked out that the way to perpetuate the loop or the trap between this existence and that.' I stopped.

By denying himself the right to a denial, Des Lewis had framed himself, farmed himself; Des had given himself one up the knot. At the same time as I was effortlessly contemplating my return ticket to Copenhagen, I shuffled my way into his silence. Seeing no potential loss in the further of the argument, I said: 'You spiked him, Des. He doesn't even remember. My question is why, but I know that's none of my business.'

Des Lewis called a halt, saying: 'You, son – you are on dangerous ground. You. Are on a hiding to nothing.'

'This is what I'm fairly sure of,' I continued. 'As you don't want to meet. What I'm absocuntinglutely sure of is this: you had it away with Mazza. You and Mazza. Sitting up the tree.'

'Who says?'

'I was told. And Des-mate? Ain't a secret anymore,' I told him. I gathered my thoughts: I'd been on the vodka since seven a.m. 'It doesn't mean you haven't got away with it: I'm certain you have. But that doesn't kill the awareness.'

Des Lewis gave me his time. 'What you want, Rene?' he asked finally.

I was prepared. 'Your assurance.'

'Of what?'

'That Dreadnought remains unchanged,' I said. 'The situation remains unchanged.'

'Excuse me?' Des coughed. 'Maybe it's better we did talk in person.'

'Too late.' I laughed. When was the last time I laughed. 'It's too late, Des,' I replied.

Opting in the natural way – the universal way – for anger in the presence of unanswerable questions, Des went on: 'What's in it for you, Rene? I'm curious.'

'Don't you see, Des?' I said to him. 'There's no choice. It's a series of loops Bugger!' The expletive was down to the fact that someone had rapped on the door to my Swiss Cottage flat. 'I'll see you around,' I said.

'Hopefully not,' Des replied.

Full of pipped trepidation, I opened the door, anticipating Alan Price or Apple Steven. It was Monelle. No question about it, this came disarming news. Were it not for one factor, I might have been on the expecting end of a gentle word, a smile, a reconciliation, or even a blowjob. The problem, the obstacle, the blockade – well, that factor had a name.

He walked in behind Monelle. It was Gary Brooker.

'Morning, girls,' I managed to say. Constitutionally speaking, I was in no mood for japes and trinkets. I was in no mood for this shit. I was in no mood. I waved them towards the armchairs.

'We're wanting to say sorry and explain,' said Monelle, adjusting her bra strap.

'Forget about it,' I told them.

'I feel like a louse.'

'So you should, Gaz,' I responded in a hallowed voice.

'Me too!' said Monelle.

'The point of your visist,' I said, closing the door on Price and Apple Steven, 'being what exactly?'

'Point being,' said Monelle, 'we've found the right thing together. Might be young, but it's good. We're in love.'

'Good's good,' I agreed. 'Good's always a nice thing to have around.'

Brooker seemed delighted with my sullen and ironic green light to his relationship with Monelle. Deposed for my ineptitude with the same, I added: 'Where do you want to go on your honeymoon? I'll pay. It's my treat.'

'Our unnymoon!' shrieked Monelle. 'I gotta do me exams first!'

It was time for them to leave shortly after that: Monelle had an appointment with her gynaecologist. Balmed with my blessing, they got ready for the twenty-storey walk down to ground level; the lift was on strike again. So impressed was I with my own maturity, guile and twang that after a quick nip of vodka, I followed them. However, I had no intention of catching up with them at the station – I am going to get her back anyway and Gary is going to die in a car accident – but I wanted to talk to a lad named Simon who looks after Dreadnought's Bentley when it's parked in the lot. Well, I say 'looks after'; what I mean is, he stands quite close to the cars at the rate of ten quid a parking session – not bad value for an overnighter, which is rare in any event: Dreadnought likes the car home in its allocated space – while rolling his joints and listening to an MP3 player.

I found Simon. I bunged him twenty notes to scratch the Bentley's lock a little bit, then to drive it somewhere quiet and crash the fucking life out of it. Dopily up for the challenge, Simon accepted the key that I had detached from the clutch in my hand and I thanked him and had a quick cigarette until he pulled the Bentley away.

There was something magical about the fact that the lift was working again when I returned to the building. I towelled the rain from my remaining glimpses of hair. Then I picked up the phone.

'Yo!'

'It's Rene. It's bad news, mate.'

Dreadnought waited.

'Someone's nicked your motor.'

'What?'

'Someone took the key from the ring and left me with the rest,' I said. 'How many fuckers can do that?'

'I see,' Dreadnought replied coolly. 'I am going to kill that fucking Ferret. Do you wanna watch? Do you wanna play, Rene?'

'Wait. It gets worse.' I stopped.

'Go on, Rene.'

'It was Frank, Dreandought. Frank the Ferret killed Mazza.'

I was cooking.

V. Bone

i

'Why would you want to go and do a thing like that?' I asked.

'*Cunts*,' said Dreadnought with a magisterial verbal swagger and a flick of the wrist, 'is a book that aims to address the culinary staple diets of many a nation, Rene.'

'But even so, Dreadnought. *Grits?*'

Dreadnought smiled. 'It's a dish considered a speciality, Rene, in several of the states of the American Deep South.'

'So's hillbilly sodomy! I know what grits are: they're otter sick!'

'That's next week.' With a grimace-like grin, Dreadnought poured us each a pint of knocked-off gin. Only visually did he query my request for a dash of tonic – or at least a slice of lemon. His own concession to the dilution process was a solitary ice-cube. We repaired to the lounge, with Dreadnought saying, 'It's only a sort of form of semolina.'

'Exactly. It's vile.'

'This from a geezer whose countrymen eat *sharks* for a midnight snack.'

'Only the perverts,' I told him. After a sip of my least favourite alcoholic beverage I gagged, coughed, put my glass on the coffee table and opened a fresh packet of cigarettes – always a moment of rarefied joy. Then I said, 'Dreadnought. I've been thinking of going back to Copenhagen.'

'For a holiday?'

'No.'

'Are you drunk, Rene?'

'Of course.'

'So at least you're telling me the truth,' said Dreadnought, impeccable in his resistance to the old wife's tale of there being nothing else to tell while inebriated but the truth. He would at least take me seriously.

To change the subject, perhaps, Dreadnought initiated a game of knuckles. We only played for the better part of an hour, but I will state for the record that I was wearying by the end. I attempted to re-ignite the subject of grits; Dreadnought was having none of it. He was in a peculiar mood. The problem was that every swipe Dreadnought made successfully was a reminder of the beating he'd lent me in the cemetery of the Church of St Nathaniel the Decisive. Bone on bone: a damaging moment.

After knuckles, to my unvoiced consternation, we had a wrestle on the Persian rug, during which I contemplated the uncomfortable notion that Dreadnought actually has a gay thing for me. Well, any port in a storm, I guess. Neither beggars nor buggers can be choosers. And I'm such a catch anyway – obviously.

We cooked grits. This type of godspit elicits from me the reaction of regressing to a childish critique that is understandable in any language: 'Yuck.' Grits and couscous and semolina and tapioca: yuck. Otter puke.

It was the first thing that Dreadnought had cooked for *Cunts*, as he had started to refer insistently to our project. 'It's a dumbed down food,' I explained. 'It's not even *food*. You'd give better to a swarm of pigs.'

'Swarm ain't right,' said Dreadnought.

'I was serious about Copenhagen,' I added.

'I know that, son. I'm noodling on it, but I don't think İ

can agree to letting you go. Not right now.'

This was a bit much. '*Agree?*'

Dreadnought nodded. 'We ain't finished.'

'Maybe we have,' I replied. 'Do you want the cliché, Dreadnought? This thing is bigger than the two of us.'

He sounded like a wheedling child. 'I want to understand.'

'You think I don't?'

'Let's cook us up a mess of grits.'

'No, let's not,' I said. 'Do you want to know my theory? I think I'm not strong enough to go any further back than the Mr Mondo scam. But it *does* go further back. When I was Lucy in that reality, there was a package I didn't want to open, do you remember? I need to go back and open it but I'm not strong enough.'

Dreadnought's face lit up. 'You *are*, Rene!' he tried to encourage me.

'Either that,' I went on, 'or it's further back in time. The English and the Danes are linked historically, as you know. And you and I – or versions of us – have always been together. Since the beginning. Maybe we were magicians; maybe we were warlords. There's no separating us. And I don't know how to get far enough back.'

I took a sip of my drink. Against my better judgement but totally with gut instinct, I lit a cigarette. Smoking had taken on a good element of discomfort, not to mention a funny taste, since having my nose broken.

'I could kick you about really hard,' Dreadnought suggested, trying to be helpful. 'Maybe if I truly knock you senseless you'll go back to the start.'

'It's a tempting offer,' I said. 'But no thanks. Why didn't you tell me you knew Des Lewis had the flashes and the visions as well?'

For a few seconds Dreadnought didn't answer. Contemplating his response he swallowed half a pint of neat gin. He belched a full atrocity. The seconds turned into a minute. Dreadnought prepared a cigar: the cutter I knew so intimately snipped and my groin gave a wince of recognition for what might have been. Still the silence. Even when the first sails of blue smoke started flapping from Dreadnought's puckered lips he refused to speak. An increasingly worrying five minutes elapsed.

'Do you want some berries, Rene?' he finally said.

This was a new one on me. What could berries be slang, code or shorthand for?

'Let's forget the cooking tonight. I've got some blueberries in the fridge. Would you like some? They're good for you,' he tempted.

'I rather think the damage has already been done.'

Dreadnought sighed. He made no effort to fetch the fruit for himself. He puffed on the cheroot and said, 'It was jealousy, Rene – ever since I was a little boy. I always wanted something the other kids had. It was my *style*, Rene.'

Unfinished though it was, Dreadnought prodded dead his cigar with an expression of distaste on his features. 'Gonna give this shit up one of these days: it's bad for your elf. The love of a father, Rene: I wanted that.' He raised his hands, palms upwards, in a gesture intended to imply he was asking the question: *what's wrong with that?* 'What's wrong with that?' he then added. 'The other kids had it. Why not me?'

I frowned. 'I thought your dad was around,' I said.

'He *was* around. He was physically present, but I knew he'd left his first wife and kid – he'd left Des – so what was to stop him leaving me and Mum? Nothing, as it turned out.'

'Yeah. Well I never had that sort of love either,' I told him.

'I know. And it stinks, Rene. *Gaw* – the fights I got meself into! Real bruiser I was!'

'You *don't* say. Fancy that.'

'Yeah well. We re-established some sort of contact over the years, and obviously he left me the shop when it was his turn to be gathered to God and that,' said Dreadnought, 'but I've always felt something that's *missing*. I knew you were somewhere, Rene, but I didn't know what you were. Where you were. Who you were. Just these fucking *visions*, as I say. No pattern. Can I be honest with you, Rene?'

'I thought you already were.'

'Mazza cheated on me a couple of times. Even left me once.'

'I know '

'Do you see what I mean! I always fucking lose what I gain!' Dreadnought shouted. 'And now I've lost her permanently to that *Ferret*.'

As despicable and pernicious a presence as Frank the Ferret was, I had set him up for Mazza's murder. In retrospect, I should have expected Dreadnought to work on Frank the way he did, but at the time I'd been surprised. And if Dreadnought's conduct had caused me surprise, my own had delivered me into a whole new world of self-disbelief. It had all flooded out: all my frustration and anger. The way he'd humiliated me, time and time again. What I've mentioned in this narrative amounts to about one per cent of the occasions on which Frank has removed my watch, my wallet, my chequebook, my mobile, my cigarettes, my lighter, my belt, a shirt button; the times he's opened my fly, even once managing to pull out my penis without my knowing it.

Why did I spare Gary Brooker? I'm still not entirely sure. I could have told Dreadnought the truth, there in his lounge. I could have said, 'Dread,' employing the abbreviation that he so detested – 'Dread, I lied. It's too late to help Frank the Ferret, but if you want to know the facts of the matter, it was Brooker who killed Mazza. But it was an accident.' I didn't. I saved him – I'm still cooking him. He's on my back burner. Added to that, of course, is the reality that I *need* him: without Brooker there's no future for Angie to despise and to take pity on him in; there's no destiny for Monelle (and how well she turns out to be); there's no Rope of Sand. I need Brooker; like the air I breathe I need sweet Gary, his dumbness, his impotence, his sandy hair, drinking, addictions and all.

'Dreadnought?' I said. 'Quick thing. Des never had sex with Mazza.'

'Good.'

'She turned him down. Repeatedly. She might have made a few mistakes along the way, but they weren't with Des Lewis.'

'I really don't want to talk about Des Lewis, Rene.'

'Okay, I'll move on. I'll talk about myself. I didn't have sex with Mazza either, Dreadnought. It wasn't me, it wasn't Mickey, it wasn't Brooker, it wasn't Charlie. It wasn't Dave Peacock, it wasn't Wrighty '

I waited. The illumination of horror filled his face. 'Say it ain't so.'

'I'm afraid it is, mate.'

'Then there's nothing I can do about it, is there?' Dreadnought said. He finished his gin. 'That Stroker's gone.'

ii

'I want you to tell me exactly how you feel. Every thought,' said Mr Drugs.

In the chair opposite sat a man named Mickey. I had just given Mickey – Mickey of no certain surname – a spoonful of his own medicine. With a damp snort Mickey had recently ingested a portion of Bone. Rather late in the day, I was finally living up to my wholly unearned reputation as a provider of dope and narcotics.

For the occasion I had opted for the cheapest location, having discarded the idea of shelling out for a room at the Dolphin Hotel. Funds are low. Dreadnought hasn't given me any pocket money for over a week. He cites temporary poverty as a result of two ostentatious (and quite frankly, vulgar and OTT) funerals and wakes in quick succession. I even believe him: these things cost a fortune. Dreadnought has suggested that I keep hold of what I collect while visiting establishments for the monthly. I eat frugally, but this drink and tobacco jones is doing my wallet no favours.

Mickey closes his eyes. 'I'm going fast I'm going slow…' There is a noticeable quantity of perspiration on Mickey's forehead. 'I'm spinning.' He frowns; he is now in some discomfort. He has lost his way; he has lost the map. When his right hand moves to his crotch my eyes are drawn to the bulge beneath his trousers. His erection strains against the fabric. He fumbles like an escapologist in a hassan sack.

Risking the fact that Mickey might clout me around the ear, I get out of my seat, cross the room (two strides) and I'm bending over in order to help him out when Mickey remembers how it's done. He frees the beast (it's a masterpiece!) and begins to work on the hood.

'She's moving inside me,' he says.

It sounds like the lyric of a love song. 'Who is?'

'I can't see.'

Sweat drips down Mickey's face; his left nostril has started to leak blood. 'She's moving her whole body inside mine,' he continues.

'Does she have a name?'

'No.'

'And what is *your* name?'

'I can't remember.'

The vision continues, with Mickey's stomach mumbling, and I am sure I can even hear the beating of his heart, until it becomes clear that Mickey is about to ejaculate. To save his embarrassment, I walk into the kitchen and allow him his moment in privacy. I will pretend I know nothing about it; I will return when he's had a chance to clean himself up.

I plan my next meeting with Brooker, knowing one important thing: Mickey's dream might not have been spectacularly adventurous, but at least when it's my turn to sample Bone I know it's not going to do me any lasting damage.

iii

Better to blame a dead man for a sin that's not worth pursuing.

That's a Danish proverb, that is.

Okay, Dave Stroker is not dead, as far as I know, but I believed what he'd said: he was not going to return to London; not in the twenty-first, anyway. Not unless he comes back as a ghost to haunt the mouldy streets. And by then I'll be long gone.

Perhaps he *did* have an affair with Mazza. To be honest (and this will sound ironic but it's not meant that way) it really is none of my business who she did or did not have it off with. There are more important anatomies to cook. Such as Brooker's.

It is with great care that I get ready for his visit to my flat – his second and possibly last visit. I think I'll move on soon: even with dispensation and a staff discount, Dreadnought is no pushover as a landlord – his rent is not low. I clean as thoroughly as a morning allows. Long overdue and quietly therapeutic this cleaning is: it gives me time to think. I am going over the questions I will use to interview Brooker when the intercom buzzer sounds. I let him into the building. Judging by the time it takes before he knocks on my door, the elevator is not working again. When he flops through into my flat, I seriously consider calling for an ambulance. He looks wasted.

'Them stairs,' he doesn't need to explain. He refreshes himself with a swift and effective regurgitation into my kitchen sink, then takes a sip from the glass I hand him. Almost immediately he retches again, a pained expression on his face. 'Jesus, Rene, what you trying to do? That's *water*.'

'I'm on a health kick. No spirits before midday. A cheeky vodka?'

We divide the bottle into two pint glasses. Brooker declines anything from my choice of mixers and instead cracks the contents of the ice tray into his glass while I finish a carton of orange juice into mine. 'You can't beat a nice lunchtime vodka,' I say.

'Cheers, Rene!'

On Dreadnought's earlier suggestion I have purchased a punnet of blueberries. Not cheap, are they? But I looked it up on the web: they really *are* good for you. And they're okay! I can eat them without feeling nauseous, which is more than I can say about most things I put in my mouth these days.

iv

Naturally enough, and entirely accurately, Frank the Ferret had protested his innocence to the accusations of car theft and murder. It hadn't done him a blind bit of good – not once Dreadnought had stopped horsing around with his tactical foreplay. I had started to worry that Frank's screams would be heard from the street outside. It was night, after all. On the other hand, the door to the walk-in freezer at Beef Encounter is pretty thick. With spores from our breaths pulsing, forming and deforming in front of our faces, we stripped Frank naked and waited for his poisonously damaged yellow skin to turn white with fear then blue with cold. Later, there was a hell of a lot of red; but first we assembled a number of tools that are freely to be found in a butcher's shop. Dreadnought removed his leather gloves but kept his overcoat on for the operation. Me, I went down to my shirt and waistcoat.

It was a surprise that Dreadnought let him live. It could be that Dreadnought is simply running out of heart for the meaty lifestyle. But that was not the most pertinent realisation I made while there in that cold box, and then in the office. In fact, it was while I was waiting for Dreadnought to finish, when I was sitting in the back office, eating a pork pie and helping myself to a heartwarming brandy, that I felt what that small freezer had briefly reminded me of. Perhaps it was the symbiosis of the chill, the room size and the concept of my waiting, along with the reality that the idea of travelling – actually travelling – into the past, as I had into my future, had been much on my mind and had been troubling me greatly, that presented me with an answer. And the answer was this: the freezer was another pressure point. The freezer made me think of the waiting room – where Mondo had showed off his card tricks. Knowing this, feeling it instinctively in the gut (I stopped chewing), I understood what I was going to do. I understood how I was going to go back there, go back to that version on my own terms: by freezing myself half to death.

The sacrifices I make for you, dear reader!

v

'How's Des, by the way?' I asked.

I had chosen my moment, I hoped, with simplistically brilliant accuracy: I had waited until Brooker had been in my flat for three hours and had gone through most of the two bottles of vodka I'd bought for the occasion of his interview. Only once, in his slurred comment that I had a bladder like a sieve, did he acknowledge that I was getting up out of my seat a lot, and I don't think he ever worked out that every time I returned to the lounge I was carrying our glasses, replenished and refilled. Or if he did, perhaps he decided to shut up and be grateful. So it was that I was able to drip-feed Brooker successive volleys of tongue-loosening booze, each of which glass had a granule of Bone floating therein, like a stowaway on an ocean liner, and slowly sinking into an ice cube. And so it was that I was able to refill my own glass with the hard stuff: I was drinking water. (It really is the hard stuff: it's hard to drink.) Prescribing one granule of Bone at a time was part of the strategy; it was so that Brooker didn't go doo-lally on me in five seconds, like Mickey had done.

'Des who?' Gary answered.

I laughed. 'Des who?' I repeated. 'How many Deses do you know? Des Lewis! Your manager Des!'

'He ain't my manager, Rene.'

'You said he was!' I was smiling.

'When? I never!' Brooker wasn't smiling.

I persevered, bluffing – always bluffing. 'Course you did!' I said, finishing my water. 'In the Slapped Rabbit.'

Brooker tried to vine-swing through a jungle of memories, a jungle of twisted, tangled thoughts, where everything looked the same and danger was present everywhere. His conclusion was this: 'Christ, Rene. I got to knock the piss on the head a smidge. Don't even remember meeting you in the Rabbit.'

'Well you'd had a few,' I agreed.

'When was this?'

'Thursday? Friday?'

'Was I with Monelle?'

'No. You had a row.'

'Christ. Well, we've been arguing like politicians. What did I say exactly?'

'It was no big deal, Gaz. You said: I've been doing a couple of odds and sods for Des Lewis. Then you said you'd been a bit naughty because you were doing the occasional job for Des before Dreadnought fired you.'

I should have been a poker player; I should have been an actor. If lying was a job – if you could open your newspaper at the Recruitment section and read LIAR REQUIRED, FULL TIME POSITION, SALARY NEGOTIABLE – you would be best advised not to bother applying: my CV would see me into the role, hands down.

'I said that?' asked Brooker.

'Yeah. Look, it's no big deal. I just asked you how Des Lewis was, that's all.'

'He's fine. Look, don't tell Dreadnought, okay?' said Brooker. Now his face wore the comical effect of italicised terror.

I improvised, gently frowning, 'About Mazza? Don't worry, mate.'

'No. About me working for Des. They hate each other.'

In the car on the way to the Bloody Chamber after Mazza's wake, it had been Brooker's double life and his involvement with Lewis that had contributed to the uncomfortable silence I'd initiated, with my question about Dreadnought and Des.

Brooker added, 'What *about* Mazza? I never laid a finger

on the girl!'

'No. But you landed a *van* on the girl!' I laughed: a reptile's giggle.

I felt sorry for Brooker at this moment.

'Look, Rene, you're a mate,' he said. 'It was an accident.'

'You think I don't know that?' I asked him sternly, pretending to wish to draw a veil over the topic. 'Do you want another drink?'

'I was only supposed to scare her.' Brooker was babbling. 'I thought she'd move faster. She did exercise for Christ's sake!'

Standing up, I plucked Gary's glass from his fingertips.

'She was supposed to move.'

'I know, Gaz-mate,' I said. 'And I told you: my lips are sealed. It was an accident. Des wanted something of Dreadnought's – he wanted Mazza – and she wouldn't agree. You were supposed to scare her. I know.'

Brooker leaned forward and rested his head in his hands. 'I'm such a cunt. I even reverse to see if she's okay and I run over…' His voice was breaking down into the badly tuned transmission of unspent grief, of unspent guilt. He started crying.

'It's okay,' I told him. I placed the glasses on the coffee table and sat on the arm of his chair to give him a big brotherly, thankful hug.

vi

There's been a palpable alteration to the horsepower and thrust of my days. But in which direction? Are things slowing down or speeding up? Projects look like they're caving in, but in fact they are simply coming to some sort of conclusion. How long have been here? Can it only be a modest seven months? I've got the seventh month itch; I want to go home. I want to walk on Knippels Bridge again. I want to go to Vestre Cemetery and visit my dad, my mum, my Uncle Hektor, my Aunt Else. I want to take the train to Helsinore and watch the heavy black birds dart around the turrets of the castle. I'm sick of the London grind, of the bomb threats, the pigeons, the smoke. So much to do, and so little time.

After I've teaspooned off the quantity of Bone I believe I will need for my trip to the freezer at Beef Encounter, I give the rest, in its original balloon, to Gary Brooker, with the express direction that he must use it very slowly, a couple of grains at a time, for best use and to avoid an early grave. I know he'll be curious to take it (and I've got to open that boy's mind somehow) but I'm fairly confident he will sell the rest. And this is good; this is to plan. It's what London always wanted; it's the gift that keeps on giving.

I make what I believe will be my final visit to the Church of St Nathaniel the Decisive, to pay my last respects. That rarest of beasts: a beautiful day! A tenderly considerate sun; a goodwill mood on the trains.

Dreadnought phoned this morning to announce that he was in receipt of some sorry news: the car insurance firm had written to him to declare that unfortunately the Bentley was a write-off. The car was dead. In high jubilation, I rode the mended lift down to terra firma, and in the car park I offered Simon the dopehead another twenty pounds and a few grains of Bone, for a job well done. Dreadnought had concluded, 'I'm sorry, Rene, but you won't be driving that car again.'

Therefore, all is going well.

I aim to visit Beef Encounter tomorrow night.

Monelle calls.

She tells me in tears that she has finished with Gary. The problem is, she confides, that half the time he is too trashed to perform in the single bed of their undeniable love, and the other half he has drunk so much that his spunk tastes funny.

All good, all good.

Dreadnought calls again.

He has, that very hour, just throttled a man with a coffee bean-shaped head for parking in the empty allocated space outside his Acton maisonette. Already he is tending that parking space like a grave.

'I need a holiday,' he concludes, sniffing like a dog lapping up water from a bowl. His lips flap through a sigh. 'When you doing it?'

'Tomorrow night.'

All good, all good.

Des Lewis calls.

'Gary Brooker's just called,' he says. 'Sounds like he's seen a ghost. I say to him: Where you been? He goes, Rene's. I go, Why? He goes, Mate. I go, Fair enough. What's pickled your gherkin? He goes, Nothing, boss What you say to him?'

'I know everything, Des,' I reply. 'I take back what I said before. You *didn't* fuck Mazza.'

'No I didn't.'

'But you tried. And I don't care because I'm not even going to tell Dreadnought. You know why not?'

'Why not?'

'Because you want me to tell him.'

'Rene?' he asks me warningly.

'I'm going home, Des.'

'I'm phoning you at home.'

'Denmark home,' I reply. 'I won't do it, Des; I won't be a part in your war against Dreadnought that isn't even a war. It's a family feud. And Dreadnought's forty-two years old! How old are you? Grow up!'

There was quite a long delay before Des said, 'I can't remember the last time someone told me to grow up.'

'You won't need to hear it again from me,' I said. 'Our relationship's over.' I couldn't resist adding, 'And it could have been so beautiful.'

Clearly he wasn't sure how to respond to that so I continued: 'It's amateur stuff, Des, for the world Dreadnought moves in. But you couldn't bring yourself to go the full step. You wanted what he has out of nitpicking jealousy and nothing else, but you're not a man of his world, Des. Why do you want to be? You're successful in your own way. Just don't be near each other: it's simple.' I end the call.

All good, all good.

Then Dreadnought calls *again*.

There is a business angle to the conversation this time. Keen no doubt to banish from my head any inferences of mental weakness on his part during the last call, he informs me with pride that in his opinion *Cooking For Cunts* is completed. It has been a juicy journey, Rene, he says, and we had some rollercoasters there, he says, but I honestly think we've done as much to it as we can, he says.

I agree.

Why not? Everything else is coming to a halt. Why not *Cunts?* Ah yes, I remember now why not. The manuscript of *Cooking For Cunts* currently stands at a page count of twenty-three pages. That's why not. And that's with the photos of the dishes inserted. As with so many facets of his life, Dreadnought has simply grown bored.

All good, all good.

Then Dave Stroker calls.

vii

The freezer door closed with a cosmic clang – the sound of planets colliding in an almighty galactic cock-up of planning. Or so my slightly fevered imagination told me. I had already switched on the light; it showed me the plumes of my breath, the racks of meat to see – the torsos, the hooked flanks, the spiked sides. Carelessly someone had left a cleaver on a shelf; it was decorated with blood. The freezer reminded me of the attic full of Dels.

I unfastened the knot in the neck of the balloon. With due reverence I sprinkled the Bone out onto a plate that I had brought from Dreadnought's office. It had a Union Jack design inside its chipped edges. I'm doing this for Queen and country, I thought.

My body temperature was dropping fast. To assist myself in this endgame project, I had drunk quite a lot of wine that my body would wish to sweat out (the cold would chill the beads of perspiration on my face), and I'd eaten nothing but a bag of pork scratchings the previous evening in the Bloody Chamber.

I licked my finger, sherbert-dipped it in the Bone and felt it effervesce on my lips – the only part of my body that still felt warm. The Bone went straight to my bones. A matter of seconds later, broken-bummed, solid-penised and absent-ankled, I dropped like a kilo weight of dung to the freezer floor. The shock of the impact sent a short spark of pain through my healing nose. Then the pain completed a dot-to-dot puzzle from one hurt or fractured, bruised or diseased part of my anatomy, to the next. The pain gave me a full physical examination, enema included. The pain popped a thermometer in my mouth and up my pipe; the pain gave me an endoscopy and laid the chilled sucker of a stethoscope to my aubergine-coloured chest. Had I not been withering from potential frostbite, that pain might have made me more worried about the condition of my body than it actually did. That pain might have given me a heart attack.

I'm on a diet as soon as I get free, I vowed as the cold burned my temples and pinched clean my nostrils of mucous. Everything felt hard.

It wasn't me who lowered my own eyelids; it was the Bone.

FLASH.

It was coming. I saw the waiting room. Blind and intuitive – nothing but – I dabbed my finger again in what was to bring me together with my other drafts, my other selves. I could smell the winter atmosphere, clean and rural. Mindful of spilling a single granule, a single morsel, I slowly licked the Bone clean off the whorls of my forefinger.

FLASH.

Cramp. A burn. Shots and images. Pain dripping.

Don't excuse me…

A lash of a leather whip.

Where was I?

FLASH.

The bright light of burning tapers in a moody darkness; a mob, the torchlights like the eyes, randomly spaced, of an impossible insect.

Where was I?

More Bone, more Bone. It was fuel – fuel for travel. 'Peter pecked a pickled pick,' a child was saying; an ugly man was calling, 'Time, gennermen, please, oh ugly ducklings.' There *once* was an ugly duckling. Flash me again, if you would, kind sir, kindest sir.

FLASH.

Drop him out the window.

FLASH.

An image of a computer diskette. A rope of sand burning like a trail of gunpowder – or a brigade of army ants, inflammable fireflies on the carpet of the night. Where?

I tried to tell myself to get my thoughts in order.

The smell of the country winter. No cars. Cows belly down to the ground. An insistence of rain. A dipsomaniacal preacher with a Bible in one hand and a Bowie knife in the other: he stabs his Holy Book on the sternum of a seven year-old, turquoise-skinned girl.

These were scenes I had never viewed before.

A whale bites a sailor from the protection of his waterside hammock. A lasso of melting stars sparkles flaringly; it catches the planet Earth, tightens and holds. A fox's head multiplies on its slender neck. A church implodes.

Where was I?

I cleaned my plate of its Bone.

That was when my troubles began.

viii

'Is this a joke?' I asked, knowing that I wasn't being jerked around. 'Where *are* you?'

'I've emigrated,' said Stroker. 'I'm calling long distance. The longest.'

'And how are you doing?' protocol dictated I should ask.

'Wish you were here. I always liked you, Rene. I know you was just doing your job. I'm calling to apologise.'

'Go on then.'

'I'm sorry, Rene. I know I must've caused you some embarrassment.'

'That's one way of putting it.'

'Sorry.' Christ! I'd be getting a call from Mazza next. I'd be getting a call from Hektor and Else. 'If you ever want to join us…'

'I can't. Are you back in England?'

'No!' Stroker cried. 'Hell no!'

'Have you made it up with your mum?'

'No!'

'Well, do that. Do that at least.' She had, after all, eventually handed over the money. 'Dave? I wish you hadn't called.' I sighed. 'Things were moving along quite nicely until now.'

All bad, all bad.

'But I understand why you did,' I said. 'At least I think I do.'

'I wanted to set you this final quiz. This will be the last time you hear from me.'

I walked over to the window. Twenty storeys up affords you a nice view of this part of London, and London is nice from afar. It is only when you make it down to the streets do you feel the forces, the magnets, the quickening of my heart-rate. Deep down I must be a really distant type of guy. Proximity is what causes me problems.

'You still there, Rene?' Stroker asked.

'I'm here. Just thinking.'

'Take all the time you need.'

I chuckled.

'What's the joke?'

'Time's the joke. Let me do some guesswork, see if we've got any common ground.'

'You got it,' said Stroker.

'And can I ask questions?'

'Of course.'

'Question one. Why did you make fun of me on the airplane? – that nonsense about travelling into the future in a spaceship made of diamonds. I mean, you knew you were leaving anyway.'

'Who said I was making fun of you?' said Stroker.

'Seriously, Dave.'

'Okay, sorry. I suppose I wanted you to know what it feels like: to be persecuted. To not have the upper hand. But more to the point, Rene, how was I to know it was going to work? What if I'd said the truth? "Rene? All my adult life I've had a dream – no, better than a dream, stronger than a dream – that one day I'll be on a plane and I will slip through time." You'd have thought I was a nutter!'

'Not necessarily. You've only told me you have a dream. Big deal.'

'Maybe I would have said premonition; I don't know,' Stroker said; 'I was frightened of looking like a tit in a trance. No thank you, darling; I'll try the iced mango if you'd be so kind.'

'Where are you?' I asked.

'Nice bar by the beach.'

'No, where *are* you?'

Stroker sounded puzzled. 'Melbourne.'

'You really *did* go to Melbourne?'

'Yeah. Where do you think I went? Pluto?'

'Not much would astonish me, Dave. So what happened?'

'I've been thinking of how to describe it, Rene, but the easiest way of saying it is: I got an earlier flight. It wasn't faster, it wasn't any less of a drag; I just come back from the bog and you're not in your seat – someone else is, a little kid. And there's a black chick in my seat. It's a completely different set of passengers! And I'm thinking: Am I going to have to spend the whole flight, wherever we're fucking going at this point, by the way, in the khazi? The stewardess goes, "Sir, can I help you?" So I have to take a gamble, don't I? She can probably smell the piss on my breath from those drinks in the bar, so I say, "Darling, I'm a bit lost. Sorry. Too much to drink." You were right, Rene? What can they do once you're up there? "Can you remind me what seat I was in?"'

'You actually had a seat?' I asked.

'Yeah! I booked myself on two flights, but I don't remember doing it. My credit card remembers, because I've checked. Two separate transactions. We arrived on schedule at eight in the morning.'

'But that's when we were due to arrive,' I said.

'The *previous* morning,' said Stroker. 'And I tell you, I had the shakes, the sweats. Immigration was a nightmare. This cunt with a chin wanted to interview me, for Christ's sake – interview me about did I live in the city or the country. They're still worried about Mad Cow Disease.' Stroker laughed. 'I brushed my teeth at Kuala Lumpur and I couldn't believe I'd got away with it. Kept expecting to see you, mate, but I was living one day *earlier*. Talk about fucking jetlag.'

I checked the date on my watch. 'So what time and date have you got there, Dave?'

Stroker mentioned the twenty-third. Not aware of what the normal time difference would be, I was nonetheless in no doubt he was living an entire day behind me. Yet the phone system was working. Why not? I thought, suddenly tired. It was too much to consider; too much to work out. 'This call must be costing you a fortune, Dave,' I said.

'Yeah, I guess. Better go.'

'One more thing, if I may. It doesn't matter anymore because if you're living your life a day ahead of me I'll never
catch you, will I? No one will. So tell me one thing.'

'Shoot.'

'You and Mazza. Did you have a relationship?'

He paused before replying. 'Yeah, Rene, she left him for
me. Soon went back. A long time ago, mate.'

'Thank you, Dave.'

'Goodbye, me old mucker.'

ix

Feeling like a gimp-footed, hunchbacked and above all
acne-pocked new arrival to a new town, I walked in the clothes
in which I'd abandoned the freezer, in the direction of the
horse-carriage waiting room. I wasn't scared. Dead-meat cold
was the air. I was Lucy. I wasn't lucky but I was Lucy.

The card tricks and teasing, the interrogation, tempta-
tion and revelation; the money changing hands, the deception:
all of these things happened naturally. I'd been here before.
Then bar-of-soap stylee, I slid through a forward snatch of
time. Lucy was saying: *I don't want to open it. I don't want to*. But
this time I was there in her presence. Browned by the filth I had
presumed I would see and feel less of, and numb and stinging
from the pneumatic cold, I was in her presence. I was urging
her:

'Open it. Open it!'

Did she see me? Scottish Tony, in another draft – Scottish Tony, Mujahid and others had seen me (Muji it was who'd
punched my lights out), but did Lucy have me in her pretty
little radar? It was hard to tell. I repeated:

'Open it. Please. It's the right thing.'

As the envelope was opened, there was the murmur of dawn: dim light, gently peeling from inside its cuff. Light leaked from within; light whirled around the broken wax seal. There was sullenness in the air. A glimpse of something just too distant to be seen. The ragged hooting of an owl. Animal noises; whistles and chirrups and growls, all moving free. The potted history, I imagined, of all that had preceded this instant of opening had been concentrated into what Mr Mondo – Mondo the Magnificent – had sold.

Faster now, with less caution, more light spilled out: an impressive, accumulative flow, there in the waiting room. We waited; we had found ourselves back in the correct place. Lucy had known to be here: her dreams had led her the way; but time had moved on since the original arrival of Mondo the Magnificent. Mondo had gone.

I felt myself, in the freezer, attempting to move my limbs in order to secure the continuity of my blood's circulation: the same exercises I had gone through on the doomed flight to Kuala Lumpur. The awareness faded.

Coldness was closing down my reactions. At the back of my skull, within the remits of the past life, I sniffed out and could see vegetation: light was streaming out now. It was a complicated present of a thousand layers, unwrapping itself. Light first, sounds; and now growth. A landscape is what I could see, growing before my eyes – verdant, lush and unbroken. A landscape was stitching itself together. Though no expert on the subject of botany, even I could tell that some of these flowers and shrubs would not be familiar to a scientist of the twenty-first; not only did they belong to a bygone era; they also belonged to an alternative version of our timestream.

There were stems of bright pink, as thick as a man's arm; fronds the pure white dazzle of a magnesium burn. Now, a glance upstairs revealed a mare's tail of wisping trailing cirrus; and downstairs, a pond plant of tiny grey flowers and shining orange leaves the shape of rectangles. Trees stood guard over the magnetic characteristics of plump shrubs and foliage. Plants kissed and fought before my eyes.

I was so far back in time that it scared me.

Wildlife joined the unravelling. With faces that resembled those of bears, long birds – as long as cars – now formed squadrons against the pulsing sky. I felt the nauseating lurch of being lifted; my stomach tensed. I was taken into the storm of ugly birds; I was buffeted and slapped by heavy wings, I was pecked, scratched and screeched at. All the while, in the air, I had the sense that I was searching for something; I was flying high – flying high above the unfolding colours beneath the flock.

Breath was a grenade in my chest, but I searched. More Bone! My examination of this existence demanded more Bone! I couldn't find what I was looking for. I swooped with the rat-brown pack, tracing for a few miles the meanderings of a blood red river.

Then I was plummeting, screaming; trees as wide as houses rearranged themselves for my ingress, to break my fall. To the palpable disgust of the forest, I made my hamfisted descent, wondering where the cold, the chill, the big freeze had vanished off to. I landed with an agonizing bump. Fat duckling. Soft ground. I bounced.

I had to breathe. Steadying my composure for what seemed to be, but what was unlikely to have been, a few seconds, I concentrated on inhaling and exhaling. Tempted backwards through time, I had found myself in a primordial atmosphere. It was difficult to draw breath. The temperature had risen but that wasn't the problem. The air was thick and stewey; there were unfamiliar gases, I was certain, in its mixture. It was breathable – but only just. It felt like an anaesthetist's mask strapped to my face.

Why was I here? If I had changed in my physical appearance to take flight I hadn't noticed, and I was definitely back in human form now. I was naked. And I was female. Pre-Lucy, alternative Lucy – and many thousands of years pre-Rene and alternative Rene – I was a woman in her birthday suit, hairy, slightly stooped and old before her years at the age of thirty-or-so; and I was searching for the man of my dreams.

This wasn't history. I was following another line altogether: a version of a primitive life. I was on a rough path through the steaming woodland. To my left, sighing shrubs; to my right, a barricade of the same, the sulphurous smells, bubbles and gases of a yellow lake. The mutated version of a fat bullfrog bounded out of the way of my heavy, wide feet.

Incapable of much in the way of predictive thought, I was nevertheless thinking that I would come across a clearing of some sort, a woodland glade. But it wasn't to be. How much time passed I couldn't say (I didn't want to know), but when I found what I sought I was still surrounded by the sigh and cackles of the forest.

The man was lying among the gnarled, hirsute toes of a tree of prodigious height. He was curled into a smooth curve, like a child sleeping and protecting himself from his nightmares. Indeed, he also slept. A beatific gentle smile on his lips; his skin softened by and rubbed smooth as a pebble in a brook. His skin sprouted not hairs but tiny flowers of various colours; the design of the blooms described a rainbow around the exposed left side of his body, from his brickish toes to his bald pate. An anatomy of horticulture, and remarkably planned: blossoms of various sizes, genera and lengths. A flower bed had altered my beloved, and my beloved was this point's version of Dreadnought.

I sat at his side, as close to his body as I could squeeze. And in order to wake him up, I started to pluck the flowers from his skin.

x

Who is shaking me?

'Rene?'

'Stop,' I mutter.

'Wake up, Rene. Wake up now. Come on, Rene. He's dead.'

It is Dreadnought's voice. Dreadnought! The realization is a shot in the arm, a shot in the heart; literally speaking, it's a wakeup call. I gag at the taste of something warm that Dreadnought has puddled into my mouth. I cough: the taste of the liquid is fiery and fierce. The drink is spat out: I feel it lapping around my chin and neck.

Groggy, yes; but I'm awake. No hospital gurney, this: I am lying, I find as I sit up, on the carving table behind the scenes at Beef Encounter. As distinct from the wood I have just vacated – ambrosial, narcotic – *this* wood smells of blood and failure. The air, too. Gone are the aromas of sulphur, blossoms and love. Dreadnought has fired up all of the pie-cooking ovens in order to raise my temperature back to normal. The kitchen is like the Corner Sauna.

'You all right, Rene?' he asks.

I don't know how to answer.

'You's going blue in there, mate. And I don't want you to perish, son. Where's your idiot mittens?' He cackles.

I croak. I reclaim my voice. 'Good to see I'm good for a giggle.'

'As ever. More brandy?'

'I'm good.' The taste of it was commensurate with a dose of poison right now. I sit up. Dreadnought's face is expectant, tight, already set.

'What you see?' he says.

'The beginning,' I answer. 'Or as close to it as I can go. I think I'm done, Dreadnought.' In a raised tone of voice I add this: 'Fuck's sake, I was picking daisies from your scrotum! How much closer do you want us to go?'

I explain, as best I can. Dreadnought thinks about what I'm saying, considers the wriggling information, and says, 'You turning poofy on me?'

'Yeah.'

'Rene?'

'Let me go home, Dreadnought. Please. I'm killing myself here.' I rub my hands together: there is dirt and frozen mud on my fingers, and it comes off in slimy maggots of rolled filth. To rid my palms of the same I clap. I roll my legs around.

'Careful.'

I'm a patient after an operation; kid gloves are all that you can use with which to touch me, treat me bend me any way you want me. 'I'm okay,' I say, freezing – my lips achatter, my limbs nearly lifeless, regaining colour.

'No you're not.'

'No I'm not. Gimme a minute.'

Once I've refused the offer of another trough of brandy, Dreadnought regards me quizzically and says, 'What? Do you fancy a coffee?'

It is certainly against type but I say, 'Yes. A coffee would be good right now.'

xi

Dreadnought wakened. His chest rolled with deep breaths, sore with the plucking. The smile on his face had turned idyllic. 'You found me,' he said. A different language: an older, archaic version of Danish.

'I found you.' But my voice was a translation – a poor translation – and all that Dreadnought could do was gurn. I delighted in picking the blooms I needed to stretch for – the ankle, the cranium – thereby dropping my body over his for seconds at a time. He drew my left breast into his mouth; he tickled the nipple with his tongue. He sucked until I started to lactate.

I took hold of his penis and it was gaining solidity. I massaged its length until it grew to its full size. Then I dipped my head towards it and I tasted Dreadnought's soil and sweat. I drew my tongue in doodles down its length; I unhooded his erection and cupped a testicle in my mouth.

His fingers reached for my warmth, and I felt perspiration in the light matt of hair on my shoulders. When I hooked my left leg over Dreadnought's face, he lapped at what gaped before him. Straddling his erection felt beautiful to the core. He sat up slightly in order to reach a fingertip to my anus and he teased me there as I slowly shifted on the hardness that seemed to be a living thing of its own volition inside me.

Dreadnought's ejaculation made me giddy. I was losing focus; losing control of my senses. I sneezed; I wriggled and galloped on what was dwindling and spastically pulsing within my own leaves. Still searching, I bundled my energy into the effort of drinking him dry. I needed his life. A warm glow broke into my stomach and ransacked my body.

'Don't leave me,' he said.

'I won't,' I said. 'I promise.'

With no fear in my body, I was lifted off Dreadnought's penis, my arms outstretched; by the hair under my arms, in my oxters, a force held me. It took me higher; my gut shrivelled. To say goodbye and farewell to Dreadnought I looked down and saw him catch a few drops of vaginal secretion in his mouth and in the bull of his right eye. He waved with his left hand. He used his right to clean his cock dry, then he raised those fingers to his tongue.

I was going. Dizzy, pie-eyed, I was soon up among the bear-faced birds, swarming with the flock. Flapped at and pecked. Cosseted and molested. An intruder; an interloper, spared death by beak on this morning of humid favours. The air now tasted sweet to my senses.

Below me, the earth shimmered as if it was a mirage. The plateau span. Spontaneously the lake rippled, the lake waved and splashed; the yellow water reached up for me, to keep me there. But I had to go. I had travelled back as far as I had the life in me to travel – to the conception – and time wanted me back to my rightful place. On the sickening return journey I spied the beasts of England and Denmark: their horns, their thorns; manes and unkempt moustaches; their plumes, their feathers, all ragged and brown.

Time was slipping away from me. I was falling, falling. I saw Katherine, I saw Mondo the Magnificent; I saw Lucy (bye-bye, cousin) and then I saw a small room of meat, a cage of butchered anatomies. And I felt the frisson of a job well done.

xii

'Got your number from Dreadnought. He seemed perplexed I'd want it.'

'So am I. You could've stolen it. You've had my phone often enough.'

'I'm not calling to argue, Rene. Just calling to ask a question.'

'Steal the answer, Frank. I'm in no mood for questions from you.'

'Did you set me up?'

'Of course I did, Frank,' I said. 'For upsetting me.'

'It was only a laugh!'

'Didn't feel that way.'

'Rene,' said Frank. 'You'll know I have some damage out on you.'

'I'll be gone, Frank.'

'Then we'll find you in Copenhagen.'

'I won't be in Copenhagen.'

'Then we'll find you in fucking Denmark.'

'I won't be in fucking Denmark. I'm going, Frank. I'm going where the sun shines brightly. I'm going where the sky is blue.'

'Eh?' Frank asked, puzzled.

Deadpan I continued: 'I've seen it in the movies. Now let's see if it's true, Frank,' I said. Tenderly I fingered the slim travel wallet in my fingers: the plastic sheath of foreign currency, purchased the day before from the earnings of this month's collection of the monthly; the leaflet of insurance advice; the return ticket that I knew I would only be using one half of. 'I have some work to finish overseas,' I said. 'I'm going to the end of the earth, Frank. He's next. I'm going to find him, I don't care what the time difference is.'

'You're losing me,' said Frank the Ferret.

'I'm done here.' I raised my final cigarette to my mouth: I was going to quit. This seemed as good a time, a moment, a potential, a pressure point, a stroke – a piece of crisis work, as any. 'I never had you.'

I hung up. I'd be gone.

Having hefted onto my shoulder the one bag with which I'd travel, I dropped the ignited cigarette on to the armchair. The petrol I'd poured there earlier helped the fire start straight away. I watched the flames while I went through a checklist of what I was carrying: my ticket, my passport, some toiletries and the clothes I had on my back.

Bye-bye, flat. Bye-bye, Swiss Cottage.

The fire was taking hold as I left the building. By chance I met Apple Steven; I said hi. I bid a slumped Simon adios. Earlier on I had called Dreadnought to lie to him about going back to Copenhagen for a short break. I was going much further than that: twenty hours or so further. I had hoped that Dreadnought wouldn't work it out and chase me to Terminal Three, but how could he? He didn't know that I'd spoken to Stroker. Or did he?

I took a last look up. There were orange dancing flowers in the window of my twentieth floor flat. This was Crisis Work. Bag on my back, I strolled to the Swiss Cottage station. This was *business*.

THE END

Notes and Acknowledgements

More than any other fiction of mine that might eventually see print, *Dreadnought Flex* is a record of time that has passed and of things that have changed. To be precise, it is a record of twelve years that have left us.

I finished the first draft in longhand in a holiday cottage in Ireland in 2005, shortly after my family and I (and our friends) had said a final goodbye to my father, who had died unexpectedly in May. Completing the novel had felt cathartic and life-affirming; the experience had felt rich. The following paragraph is how I imagined the Acknowledgements would read, at the time.

> *Forgive me, if you will, for the liberties I've taken with the geography and protocols of Heathrow Airport and with some of the geography of West London. My mountain-shaped thanks to Paul Meloy, M.F. Korn, Joel Lane, Gideon Keren and David Farrer; also to Alan David Price and D.F. Lewis. Heart-shaped thanks to my mother, to Jackie — and especially to my dearly missed father, who died while this book was in progress. (Rest in peace, Dad. God bless.) And to the one man who assisted more than any other, I'll offer a salute. With good behaviour, he'll be out in seven years.*
>
> *D.M., Garricullen, Co. Wexford; Leighton Buzzard, Beds.*

The friends I thanked then remain thanked now, of course, although Joel is no longer with us: like my father, he was taken far too young, and with no warning, in 2013. The man I refer to in the final two sentences has almost certainly been released from prison by now. I hope he has remained on the outside of those walls.

For various reasons, the novel was not submitted in 2005. It was not submitted in 2006 either, or in any other year before now. That early draft was not so much as touched until 2015, when I dared myself to take another look.

Largely as a result of the enthusiasm that Charlie Franco of Montag had shown for the publication of my previous work, I started to put *Dreadnought Flex* through its paces in late 2016. Charlie was one man who helped this book recover from its depression. My dear friend Paul Meloy – one of the few people to have read the earlier draft – was another. Paul has always loved Dreadnought and has wanted him – and his story – to see the light of day for many a year. Thank you, both, in different ways, for encouraging me to confront what my heart had jailed in a previous decade.

It was while re-reading that raw first draft (and not while writing it, if memory serves) that I acknowledged the influences of Martin Amis – the voice he used in *London Fields* – and Peter Høeg – the voice he used in *Miss Smilla's Feeling for Snow*. Rather late in the day, I would like to thank these two authors for two of my favourite books ever.

I would also like to thank Steven Stapleton of Nurse With Wound for permission to use a piece of art from his *Homotopy to Marie* recording that I had in mind all the way through writing this book. Mr Stapleton is a genius.

From the time I was thirteen, Sheila Furnell encouraged my writing to develop. As the wonderful Thomas Harris once wrote of someone in *his* life, it is too late to thank Sheila, but in this moment of completion I would like to say her name.

About the Author

David Mathew is the author of the novels *O My Days*, *Ventriloquists*, *The Parry and the Lunge* and *Dreadnought Flex*, among other works. His shorter fiction is collected in *Sick Dice* and *Panic Soup*. A full-time academic in the Centre for Learning Excellence at the University of Bedfordshire, UK, he has a PhD in Higher Education and Psychoanalysis, and his academic work is published in the books *Fragile Learning: The Influence of Anxiety*, *The Care Factory*, and the forthcoming *Psychic River: Storms and Safe Ports in Lifelong Learning* and *Long Lessons: The Endurance of Anxiety* (a follow-up volume to *Fragile Learning*). He is a keen student of psychoanalysis and human behaviour, as well as of group activity. He lives in the south-east of England and enjoys hiking with his dog and the musical genres of jazz fusion and post-rock (although not at the same time).

www.ingramcontent.com/pod-product-compliance
Lightning Source LLC
Chambersburg PA
CBHW021219260626
47172CB00002B/499